Addressed to kill

It is Christmas time and there is a need to be afraid. Cheryl Towlson's frenzied screams go unheard as they echo across the pitch black woodland. At dawn she is found raped, having been strangled with her own tights.

Hours before, Cheryl had received a mysterious, threatening phone call. The callous voice had used a pet name only known to her ex-boyfriend. But had the rejected Patrick been the caller?

As D.I. David Stark's motley team of detectives – under pressure both professionally and compassionately – swing into action, another young woman, unconnected with Cheryl, is violated with similar cunning and ferocity. Her perverse attacker also has intimate knowledge of her private life. How can this be?

Dave Stark begrudgingly announces that 'Christmas is cancelled', and the seemingly fruitless investigation is given a bizarre twist, courtesy of The Royal Mail. It is only when someone close to the detective inspector becomes a potential victim that the trap begins to close on the unlikely perpetrator of a series of horrific attacks on young women. In a disturbing and emotional climax the atrocity of rape leaves a scar on the minds of all involved.

Keith Wright is a serving CID detective and his professional knowledge of police investigations coupled with a formidable talent for storytelling combine to make his third novel a 'must' for all crime fiction enthusiasts.

Also by Keith Wright

One oblique one (1991)
Trace and eliminate (1992)

ADDRESSED TO KILL

Keith Wright

Constable . London

First published in Great Britain 1993
by Constable & Company Ltd
3 The Lanchesters, 162 Fulham Palace Road
London W6 9ER
Copyright © 1993 by Keith Wright
The right of Keith Wright to be identified
as the author of this work
has been asserted by him in accordance
with the Copyright, Designs and Patents Act 1988
ISBN 0 09 472100 9
Set in Linotron Palatino 10pt and
printed in Great Britain by
Redwood Press, Melksham, Wiltshire

A CIP record for this book
is available from the British Library

'Give me a child until the age of seven,
and I will give you the man.'

For my Mum

1

'A violently active, dominating, intrepid, brutal
youth – that is what I'm after.'
ADOLF HITLER

Cheryl Towlson fought her way through the mass of writhing
bodies, which gyrated rhythmically to the strident beat of Slade's
'Merry Christmas Everybody' emanating from the hi-fi speakers
in each corner of the living-room. Cheryl was easily seen, despite
the dim light, because of her eye-catching blonde hair; she
twisted and turned in between the masses, avoiding the legs and
feet that shot out at her in the name of dancing. She moved
awkwardly in her tight-fitting mini-skirt, her breasts crammed
into a white cotton top which displayed the deep valley of her
cleavage.

She had moved into the flat with her friend Barbara a few
months ago and they had decided to hold the housewarming-
cum-Christmas party on the spur of the moment. Cheryl wasn't
superb-looking, average really, her nose a little too large and her
eyelashes very blonde; she felt, somewhat mistakenly, that
smearing make-up on her face in a seemingly reckless fashion
would disguise her anaemic appearance. At nineteen, one is very
appearance-conscious. These were heady times for Cheryl. It was
the start of the rest of her life, free and easy, out in the big bad
world for the first time and enjoying every minute of it. All her
hopes and dreams had yet to be fulfilled. Who knew what the
future would bring?

A young man with short cropped hair and stubbled face met
her in the hallway and took hold of her around the waist.

'Cheryl, my darling, how are you?' he slurred, his drunk-
enness apparent.

She wrested his hands off her and turned to answer the door. 'Merry Christmas!' Two more girlfriends entered the throng.

'Hiya, Jane, hiya, Marion.' Cheryl beamed at yet more guests.

They hugged each other as if they had been lifelong friends, instead of the casual acquaintances they were.

'Sorry we're a bit late, Cheryl, but we got talking in the pub, you know how it is.'

'That's okay. I'm not sure if anyone else can fit in the living-room, they've gone absolutely barmy in there. It's going really well.'

'Great.' Jane's face lit up with excitement. 'Point us in the direction of the booze and the fellers, and leave us to it!'

A girl's scream could be heard from the living-room, followed by raucous laughter.

'I see what you mean,' Marion observed.

Cheryl stood in the doorway and could see Barbara over on the far side of the room, barely visible in the murky light that was intermingled with layers of smoke and the cavorting horde. Barbara was slightly older than Cheryl, darker skinned, slim and with black velvety shoulder-length hair. She waved and smiled. The party was a success. Cheryl watched as a man approached Barbara and distracted her attention. It was Dave Lampton, 'a real dish', as Barbara had described him. She was right. Barbara always seemed to get the handsome guys. Cheryl looked around the room to see if there were any decent men left for her to home in on.

A repetitive bleeping noise crept into Cheryl's ears. It took several rings before she realised it was the telephone. She spun around and took the call in the hallway.

'Hello! Thanks for calling the madhouse!'

She could hear nothing. She stretched over and closed the living-room door, shutting out some of the din.

'Hello,' she repeated.

She sat on the stairs and felt her tight skirt dig into her stomach. She threw her hair back and placed the white plastic close to one ear with a finger in the other.

The voice sounded croaky and a trifle odd. 'I want to speak to Cheryl.'

'This is Cheryl. Who's that?' She didn't recognise the voice.

'Guess who this is?'

8

'I don't know. Come on, stop messing around, I'm in the middle of a party. Who is it?'

'If I was to say "Honey-bun" to you, would that give you a clue?'

Cheryl sighed. 'Oh, Patrick! This is not the time. You knew I was having a party tonight, and you still have to ring. There is nothing more to discuss. It's over. We had a good time for six months, let's not spoil it now, for God's sake!'

'What if I was to come over and rip that lacy camisole I bought you right off your gorgeous body?'

'You're drunk, what's the matter with you?'

'Nothing that a good fucking wouldn't mend, you fucking slut!'

Cheryl was stunned. She struggled for some riposte but instead slammed the phone down and held it in place. Her heart was beating faster. The phone rang again. She picked it up and immediately replaced it. Then she unplugged it.

When she had told Patrick last Thursday that their relationship was over, he had seemed to be fatalistic about it. He must have known the end was coming. This new behaviour was most out of character, or at least she thought it was. She returned to the party, her thoughts her own as she wandered into the kitchen. Barbara was pouring some drinks and turned to face her flat-mate.

'Another G and T, Cheryl? Hey, what's the matter?'

'Oh, nothing really. It's Patrick. He's just rung up, drunk, swearing at me. I've had to unplug the phone.'

'You're joking, aren't you? I didn't think he had it in him. What did he say?'

'He called me an effing slut. Nice, isn't it? I mean, what does he expect me to do when he calls me that, take him back?'

Barbara wasn't one to mince her words. 'The little shit. Are you sure it was him and not somebody messing around?'

'It was him all right. He mentioned the camisole he bought me and he called me by the name he always uses.'

Barbara's face broke into a grin. 'Oh, did he now? What's that, then?'

'I'm not telling you.'

'Oh, go on! Don't be a misery-guts. Come on, what is it? Luscious Lips, Pussy Galore, Sexy Bum . . . ?'

Cheryl playfully hit Barbara on her shoulder and took the gin and tonic. 'Just shut up, will you! I'm not telling you and that's it. Don't you start hassling me as well, I've got enough on my plate with Patrick throwing a wobbler on me.'

'Well, don't let that weasel spoil the party for you.' Barbara pursed her lips and looked thoughtful. 'Let's see. I prescribe a double dose of alcohol in copious amounts until your legs give way, at which point your emotional troubles will be considerably lessened.'

Cheryl laughed. 'Sounds like good advice. I shall tackle Patrick about it tomorrow, though. He's not getting away with that!'

The bar at Radford Road police station was full. It was not over-large but it was tastefully decorated with a few aesthetically pleasing prints on the wall and an array of various police shields festooned across the top of the bar.

Detective Superintendent Wagstaff, complete with 'Wing Commander' handlebar moustache, surveyed the scene as he mouthed a fat cigar. He had served thirty-two years with the Nottinghamshire Constabulary, 'man and boy', but it was time to part company. His 'retirement do' now heralded his departure. There was a very good turn-out and the organisers had had to open the plastic dividers allowing the crowd to spill out on to the dance floor to ease the congestion.

David Stark, Detective Inspector, leaned against the wall, close to the bar, clutching a pint of lager. In his forties, Stark looked surprisingly young for his age. He stood over six feet tall, was slim and wore a well-pressed, grey double-breasted suit. Earlier, at home, as he had groomed himself in the mirror, he had noticed that there were streaks of grey starting to creep into his jet black hair, which gave him cause for some concern. His wife, Carol, had accused him of being vain, but quickly reassured him that it made him look more distinguished, which he begrudgingly accepted.

The hubbub of a hundred conversations was broken by a resounding banging of a tray on to the bar. Nobby Clarke, Detective Sergeant of the parish, was the cause of the distraction. His bulky figure and fringed hair became more visible as he stood on the bar footrail and bellowed, 'Can I have your attention, *please*?'

Only a few idiots at the back continued talking.

'Thank you at the back!'

There was quiet and Nobby continued his introduction. 'Can I please have your attention in order that David Stark, our beloved Detective Inspector –'

Cackles and jeers.

'Thank you. So that our beloved Detective Inspector may say a few words. Thank you.'

'I hope it is a few words an' all!' a wag shouted from the back.

A space had developed between Stark and the rest of the crowd. Normally an officer of greater rank than he would have made the speech, but Wagstaff had insisted that David do it as a mark of the respect he had for his inspector, both as a policeman and as a man. Stark placed his pint of lager on the bar and toyed with a piece of paper as he began his monologue.

'Thank you, Nobby, for that decidedly inauspicious introduction. It's my honour tonight to say a few words about Mr Wagstaff, and I mean it when I say that. Mr Wagstaff will be sadly missed –'

Wagstaff interrupted. 'Ehup, I'm not dead yet, you know!'

'Come on, sir, it's bad enough with this lot of barrackers without you joining in.'

'Sorry, David, carry on.'

'Now, I won't bore you –'

Cheers from the back.

'Thank you, and I must be somewhat limited in my few stories as there are ladies present –'

'Where?' came the shout.

Despite the usual shouts and interruptions, Stark continued unabated. 'Mr Wagstaff joined the force on 2nd July 1960, probably before a lot of you were even born . . .'

Stark glanced at Ashley Stevens, a young detective constable, immaculately dressed as ever with a gold bracelet dangling from his wrist. Ashley smiled and raised his glass.

'. . . The force he joined was not the one we have today. He joined the Nottingham City Police.'

Some cheers from the old stagers.

'He did contemplate joining the County force at the time, but there was a height requirement. Mr Wagstaff was *over* five feet three and as we know that immediately disqualified him from the County Police . . .'

11

Hisses from some quarters.

'Anyway, he rose rapidly through the ranks and in fact was promoted into the rank whilst remaining on the CID on each occasion, a rare feat and one that would be unlikely to happen in this day and age. I've had a chat with a few of your former colleagues, sir, and they have asked me to remind you about your use of handcuffs –'

'Here we go . . .' Wagstaff smiled.

'Now, I'm not saying you have been unlucky, sir, but I was told that when you went to a large pub fight as a probationary PC all those years ago, you used your initiative and handcuffed one reprobate after a bit of a scuffle, but as the fight was still going on you were anxious to help your colleagues. So to free yourself for action you handcuffed your prisoner to the steering wheel of the police car, which in essence wasn't a bad idea. However, you made one simple error, sir: you left the keys in the ignition! And I can only imagine your horror as you watched helplessly when the police vehicle was driven off, handcuffs and all, by your "prisoner" . . .'

Whoops and laughter.

'We did catch him though,' Wagstaff shouted in defence.

'Yes, I understand so, sir. In fact I checked up – he was released from intensive care only last week . . .'

More laughter.

Stark continued his speech in a similar vein. He presented Wagstaff with his customary engraved tankard and the gift Wagstaff had requested, when asked: an aquarium, minus the fish of course – a cumbersome offering.

Wagstaff said his piece and thanked everybody.

'It is with some regret', he concluded, 'that I go but it is a young man's job today; and talking of young men, I had better introduce you to my successor – Detective Superintendent Bill Wormsley, who at forty-two is considerably younger than my good self.'

Wagstaff indicated the man standing next to him. Bill Wormsley was shortish and stout in build. He had a weathered face that appeared dispassionate; there were no laughter lines visible but on this occasion he did make an effort, although his smile degenerated into a kind of sneer.

'Thanks a lot,' he muttered. He spoke with a gruff voice and largely in monosyllables. A first-rate detective with a reputation for never leaving a stone unturned, he was however noted for his aloofness with the lower ranks.

'I can only hope, Bill,' Wagstaff continued, 'that the lads treat you as well as I have been treated.'

There was much laughter, and Wagstaff signed off with a 'Thanks again and Merry Christmas.'

The conversation grew quickly, interspersed with sporadic laughter that resounded around the confined bar area. Stark was surrounded by some of his detectives.

'Good speech, sir,' Steve Aston offered, as he sipped an orange juice. Steve was a ginger-haired youth and a devout vegetarian.

'Thank you, Stephen. I don't relish public speaking, I assure you.'

'Good speech, sir.' Ashley mocked his colleague's slightly higher voice. Ashley was a confident young man, with a considerable private income that was reflected in his clothing, jewellery and Toyota Celica sports car.

'Get knotted, Ashley. No one can say anything with you around, can they?'

'All right, touchy. It's a shame old Wagstaff is going. He was okay really, wasn't he?'

Nobby, ex-paratrooper, hard as nails, and not a man to cross, spoke candidly: 'Yes, one of the old school. I reckon this new bloke'll be a bad bastard, though.'

Stephanie Dawson spoke. 'Why, what do you mean, Nobby?'

'Well, I was talking to Des Brandon at Newark the other day and he says Wormsley is a right double-dyed git!'

Stark interrupted. 'It's always the same when you get a new gaffer. I've heard similar stories, but let's give him a chance, shall we? You never know, he might have turned over a new leaf.'

Nobby wasn't convinced. 'Yeah, and pigs might fly as well.'

Steph toyed with the gold chain that separated her pronounced breasts. Stark referred to her as his 'Beautiful Blonde Bombshell'. She wore a tight-fitting suit that attracted the stares of all those around her and, unlike some of her younger feminist colleagues, she loved it.

'At least we are off over Christmas. I've finished after tomorrow for four days and I don't know about anybody else but I'm going to make the most of it.'

Ashley grinned. 'I bet you are!'

Steph fluttered her eyebrows exaggeratedly.

'Whatever do you mean, Ashley?'

The group laughed. Nobby leaned past Steph to reach for his drink on the bar. As he did so he rubbed his hand along the contours of her backside. Had it been anybody else she would have flinched but Steph and Nobby had an 'understanding'. She smiled at him. Nobby raised his glass.

'Ah well, have a nice Christmas, everybody.'

'Cheers!'

Cheryl had her head in her hands as she sat on the settee. Morning had broken. Her hair was straggly and her legs were pale and 'goose-pimply' where they were exposed beneath the white cotton night-shirt with a picture of Mickey Mouse on it. There was devastation all around. Discarded cans of lager, some partly full, and compact discs were in a state of disarray. She noticed that the hi-fi was still turned on. Her brain was throbbing, numbed by alcohol; in the throes of dehydration, her mouth was dry and her throat sore. She peered through squinted eyes at Barbara who drew on a cigarette as she sat in the corner of the room, before barking out a cough and swallowing the phlegm.

Cheryl spoke first. 'Good party, huh?'

'Yeah, brilliant. What time did we go to bed?'

'Twenty to four, I think.'

'Jesus. What time is it now?'

'Half nine.'

'You're late for work, Cheryl.'

'It's okay, they said I could go in a bit later. I suppose we'd better make a start at clearing this mess up.'

Barbara groaned. 'Oh God, let's leave it till next Christmas.'

Cheryl struggled to her feet. 'Come on. We can make a start on it, at least.'

The two girls ambled around the room, collecting cans and pausing to groan when they bent their heads to pick up the mess, as the blood invaded their skulls.

Barbara grunted out an attempt at conversation. 'Did I dream it or did Patrick ring up last night?'

Cheryl sighed. 'It was no dream, more like a bloody nightmare. He rang up all right.'

14

'What's up with the bloke? Anybody would think he owned you!'

'I know. I'm going to speak to him later and give him both barrels. I hope he's not going to be a pain in the neck over our separation.'

Barbara was philosophical. 'It'll wear off. I had a similar problem with a bloke I went out with. They soon get the message.'

Cheryl threw her hair back, a habit of hers which she immediately regretted as she steadied herself on the wall, her head spinning. 'He'll get the message all right!'

The briefing of a senior officer every morning is referred to somewhat sarcastically as 'morning prayers'. It takes some poor detective constable at least an hour, at seven in the morning, to sift through the scores of teleprinters and compile the information in the relevant files for the gaffer to peruse in comfort, and woe betide the DC should he miss something. It's a horrendous task but the importance of a morning briefing is self-evident in the day-to-day smooth running of the CID. Its importance can also be borne out, days later, when a matter suddenly becomes of relevance and pieces fall into place.

It was Detective Inspector Stark who knocked on the door of Bill Wormsley's office on the second floor of Nottingham police station, and walked in. He was clutching a large notepad. The early morning DC had already briefed Stark, whose turn it now was to complete the Chinese whispers with Detective Superintendent Wormsley. The office was not over-large and consisted mainly of a desk, a bookcase behind that, and a couple of plastic chairs against the wall. Wormsley had already changed the office and stamped his personality on it. There was a rubber plant in one corner and an array of cacti stretching across the window sill. Wormsley greeted Stark heartily from his comfortable office chair – grandiose in comparison to those used by his visitors.

'Ah, David, good morning. I take it you've come to do the runners and riders for today.'

'Morning, sir. Yes, there's a fair bit to brief you about but I've tried to trim it down for you.'

'Right. I enjoyed Mr Wagstaff's retirement do, I must say.

Enjoyed your speech too.' Wormsley looked thoughtful before continuing. 'I don't think we've ever worked together, have we?'

'No, sir, I don't think we ever have.'

'Well, Mr Wagstaff speaks very highly of you, and I'm sure we'll get along well. When I get a chance, we'll have a proper chat about the sub-divisional CID and the changes I have in mind. Give me a chance to get sorted out and I'll get the two other DIs from the other nicks on the division over here for a meeting.'

'Fine.'

Wormsley placed both his hands together, as if in prayer, resting them on his pursed lips and peering at Stark as if trying to weigh him up.

Stark shifted slightly in his seat and opened his notepad before speaking. 'I'll go through the morning briefing as I used to with Mr Wagstaff, shall I? And you can tell me if you want any more or in a different format as we go along.'

Wormsley smiled. 'That sounds like an excellent idea, David.'

Stark was caught a little off balance by Wormsley's hail-fellow-well-met attitude, which didn't quite ring true.

Wormsley rose and stood with his hands resting on the window sill, looking out of the window at the layer of early morning frost that glistened on the lower rooftops as the winter sun began its attack on the icy covering. He was not a tall man but his silhouetted figure displayed the broadness of his frame.

Stark began the briefing to Wormsley's back. 'There are two locked up overnight. One is a drunk driver and the other is in for a domestic ABH. Nothing for us – Uniform will sort those out, obviously. There are three on the prisoners' list for yesterday – it must have been fairly quiet.'

'Yes, I've seen those. Shoplifters and a burglar.'

'Yes, the burglary was more a domestic, argument over the hi-fi as usual, so it's nothing special.'

'Right, okay. Any major crime on the sub-division?'

'No murders or rapes overnight – just an indecent assault at Bulwell around seven o'clock.'

'What are the circumstances of that?'

'She came out of the back of the Food Giant supermarket and she crossed over the railway lines at the back to get home. A youth in his teens knocked her down and had a feel of her breasts and her vagina before running off.'

'Did he feel her over her knickers or did he actually insert fingers or what?'

'It was over her knickers. The lad didn't have the chance to do a deal else. She put up quite a fight, I understand.'

'Good. Who's dealing with that?'

'Dave Stringer. He's a good lad. I think they've got somebody in mind for it. He's done all the necessary – I've had a look at it.'

'Mmm, okay. What else?'

Stark was aware of Wormsley ambling back to his desk and sitting down. The chair unfortunately made a friction sound that Stark initially confused with Wormsley passing wind. Stark coughed away a laugh, before continuing.

'There's three sudden deaths on the patch overnight. All old people, natural causes, no suspicious circumstances. Winter's here again and they're dropping like flies.'

Wormsley leaned back in his chair and placed his hands behind his head as he reclined. 'Any "Missing From Homes"?'

'Yes, Claire Jackson and Terry Smith. They abscond regularly from the local children's home at Bulwell. No sooner are they found and returned than they go walkabout again. The social services can't control them.'

'How old are they?' Wormsley frowned.

'Both fourteen.'

'Are the kids being spoken to properly by us each time they are found?'

'Yes, but it's like talking to that wall, though. You're wasting your time with them. They literally just tell you to fuck off or sing stupid songs as you try to talk to them. I've spoken to the lads about it. What can you do?' Stark asked rhetorically.

'Can't we get them into a secure unit?'

Stark laughed. 'I'm sorry, sir, but the secure units are overflowing and even there they can do more or less what they like. They can walk off whenever the fancy takes them. The number of proper "secure units" you can count on one hand, and there are waiting lists for those with kids far worse than Claire and Terry.'

'So they just run wild and rob and steal and do what they bloody well like, then?'

'In a word. Yes.'

'What a bloody state of affairs.'

17

There was a pause. Wormsley broke the silence. 'Any burglaries?'

'Yes, there's a dozen on our patch, about the norm for over-night, mainly commercial premises. Nothing of high value.'

'Get those two "Missing From Homes" checked against any fingerprints found, will you? I'm not trying to teach you to suck eggs, but you know what I mean.'

'Yeah, okay, but I would think that they would be down the Green at blues parties or "raves" all night.'

'You're probably right, but they need money to buy their dope with, don't they?' There was a strident tone to Wormsley's com-ment. He wasn't used to being queried – just obeyed.

'Yes, okay, sir.'

Wormsley twisted his chair and stared out of the window again. 'Any crime circulations in the force area?'

'Yeah, there's three or four, none on our sub-division but two on Radford Road. Their DI Phil Dowty will give you a ring if he hasn't already, and fill you in with those. Night Crime Patrol went to them so they should have been started off all right.'

'Anything else I need to know about?'

'Not really. No doubt we'll have a more general chat at the meeting of all the DIs when you've got settled in.'

'Yes, okay. I've had a bit of a look at Hucknall and there are a couple of points I'd like to know about. One is the wages job a fortnight ago when the sawn-off was used. I'd like to see all the actions on that enquiry and know what the update is because that's going to go stale unless we get something more substantial on it.'

Stark nodded before Wormsley continued. 'And the other thing is the spate of burglaries we are having on Ruffs Estate. We are getting hammered with daytime burglaries around there. There have been forty-seven in the last three months. Who's looking at those? Anyone in particular?'

'Barry Marsh is collating all the information on those, sir. He's new to the sub-division, a Welsh lad. Do you know him? He came from West Bridgford. He's shaping up nicely. I'm keeping my eye on it, I assure you.'

'That's good to hear, David. I'm a big one for keeping an eye on things too.' Wormsley smiled, but it wasn't the sort of smile that endeared one to him.

The telephone rang and Wormsley was quick to answer. 'Superintendent Wormsley ... Hello, Phil. No, it's okay, we've just about finished. Hold on a sec.' Wormsley turned to Stark. 'It's Phil Dowty. I don't think there's anything else, is there? Tell the men I shall call in on them later.' The detective superintendent raised a thumb at Stark. 'Thanks a lot, Dave. See you later.'

Stark rose and left the room. As he walked down the stairs he realised that Wagstaff's days were well and truly over. Gone were the days of, 'I'll leave it with you, David. Just keep the wheel on!' It looked as though Wormsley was going to stick his big nose in far more than old Waggy had. The winds of change were blowing through the corridors of Nottingham police station. Stark shivered with the draught.

It had not been a good day for Cheryl Towlson. Her head had been throbbing. What with the party last night and Pat's malicious phone call, she had barely been able to concentrate all day. Cheryl worked for a finance company and the excessive spending that Christmas entails had brought on a last-minute clamour for loans from desperate people resorting to desperate measures. She had contemplated confronting Pat about the call, but now all she wanted was just to get home and lay her head on a soft pillow for a couple of hours. She felt sure she would be okay after that. Barbara had suggested they go into town later for a few hours, 'hair of the dog' and all that, but the idea of more alcohol made Cheryl want to vomit.

Her beige raincoat was really insufficient for the cold temperature, with only a cardigan and blouse underneath, but an overcoat would have to wait until her own financial situation improved. The effects on her social life of sharing a flat with Barbara were exciting, but they did tend to wear a hole in the pocket. Her hairstyle had collapsed and her skin felt sticky, after-effects of last night's drink made worse by walking home.

The welcoming sight of light shining from her flat window through the branches of the trees in the distance comforted her. The journey was drawing to a close, and the warmth of the room and a hot cup of tea were long overdue. Cheryl had never enjoyed the early darkness that winter brings. She toyed momentarily with the idea of walking the longer way home, literally around the houses, but her tiredness dictated that she cut across the railway line and through the copse to the back of the flat complex.

Cheryl negotiated the rough terrain and concentrated as best she could on the ground in the darkening surroundings. She stumbled and twisted her ankle as she stepped in a hollow, causing her to hop a couple of steps.

'Bloody hell!' she cursed.

Cheryl had barely got the words out and regained her balance before she was hurtled sideways and crashed into the under-growth, banging her elbow on the frozen soil. A hand quickly covered her mouth and nose and she became aware of a weight crushing her against the ground. A face drew close to hers as she struggled to breathe.

'One sound, Honey-bun, and you're fucking dead! You're mine, baby, all mine, so keep your fucking gob shut!'

Terror flooded into her and she froze – paralysed with fear and surprise. Her chest heaved as she struggled to take in air and comprehend the enormity of the situation. She wanted to speak, she wanted to kick out, but she couldn't; she felt helpless and her assailant knew it. She was instantly overwhelmed by the man's strength and nastiness. The hand over her mouth and nostrils was removed and she gulped in air.

It was a hard punch that rocked her head to the right and immediately bruised her jaw. The effect of the punch and the nightmare scenario heightened her dizziness and she almost allowed her mind to swirl into unconsciousness. Only the sur-vival instinct forced her to fight the pain and she stared up at the monster who contemptuously leered down at her. He was a young man with dirty skin and greasy brown hair that hadn't seen a comb for a couple of days. His eyes were wide and staring, and he breathed heavily. He was enjoying it.

Her mind raced with what to do – scream, fight, scratch? – but she couldn't move, couldn't speak. She just lay there debilitated and afraid. She began to sob. She felt a dull ache in her stomach brought on by terror, a feeling she had had as a child when discovering for the first time that she was separated from her mummy and was now lost. She experienced the blind panic that reduces a normal person into a shivering quarry, fate having

20

thrown her to the lions. She was alone – God, she had never been more alone. She began to cry and beg.

'Please, please don't hurt me! Honest, I won't do anything, I promise, honestly!'

The maniac clutched at her throat and squeezed hard. She put her hands on his in a vain attempt to alleviate the constriction. His hands were gnarled and callous, matching his temperament.

'You do as I say or you're fucking dead, bitch!' His adrenalin was on a high and he gasped out more abuse. 'What are you crying for, eh? You mardy fucking cow, you're all the same, the frigging lot of you!'

Cheryl couldn't see much of her attacker, but she could smell him: a disgusting mixture of alcohol and halitosis that she couldn't evade. The foul stench polluted her mouth and lungs. She felt sick, she felt desolate, she knew she was at the mercy of this stinking and repulsive man who for some reason had chosen her. Why her? He had called her 'Honey-bun'. Only Pat called her that. What the hell was going on?

In a matter of seconds her world had been turned upside-down, and shock and confusion pervaded her senses. Cheryl felt him tear at her blouse, ripping it off to expose her bra. The cold air made her shiver all the more. She felt ashamed and she instinctively crossed her arms over her bare flesh, but in her heart of hearts she knew all resistance would be futile. He released his hold of her throat to undo the bra, and she screwed her eyes up as he slobbered over her breasts, which heaved as sobs wracked her body. He smeared saliva over her chest with his tongue and she shivered in revulsion. She was helpless, too frightened to move, she knew he meant it. Cheryl knew he would kill her. She had to switch off, numb her senses. Don't upset him, it will be over soon. Oh my God!

'You are going to get the best fuck you've ever had, baby. I swear you'll love it!'

The sick mind was in its element. She felt him fumbling with her knickers and she attempted to cross her legs. He punched her again, not as hard but hard enough. He grabbed her throat, causing her to gurgle.

'I fucking warned you, you cow!'

He squeezed harder and she grunted as if to display her submission. She opened her legs and her humiliation was exacer-

21

bated as she urinated uncontrollably. He roughly pulled her tights and knickers off, the urine serving only to feed his tortured mind and excite his quest for power and control. He punched her again and hurled further insults, mocking her incontinence. He wasn't put off.

Her attacker was a bastard of the highest order. He bullied her, violated her and forced her to do the most degrading acts. She found her acquiescence shameful and repugnant but she had no alternative but to comply. She felt sick, but the nightmare continued. Fear of death enforced her subservience, but failed to quell her revulsion. He had fantasised over this moment for days. He disliked women, he was angry, he was a coward, but now he could get back at women. She had to do whatever he commanded. He was running the show and she must suffer. In his distorted mind he considered she was the same as all of them, a bitch, and now, merely because he was stronger and more threatening, she was his to play with and abuse.

As the minutes wore on Cheryl tried to formulate a way out of the confusion and living hell. Her mind was racing yet her movements seemed to be in slow motion. It was as if she was watching it all from another place. She knew it wouldn't last for ever and that soon her life would be in mortal danger, when he had finished with her. She couldn't think at first, but he was still there and he wasn't going to go away. She was going to die! She concentrated on his every move, attempting to read the best way to react, the way that could mean survival for her.

As he ravaged her brutally she decided to grunt and moan as if she were enjoying it. If it saved her life, she would do anything. She must not upset him. It was a life-threatening situation and she must survive. She thought of her mother and father and Barbara – what would they think? What should she do? Dare she risk a scream? No way. If it failed he would be annoyed and she would be dead.

It wasn't long before the bastard had finished and he ripped off her thin gold necklace.

'A souvenir of our special day!' he mocked. 'And you'll always know I've got something to remember you by.'

Cheryl's eyes were wide and staring, her whole body trembling as the man fell off her.

The post-ejaculatory mood swing began to take effect and he

lay quiet next to her. Cheryl listened to him breathing, his arm across her chest. Would he fall asleep? But the temperature seemed close to freezing point. Could she escape? The cold earth clung to her semi-naked, sweaty body. She was shivering, and struggled to control her breathing and crying. She waited. She didn't know what she waited for, just a chance, any opportunity to get away. She was gaining more strength and strained to hear a sound, a hint of people nearby who might help. If they were close enough she could survive.

He had not fantasised about this part of the proceedings – the aftermath. It would soon be time for him to go. Or would he take her again? Maybe. He revelled in the control he had over her and began to taunt her to enhance his power and the obvious fear she had of him.

'I know everything about you, Cheryl. We even spoke on the phone, you thick bitch.'

God, he knows my name, he does know me, oh hell!

'If you tell the police about this you are fucking dead! I'll be back, understand? And you will be dead!'

'I won't. I promise I won't. Can I go now? Please!'

'Maybe. I haven't decided yet. Perhaps I'll treat you to some more cock. How's that? You seemed to enjoy it. You did enjoy it, didn't you?'

'Oh yes. I was frightened at first, but it was great, honestly it was. I won't tell anybody, I swear. I swear to God!' She did not look at the man. She was afraid he would see the obvious lie in her eyes.

'You're lying; you cow, you were faking it, weren't you? Admit it.'

'No, you were good, honest.'

'So what do you want to fucking go for, then, eh? Do you think I'm thick or summat?'

'I'm cold now, that's all.'

The man's hand felt Cheryl's tights next to him and he knelt over her, straddling her semi-naked body. He held her tights and wrapped them around her neck and lifted her head towards his groin.

There was a sound. Voices. Somebody was coming. His bravado failed him. It sounded like men approaching. Somebody was definitely coming. He was going to be caught. Fucking hell! He pulled at the tights, choking Cheryl.

'Don't you dare!' he threatened in a whisper. 'Don't you dare make a sound!'

He didn't look at her. He looked away, towards the sound of the approaching figures, and pulled at the tights with all his strength. Now his fear fuelled the adrenalin that pumped around his strong arms and the increasing intensity of his heartbeats caused him to tug repeatedly at the tights with a venom born of both fright and disregard. He could feel her jerking and thrashing, twisting around on the dank soil. He leaned his body on hers to quieten the sound of movement. Cheryl went limp and became heavy, her eyes half-open and glazed, her tongue bulbous in her mouth. He carried on pulling at the tights. He couldn't risk discovery. She might be pretending.

She wasn't.

Barbara turned off the television set and frowned. It was five past one in the morning and still no sign of Cheryl. Barbara was extremely tired but her exhaustion was masked by concern for her flat-mate.

'She could have bloody rung me!' she said out loud. 'I bet she's gone back to that dickhead Patrick. I knew she hadn't got him out of her system!'

Barbara went into the hallway and sat on the stairs in front of the telephone. She stared at it, and nibbled at her bottom lip, unsure what to do. She ran her finger down the telephone book and stopped at Patrick's name, written in red and underlined by Cheryl in the excitement their first encounter had engendered. She dialled the number. After a dozen rings it was answered.

'Hello?' The voice sounded guttural and tired.

'Hello, Patrick?' Barbara curled up on the settee, and pulled her nightgown over her feet.

'Yes, who's that?'

'I'm sorry, Patrick. It's Barbara – Cheryl's friend. Is Cheryl with you?'

'No, she isn't. Look, if this is some kind of joke, Barbara, then I don't think it's very funny. It's one o'clock in the morning, for Christ's sake!'

'I'm sorry to bother you, but I'm worried about Cheryl. You see, she hasn't come home yet since she went out to work this morning and I thought she was going to see you. She usually rings me if she's going to be late and I've not heard a word from her.'

'Well, that problem is not my problem any more and you're welcome to it!' The phone went dead.

Barbara sighed. Now she'd put her foot in it with Patrick. Cheryl would love her for this. Well, Cheryl ought to have bloody rung!

Barbara stepped wearily up the stairs and took her dressing-gown off before collapsing on to the bed. She had hoped for an early night after the party. She faded into sleep very quickly.

When the phone rang, Barbara shrugged herself awake and half fell down the stairs. She picked it up and there was a pause before the line went dead.

'Now what?' She waited for a minute or so but the phone did not ring again. She felt alone and confused.

'Oh, Cheryl, I'll bloody kill you when I see you.'

2

'Christmas comes, but once a year is enough.'
ANON

The bedroom was cloaked in darkness. A man and woman lay motionless in the bed, its quilt in a state of disarray. Gusts of wind caused the walls of the house to creak under the strain as they were battered incessantly by the blasts of winter.

A hairy foot protruded from underneath one side of the cover and, in contrast, manicured, painted fingernails hung down from the far side, close to the pillows. In the distance, outside, the noise of a car alarm and the subsequent clunk of a car door being closed fell upon deaf ears. Dave Stark turned over and placed his arm over Carol's curled-up figure.

A crooning voice suddenly broke into the relative quiet of the room, in the middle of a Christmas melody. The radio alarm clock, the cause of the seasonal awakening, displayed 06:45.

'Sleigh bells ring, are you listening? In the lane, snow is glistening. A beautiful sight, we're happy tonight . . .'

David Stark opened one bleary eye. He croaked aloud, in unison with the singer: 'Walking in a Winter Wonderland.'

He stretched his body, issuing groans and distorted gurgles as his muscles lengthened. He closed his eyes again but received an elbow in his ribs.

'Don't go back to sleep!' Carol muttered wearily.

Dave leaned over and turned the radio off, and his bedside lamp on. The dull wattage of the lamp caused him to screw his eyelids tightly together, as the light attempted to steer past his pupils and invade his brain. He allowed it in gradually by squinting his eyes, but remained prostrate on the mattress.

'Come on, love, you'll be late for work,' Carol urged as she held on to the semi-sleeping state she hoped fully to embrace once her husband had arisen.

Why was she always so bloody sensible? There was a pause because it was an effort for him to speak.

'But it's Christmas Eve. A man should be in the bosom of his family, not rushing out to work.'

Carol leaned on to her elbow and stared down at the unkempt specimen of manhood at her side. His face was pale and there was a hint of bags showing beneath his eyes. She matched his squint in the glow of the lamp and frowned as she spoke. 'Ye gods! Is that the man I married?'

'It's not too late for an annulment, you know,' Dave replied, sleep now beyond recall.

Carol continued unabated. 'And as for being in the bosom of your family on Christmas Eve, Detective Inspector bloody Stark, I don't know how you've got the nerve! I think in the twenty-one years we've been married, we have managed one full Christmas together.'

'All right, for God's sake! It's going to be different this year. I'm off after five o'clock tonight and I'm never going back.'

Carol laughed sceptically. 'If only it were true.'

'Well, I'm off for three days now, anyway.'

The two embraced and Carol rested her head on his chest.

'I've really been looking forward to this Christmas. We'll be like a normal family for once. It'll be good for the kids too. They might have enjoyed it more ten years ago, but better late than never.'

Dave laughed. 'Judging by the schedule you've got planned for us all, it'll be more hectic than if I were at work.'

Carol took hold of Dave's scrotal sac and slowly started to squeeze.

'Say that again, Dave. I don't think I quite heard it right.'

'I said I'm really looking forward to our Christmas together.'

She removed her hand. 'I thought that's what you said. Come on now, get up.'

Dave groaned. 'All right, all right, I'm getting up, just give me a minute.' He closed his eyes again. He began to caress Carol's breasts and edged his hand down towards her . . .

'Oh no, you don't! It's not quite Christmas Day yet.'

'Bloody marvellous, isn't it? I tell you what, the way we're going, you're not far off the truth either.'

'Come on, Dave, get off to work. I want the bed to myself.'

'Now we're getting to the truth of the matter. It's nothing to do with me being late; you just want to sprawl out.'

'So what? It's not a crime, is it?'

Dave rolled on to his side and placed his feet on the floor, so that he was sitting on the side of the bed.

'No, but it ought to be,' he muttered.

He stood and shivered in the cold. 'Where's my robe gone now? I left it –'

Carol finished the sentence for him. 'On the bedroom floor last night. Yes, I know. No wonder the kids' rooms are a tip. They take after their father.'

'Come on, it's cold. Where have you put it?'

For a man in his early forties, he had retained a muscular physique: the shadows on the contours of his body rippled as he peered around the room. Carol was laughing from the comfortable warmth of the bed, her chin resting on the edge of the mattress. Her light brown hair was short, and the wisps of hair curling in front of her ears, twinned with a devilish smile, gave her an impish look. Unfortunately the room was very cold and Dave's manhood recoiled as the cold air reduced his pride and joy considerably. He reached down to protect his nether regions.

Carol was giggling. 'Forty-three years old and still playing with it!'

'Shut up.' He laughed, and walked around the bed, seeking out the warmth of his robe, which he had spied on the peg at the back of the door. He wrapped the towelling around him and headed off towards the bathroom.

Carol drew the quilt over her head to gain warmth and some respite from Dave's throaty warbling which now emanated from the bathroom.

'In the meadow we can build a snowman . . .'

It was more a sense of duty than desire that prompted Albert Hudson to struggle down the gravelly path at the rear of Buckingham Avenue. The harsh wind buffeted him along and drew swirls of dust into the dawn sky. The clouds were animated and grey as they tumbled through the atmosphere seeking out another victim to rain on. Occasionally Albert would clutch on to his cloth cap and pause in the shelter of one of the larger trees that formed the perimeter of the estate and segregated the road from the railway line. It alleviated the cold and afforded him a few moments to catch his breath.

Since the death of his adored wife Amy he had grown more attached to Sal, his Border collie, who had almost seemed aware of the sadness and grieving Albert had endured. He rested on his carved walking stick and stooped to peer through the trees. He whistled out a shrill sound.

'Come on, Sal,' he shouted.

The bitch had disappeared among the trees and, unusually, did not respond to her master's voice.

He tried again. 'Sal!'

There was still no response. He trooped onward and down a small path, hewn from the locals' footsteps over recent years. He muttered to himself, distressed at the lack of obedience his beloved dog was showing. Suddenly he caught sight of her black and white fur just to one side of the path and noticed that she was tugging at something. He stepped into the trees, and the reason for Sal's disobedience exploded into his vision. He froze on the spot, his mouth gaping and the cool air forgotten. He swallowed and took a tentative step towards the dog before stopping again as if the apparition might harm him. His gaze was fixed on the Border collie, astonishment paralysing him momentarily.

Sal was tugging at the ligature that was still wrapped around the dead girl's neck. Each tug rocked the stiffened body, now solid with rigor mortis. The old man stumbled towards the grotesque figure and yanked Sal away.

'Sit and stay!' he ordered. A tremor in his command betrayed his shock.

Albert stared at the semi-naked figure of Cheryl Towlson.

The wind had ruffled through her clothing and thrown dust into her gaping mouth: it had settled on her protruding tongue. Albert sat down on an overturned tree trunk, his body loose with incredulity and sadness. His stomach churned as he took in the macabre sight, and he lit a cigarette. He had had a hard life and encountered much adversity but the image before him rocked him to the core.

It was apparent that some wild animal or perhaps a dog had eaten away at her hand as several of the bones were exposed beyond the red-painted fingernails; her eyes had been gouged out of their sockets with pieces of skin and flesh ripped away around the edges. Despite the gross disfigurement, Albert thought he recognised the girl, which exacerbated his horror. She had always seemed so pleasant whenever he had seen her on the estate. She had often smiled and said hello, occasionally pausing to pat Sal.

He sighed and drew deeply on his cigarette, clinging on to Sal's collar and stroking at her neck with his finger.

'Oh dear, Sal,' he said aloud, 'what have we walked into here, my old gal?'

The collie panted and blinked her eyes at Albert. He stubbed his cigarette out and headed off towards the estate as fast as his ageing legs would take him. He hurried Sal along by tapping her with his stick.

He knocked loudly on the first door he came to.

David Stark had been informed of the murder immediately upon his arrival at work. As usual he had taken the news with a degree of resignation. Stark usually revelled in major enquiries. It was the ultimate challenge, to catch the perpetrator of the ultimate crime – murder. It was just a shame it was Christmas Eve!

Stark had had a chequered career. He had done well for a man with no great academic achievement. Common sense, resolution and excellent detective ability had enhanced his standing in the eyes of his senior officers. He got results and that was what counted. It was fair to say that his family had suffered over the years and he did have an underlying feeling of guilt about that; but other than return to the uniform branch, he was stuck with the ramifications of being a detective inspector: late-night call-outs, engagements cancelled and long hours. Stark was a copper's copper. He did not need to wield the big stick. His easygoing personality and management skills made his detectives want to work for him, and a CID office with a contented atmosphere, to him, meant a successful office. His last spell of 'acting up' in the next rank had gone well, he had thought, but as yet no substantive promotion had come his way. The head of the CID was aware of Stark's abilities but quite clearly did not like him. He had criticised Stark for being too close to the lower ranks and not 'distancing' himself sufficiently. As ever, Stark had made his feelings known. He simply did not agree with that way of thinking. As long as the men were doing the work and were loyal, there was no need for him to rant and rave. He refused to become a clone. He enjoyed a laugh with the lads and since any change would mean he was being false, such a change was not on his agenda, even if the Detective Chief Superintendent considered it a failing in his make-up.

Stark's mind was full of different phrases as he drove to Buckingham Avenue, considering different ways to explain to poor Carol that he wouldn't be cutting the turkey again this year. His heart sank. He was suffering from a mixture of exhilaration and anticipation on the professional side and disappointment and consternation on the personal side. Yet again he would have to let his family down. You can't turn your back on murder. It was just sod's law.

As he got out of the car he attempted to throw off his personal thoughts and focus his mind on the job ahead.

'Merry Christmas, sir,' Mick Molesworth shouted to Stark as he approached the scene. Stark glowered at the uniformed sergeant, steam issuing from his mouth as he spoke.

'Yes, Merry Christmas to you as well, Mick.' He managed to smile before continuing. 'Where is it, then?'

'Over there, sir, you'll see the red tape. Come on, I'll take you over there.' The sergeant led the way.

Stark stepped through the undergrowth along the cordoned-off trail that had been established as the route for the police. It was a route that did not display any signs of the attacker having used it. By definition it was rough terrain. Stark battled with the nettles and shrubs to catch sight of the corpse. Nobby Clarke, his detective sergeant, followed behind.

Stark came to a halt and automatically put his hands in the pockets of his Crombie woollen overcoat. He said nothing but surveyed the scene. He noticed the obvious signs of wildlife interference and the ligature around the poor girl's neck. He noticed her knickers to one side of her; her raincoat and shoulder bag with a bright metal buckle lay about three or four feet away.

The shoulder bag was not open. He scanned the immediate area around the body before speaking to Nobby, now at his side.

'It's at times like these that I miss my pipe.'

Nobby's well-weathered face displayed a wry smile. 'Don't succumb now, boss, you've gone over a month without it.'

Stark looked thoughtful and strained to look beyond the body. He fumbled in his overcoat pocket and produced a packet of Polo mints. He thrust the sweets toward Nobby but the offer was declined. 'There's one thing that bothers me about all this, Nobby.'

Detective Sergeant Clarke blew into his hands and rubbed them, before responding. 'What's that then, sir?'

Stark turned and stared Nobby straight in the eye. 'How the fucking hell am I going to tell my missus about it?'

'Rather you than me, sir.' Nobby laughed.

'You'd better shout the rest of the lads up and tell them from me. Christmas is cancelled!'

'Yeah, okay.'

Nobby returned towards the line of police vehicles. Stark spoke out of the corner of his mouth to Mick Molesworth, who had stayed with him. 'Oh shit! That's all I need!' He could see the stocky figure of Detective Superintendent Wormsley barging past the young PC who had been instructed to keep a log of all those in attendance.

Wormsley got in first with his instructions to Mick. 'I want the police surgeon, Scenes of Crime and Forensic informed and travelling now!'

'Okay, sir, I'll arrange that straight away,' Mick replied.

Stark caught his arm. 'Don't bother, Mick. I already arranged that, mate, before I left the station.'

'Oh, right, okay then.' Mick ambled off and left Wormsley and Stark together.

Stark apprised Wormsley of the situation. 'It looks as though she's been dead some time. The uniform lads have done a good job of things, it's all set up nicely.'

Wormsley was not so impressed and was terse in his reply: 'That's what they get paid for, isn't it?' He craned his neck and studied the scene, before offering a more mellow comment. 'You know, David, I hate outdoor murders. You're battling against the elements all the time. It's starting to rain now, for Christ's sake.'

'Yeah, good, isn't it? I'll arrange for a tarpaulin or tent or something to get the scene covered.'

'Yeah, and do it quick, will you? I would have thought you might have considered that along with the basics, David!' There was acid in Wormsley's comment.

Stark swore in his head as he made off back along the route. 'Piss off' sprang to mind. He radioed for the tarpaulin and joined Nobby who was talking to the old man, Albert Hudson.

'So you haven't moved anything or done anything then?'

'No, lad, I've told you. Sal here was tugging at the thing around her neck and that's it. I've not touched owt else.'

Stephanie Dawson and Steve Aston drew up in a CID car, and Stark met them.

'Looks like your Christmas plans have gone down the Swanee, Steph. I think this one's going to be a runner. Will you get the details of all the bystanders and cars nearby, as a starter? Eh, and watch it – Wormsley's sneaking around, giving his orders.' He winked at Steph and slipped into his best Nazi accent. 'And as you know, orders must be obeyed!'

Stark was puzzled at Steph's reaction. Her eyes were wide and staring and looking beyond Stark. He turned around to find Wormsley standing at his shoulder.

Wormsley spoke. 'You heard what the DI said. Get on with it, then.'

Steph grinned and walked away.

The white Transit van of the Scenes of Crime Department arrived conveniently to distract from the awkward moment. Stark walked quickly towards it. Two Scenes of Crime officers got out of the front. Stuart Kirkland and Mandy Eastman had a long and arduous task ahead of them and their grim faces were indicative of the concentration that was necessary for such an important role. Stark briefed them as they donned their white overalls and plastic shoe coverings, before traipsing down the red-taped 'murder aisle'. They clutched cameras and tripods and large metal cases. Detective Sergeant Stuart Kirkland held a video camera and before long began his morbid film, starting with the surrounding area and possible approaches to the scene. He used the zoom lens to facilitate the filming and prevent him trampling over any minuscule evidence as yet unseen to the naked eye.

Much to the annoyance of Stuart, Wormsley insisted on trying to 'direct' the film. He persistently butted in and generally made a nuisance of himself.

'Don't forget the bag . . . Zoom down on to the approach . . . Get the railway line at the back in . . . Go past the scene towards the estate . . . It looks like there are footprints there, look . . . Get that tin can in and that fag end . . .'

Stuart was recalcitrant and spoke his mind. There was a long day ahead and he needed concentration, not interruptions. 'Look, Mr Wormsley, at the last count I have been the Scenes of Crime officer at twenty murders . . .'

Stark had anticipated friction and tried to make light of it in an attempt to avoid the inevitable confrontation. 'Oh, happy twenty-first!'

The joke was lost and Stuart continued. '. . . So can I please do my bit and we can then discuss it when I've finished. If there's anything you want then, I will gladly do it, if I've missed it.'

Sergeant Kirkland had underestimated the man he was talking to. Wormsley had no intention of being spoken to by a detective sergeant in that vein. He stuck his square chin up and his top lip stretched across his teeth. His response was unerringly grandiloquent. He poked his finger at Stuart to emphasise his tirade.

'No. You look. I'm the senior investigating officer appointed to deal with this murder case. You are a detective sergeant, and if I decide I want something doing, I will tell you, and by Christ, pal, you fucking do it without question! Understand?'

Stuart scowled and turned away, back to his video camera. He shook his head in disgust.

Stark looked heavenwards. How to win friends and influence people!

There was a fracas over on the far side of the crime scene, and Stark's attention was drawn to a group of young boys of around twelve or thirteen who were remonstrating loudly with Sergeant Mick Molesworth.

'It's a police state, that's what it is. If we want to go into the wood, we will do and you can't stop us! I'm going to complain about you, I am.'

The boy didn't see it coming, but his head jerked to one side as it was struck by the open palm of the sergeant.

'Complain about that bugger, you little bleeder. Now get lost!'

The boys ran off, the mouthy one clutching the side of his head.

Stark sighed and mumbled to himself. 'Merry bloody Christmas!'

It was as if there were a stranger in Barbara's room. As the veils of sleep were peeled away, she could hear voices outside and then tyres on gravel. Her eyes opened wide and the walls of her bedroom were strobed with blue light, which ironically shone intermittently on a photograph of her and Cheryl taken on holiday in Spain the previous year.

Within a second she was at the window. She could see the line of police cars and other vehicles stemming all the way back to the main road. A small crowd of onlookers huddled together close to a group of uniformed policemen.

She turned and ran into Cheryl's room, almost knocking the door off its hinges as she entered.

'Cheryl?'

The bed had not been slept in. She raced back to her bedroom window and her eyes traced two parallel lines of red police tape, but the trees obstructed her view of the focal point. Her familiarity with cop television programmes indicated to her that there had been a murder. Her heart raced, and she bit at her fingernails. She threw open the window and before she knew it she was shouting down at those assembled.

'Excuse me, I'm scared. My friend hasn't been in all night. Is everything all right?'

A man in a Crombie overcoat, obviously a detective, glanced up at the window and became aware of several curtains twitching from the block of flats. He homed in on the girl on the second storey with the window wide open, and he could see the worry quite apparent on her face as she leaned out precariously. He put his hand to his mouth and returned the shout.

'I'll send somebody up to see you, love.'

She let the curtain drop and leaned with her back against the wall. She closed her eyes.

'Oh, please God, not Cheryl.'

She gathered her thoughts and laughed somewhat unconvincingly. 'Don't be silly, Barbara, of course it's not Cheryl.'

Curiosity got the better of her and she peered through the gap in the curtain again. A man was walking towards the flat complex. Barbara went to her wardrobe and hurriedly began to dress, her mind flickering through a host of nightmare images, which she attempted to chase away with reasoned arguments. But the nightmare did not go away.

Steve Aston had a lot on his mind. He was a fairly inexperienced detective. He muttered to himself the instructions Stark had given him. 'Go and see the woman at the window, then when you've finished that, follow the body down to the mortuary, along with a Scenes of Crime man, when the undertakers arrive, and take possession of all the deceased's clothing. Wait for the pathologist and then stay with "it" throughout the post-mortem.'

Steve bit at his bottom lip as he approached the flat complex, his bright ginger hair now tousled in the annoying breeze. He wore a multi-coloured ski jacket over his suit which at first glance gave him a bulky appearance, belying his thin frame. Steve was a little under-confident for a man in his mid-twenties. Nobby Clarke hadn't helped him. Nobby had made it quite clear that he thought Steve shouldn't be on CID. Steve was a vegetarian, he didn't drink alcohol and he was a little timid, not quite following in Nobby's footsteps!

'He ought to be a bloody vicar, not a detective!'

Nobby's cruel words had haunted Steve and created a barrier in the development of his confidence, which some of the other DCs played upon, and took full advantage of. Steve was determined to prove them wrong. He wouldn't make a mistake, he wouldn't give them the satisfaction.

He knocked on the door of number 16, Buckingham Avenue. The hard wood caused his cold knuckles to throb and he placed his hand in his pocket. He produced a white handkerchief and blew hard as the door was opened. He spoke through the cloth, giving him a nasal tone.

'Hello, love, I'm from the CID. Nothing to worry about. I wonder if I could have a couple of minutes of your time?' While trying to replace the handkerchief, he began fumbling with his wallet for his warrant card, the handkerchief flapping in the breeze.

Barbara spoke, her face solemn and concerned. 'It's all right, I saw you out the back. I know who you are. You'd better come in.'

36

The two stood rather awkwardly in the hallway. Steve attempted an ice-breaker. 'Oh, it's a lot warmer in here, that's for sure.'

Barbara remained pensive and stared at the callow youth. Steve got down to business. It never really occurred to him that Barbara could be connected with the goings-on in the wood. He had already decided she was a nosy parker after the first hint of gossip. He had not read her face well at all, but then he was not one for looking anyone full in the face if he could avoid it.

'There's been a –'

'Murder.' Barbara finished the sentence for him. 'I know that much. I'm not daft, you know. Who is it?'

'What do you mean?' Steve asked the wall.

'Who is it that's been murdered?' She remained restrained and fought off the overwhelming feeling of panic that engulfed her. If she ignored the thought that it could be Cheryl she felt certain it would not be her.

'I don't know.'

Barbara snapped. She was already annoyed by the spectacle before her. This was not the pre-conceived image she had had of a detective, and his bumbling, seemingly shy behaviour served only to frustrate her even further.

'What do you mean, you don't know? You're a detective, aren't you? Of course you know!' She was shaking.

Steve scrutinised Barbara, her hostility forcing him to meet her stare, and he decided that she was either a nut case or there was something amiss. He looked puzzled.

'Are you all right?'

Barbara swallowed hard. 'Of course I'm not all right. I'm worried it could be my flat-mate down there. She hasn't been home all night, you know. Not that that is particularly unusual – I mean, she's a young girl, why shouldn't she stay out all night? I'm not criticising her. I just wish she had rung or something, that's all.'

'Well, it is a woman that's been killed, but don't worry – I'm sure it won't be her. What does she look like?'

Barbara touched her hair. 'She's got very blonde, short hair. God, I don't know, she's got a biggish nose, and blue eyes, and she always wears a gold necklace her mum bought her for her birthday. The woman – you know, the victim – she doesn't look like that, does she?'

'Well, she does, although I don't think she had a necklace on, but I did only have a brief look at her.' Steve chomped on a Polo mint which he had gratefully received from Stark.

Barbara grasped at the one thing that discounted Cheryl. 'No necklace. Oh, thank God!' She sighed. 'For some reason, I thought it was going to be her. I don't know why, I just did. Oh, thank you, God.'

Steve gulped. 'Can you remember what your friend was wearing?'

'Yes, let me think . . . A beige raincoat, a blue cardigan, a white blouse, at least I think it was white, and a shoulder bag with a bright metal clasp.'

Steve went a whiter shade than his normal anaemic appearance. He was stuck for words.

Barbara saw it in his eyes. Her tears welled up and her trembling intensified. 'She hasn't got . . . I mean the woman that's dead . . . she isn't, she can't be . . .'

Steve did not need to reply. She bit at her nails and screwed her eyelids tightly together, forcing out a tear. She slid down the wall on to the floor and sobbed – heartrending sobs that reverberated around the flat.

Steve stood and watched, his arms hanging at his sides limply.

'I'm sorry, love,' was all he could muster.

3

'I got the bill for my surgery. Now I know what
those doctors were wearing masks for.'
JAMES H. BOREN

A dozen or so Christmas cards were festooned on the notice-
board of Nottingham CID office. A vain attempt by some of the
younger DCs to adorn the room with the odd piece of festive
décor had resulted in two silver stars hanging from the ceiling
and the almost obligatory two round balloons with a long phallic
one in the middle, now dangling limply from one corner. There
were eighteen desks crowded into the room, one for each detective. They were assembled in four clusters, denoting each individual 'shift' of men. Accounting for abstractions and leave and
sickness, there were only usually about eleven detectives left in
total who were available to work on a day-to-day basis. Two of
the shifts were on days and one was due to work afternoons. The
other shift were day-off.

One of the Nottingham detectives, Jim McIntyre, of Scottish
descent, leaned back on his chair, fag in mouth, dropping ash on
to the floor as he continued his annual derogatory observations.
He was overweight, with a pock-marked face and an ill-fitting
suit. His audience of four detectives had heard similar derision
from him in previous years.

'I'm just saying that I think Christmas is not only a waste of
time, it's a bloody *expensive* waste of time. Everywhere you go,
there are drab people walking the streets, spending money they
haven't got on presents nobody wants.'

Ashley Stevens toyed with his gold ring, smiling at Jim's scepticism. He offered his contribution in a vain attempt to change the
subject.

39

'It doesn't look as though there is going to be much Christmas cheer in this office anyway, with a murder running.'

Jim was in full flow. 'Screw the murder. I want somebody to tell me how, simply because we get into the middle of December, nobby greens, potatoes and every toy on the market increase in price.'

Grant Donaldson, the only black detective in the office, ignored Jim and concentrated on writing a statement for a crime prosecution file that was long overdue for submission. He had never liked Jim, who he thought was racist, ignorant and beyond his time as a detective. A dinosaur who was bigoted and beyond any sort of change or compromise. A fair description, really.

Ash was drawn into another reply. 'What are you talking about "nobby greens" for? For Christ's sake!'

'You go down to Harold's shop on the Main Street now and I bet you –'

Ash groaned.

'No, let me finish. I bet you, right, that there is at least three pence on the price of Brussels sprouts.'

Jim spoke with such conviction about his nobby greens that Barry Marsh could not help but laugh. Barry was new to the office, having transferred from West Bridgford. He had a distinct Welsh accent and had quickly endeared himself to his peers because of his quick wit and easy temperament. He saw an opportunity for ribaldry. It was easy with Jim, who was not the most intelligent man on the force.

'Yes, you're right, Jim, but I bet you that if you were to measure each Brussels sprout, you would find that they are bigger in circumference by at least a millimetre and that overall you are still getting value for money. But you must check your carrier bag after you have emptied them in case a leaf or two has fallen off, otherwise you may be losing out.' Barry's face was deadpan.

Jim frowned. There was a pause. Grant was giggling. Jim looked at Ashley. 'Is he taking the piss or what?'

Barry stood up and placed an arm around Jim's shoulder. 'I wouldn't take the piss out of you, Jim, now would I?'

Jim shrugged him off, obviously hurt. 'I was only passing a comment, that's all. Sorry for breathing, I'm sure. But I still think I'm right.'

There was a slight lull in the conversation. Barry went to put on the kettle, which was kept on a counter that ran down one wall of the office.

Charlie Carter joined him.

Charlie had many redeeming features, one of which was that, although he had the most service in, with seventeen years as a detective, he was not averse to joining in and making a cuppa for the lads. Charlie was as keen to detect crime today as he was the day he joined, which forged a bond of respect from the younger element in the office. He always had time to help out the lads if they had a problem. He was something of an enigma at the station, where there were many stories of his past exploits.

Barry went around the office collecting dirty mugs that were still on desks from the night before. He placed them on the tea-stained tray and spoke to Charlie, although his question was directed towards the body of the office.

'Have you seen the Chief Constable's latest order?'

'No, I haven't mate. What's that?' Charlie asked.

'Three pints of lager and a bitter shandy!'

Charlie laughed. 'Why are you such a prat?'

'I don't know. It comes naturally, really.'

Barry's Welsh twang continued the usual trivial conversation.

'Hey, Ash, have you told your beloved that Christmas is cancelled this year yet?'

Ashley was loath to allow his reputation for numerous assignations with the opposite sex to be smeared. 'Which one?'

'Don't give me that. How long have you been seeing Christie? Six months?'

'It's seven months, two weeks, three days, twelve hours and . . .' He looked at his watch. '. . . sixteen minutes. On and off.'

Barry laughed. 'Yeah, it would be on and off with you as well, wouldn't it?'

'No, I've not told her, what's the point? We don't know who's going to be working on the murder yet, do we?'

Grant, who had been on the CID almost a year, joined in: 'Surely all of us will be, won't we?'

Charlie spoke with experience, a twinkle as ever in his eye. 'Don't bet on it, mate. Somebody's got to stay and hold the fort. Day-to-day crime won't stop because we've got a murder running, you know.'

'No, I suppose not.'

41

Barry was honest. 'I hope I'm on it. I can hand that bloody pile of undetected house burglaries on the Ruffs Estate over to some poor bugger then.'

Ash spoke. 'Haven't you detected those yet? Come on, Barry, get a grip. All daytime burglaries, same MO, it's got to be the same lot that's doing them, surely?'

'Well, I'm open to suggestions, Sherlock. It's not the usual lads. There's only one set of prints that have been left and I've checked over thirty names and it's none of those.'

Charlie smiled wryly. 'You'd need to check three hundred names and even then you might miss him.'

Barry sighed. 'Yeah, tell me about it. Anyway, when I get seconded on to the murder enquiry, Ashley, you can show me how it's done. I'll hand it all over to you. You can be my beneficiary.'

'Oh, no, you won't, but I do promise you, as a token of my friendship, that you can have my theft of mailbags, when I get seconded to the murder.'

Barry emphasised his Welsh accent. 'Yocken, boyo, yocken.'

'What do you mean, "Yocken"?'

'It's an old Welsh phrase, mate. Yocken. I'm surprised you've never heard of it. It's better placed in front of another word.'

'Oh yes, what's that?'

'Yocken bollocks!'

The room exploded into laughter, interrupted by the telephone ringing.

Grant reached over to answer it.

'This is it, this is the call,' Barry said excitedly.

Grant waved the others away as they crowded around the phone.

'Yes, sir . . . right . . . Ashley and Barry, yes, okay . . . half an hour . . . what, at the scene or at Sherwood Lodge?'

Ashley and Barry were beaming at each other – a chance at last to be relieved of the mountain of paperwork that had built up in recent weeks, despite the fact that some other poor sod would have to do it.

Grant continued. '. . . Charlie, yes, he's here. Right, okay then, sir. Cheers.' Grant replaced the handset.

Barry shook Charlie's hand. 'Looks like you're coming too, pal.'

42

Grant turned around and made his announcement. 'That was Stark. Ashley and Barry –'

Ash interrupted. 'Yes, where have we got to go?'

'Ashley and Barry are to remain at section while the rest of us go on the murder!'

Steve Aston battled with the CID car. The wind was now joined by hail and he struggled to see through the windscreen as the flakes lashed down on to the Ford Fiesta. He could barely see the hearse in front.

Steve had been happy to leave Barbara back at the flat, safe in the capable hands of Detective Policewoman Stephanie Dawson. He knew that he did not have the capacity to handle grief as capably as Steph.

He negotiated the ramps that were spread along the length of the road that swept through the grounds of the City Hospital. He parked close by the rear door of the mortuary and quickly ran across the car-park in time to stoop under the metal shutters as they were raised. The hearse had backed up to the shutters and Tony, the mortician, hastily wheeled up an elevated 'stretcher' to meet the corpse.

Tony, in his early thirties, could be said to lack an interest in personal hygiene. His dark hair was straggly and not a little greasy and his fingers were nicotine-stained. He wore a white cotton waist-length coat that was fraying at the cuffs. He nodded to Steve.

'Lovely day.'

'You're joking, aren't you?'

'I'm bloody not joking. Every day's a lovely day while you're still pulling breath.' Tony smiled.

The mortician dragged the bagged-up corpse on to the stretcher and pushed it forwards away from his body, forcing it to free-wheel along the concrete floor. The momentum of the stretcher eventually slowed and it came to a standstill opposite the wall of 'body drawers'.

Steve hated the mortuary. He had been several times and his opinion of the place and of the staff had not improved. Especially Tony – he seemed actually to enjoy his job, and his crude references and jocular approach made Steve feel ill at ease. Some detectives seemed to be at home there. Not Steve.

Tony waved a gleeful farewell to the undertakers and started to unzip the bag.

'What have we got here then?'

'It's a murder job, a young girl. She's been raped,' Steve informed him.

'Oh aye. Was she worth it, then?'

Steve shook his head. 'God, you're sick, you are, Tony.'

Tony finished unzipping and gazed down at the ravaged face of Cheryl Towlson.

'Mmm, not bad. Not my cup of tea, but there you are. It takes all sorts to make a world, doesn't it?'

'You can say that again.' Steve sneered, making his disgust apparent.

'Don't you like it here, my pal?' Tony asked, slapping the young detective on the back.

'Not really. It stinks, it's full of corpses and it has an atmosphere.'

'Well, what do you expect to find in a hospital mortuary – subtle lighting and background music?'

'No, but you know what I mean. All those drawers there, full of bodies, you can't see them but you know they're there. Old people, kids, car accidents. It's horrible.'

'You ought to have a look in that drawer at the bottom, that's my bits and pieces drawer. Full of arms or bits that have fallen off. We had a head in there last week. No body, just a head.'

'Do you mind?'

'No, I don't, as a matter of fact, but then again, it's not my head, is it? Are you coming for a cuppa? The butcher won't be down here for a while yet.'

The two walked towards an annexe room that was shielded by net curtains. Tony switched the kettle on. He was smiling. He did exaggerate his image a trifle to the likes of Steve, but he enjoyed the looks of revulsion his attitude generated from those unable to comprehend the reason for it.

The two men sat down and Tony lit a cigarette. Two more different people you wouldn't find.

'Smoke?'

'No, thanks.' Steve shifted in his chair. 'How long did you say the pathologist would be?'

Stark stood, hands in pockets, bending over at the side of the two crouched figures. The burst of hail had abated, but the continuing drizzle was sufficient to cause annoyance. The two Scenes of Crime officers were somewhat more comfortable under the tarpaulin as they photographed an indentation that was quite apparently a footprint. There was a distinct wedge cut in what would have been the upper part of the sole of one of the shoes. Stark was pleased at the job Stuart Kirkland had done. There was a chill in the air, and Stark's teeth were starting to hurt with the biting cold. Stark turned and caught sight of Nobby, bidding farewell to Albert. A thought crossed his mind. He hoped he was wrong. He churned his legs into action and the muscles warmed in response, as he jogged over to Nobby. He took hold of Albert's arm.

'Excuse me a second, please.'

'He's just said I can go home. What's up now?' The old man was tired and drawn, his wrinkled face sagging under the weight of the morning's events.

'Nothing's up. I just want to have a look at the soles of your shoes, if I may.'

Steam issued through the man's yellowing teeth. He let out a sigh and frowned.

'Aye, all right, youth, if you must.'

Stark took hold of each shoe as a blacksmith might with a horse. He examined the left sole and then the right. The right sole had a distinct wedge cut into it. The footprints at the scene were those of Albert!

'Bloody hell.'

'Is something wrong, then, or what?' Albert asked, slight concern furrowing his already wrinkled brow.

Stark sighed. 'No, nothing's wrong. Forget it. There was a footprint at the scene and unfortunately it happens to be yours. I was kind of hoping it would be the killer's. Never mind. Thanks for your help.'

Albert clucked at Sal, his Border collie, and trundled off into the cold. He stopped and coughed up some phlegm that was quickly dispatched on to the soil.

Wormsley appeared from nowhere, as was his wont. 'Anything else turned up, David?'

'No, sir. The bloody footprint is the old man's. You know, the bloke that found her.'

Wormsley again stuck out his square chin, an almost comical habit of his. 'How old is he?'

'He's about eighty . . . Here, you don't think? . . . No, I can't see it.'

'I'm just saying that he should be revisited. It might not be him but he might know something. It's basics again, David. We have a murderer to catch and that's exactly what we will do – catch him.'

'I know. I'm not arguing with you.'

The two men stood hunched over slightly in the bitter breeze. Nobby shouted over to Stark, from the back of the houses.

'Are you there, boss?'

'Yes, Nobby?'

'Special Ops are here. Can they start house-to-house?'

Stark glanced at Wormsley. The DI strolled towards the group of uniformed men and, to his dismay, Wormsley remained in tow. Stark gave his instructions.

'Make a start on this row of houses, lads, can you? They'll have to be done again, but let's just make sure that there is nothing staring us in the face in the immediate area. Half of you can start searching around the scene now SOCO have finished. DS Clarke here will tell you the brief scenario.'

Stark turned to speak softly with Wormsley. 'What time shall I tell them to attend the briefing? I take it we are going to set a Major Incident Room up at Sherwood Lodge?'

Wormsley spoke to the men. 'Back at Sherwood Lodge for 11.30 a.m. for a full briefing. Nobby, stay here and supervise. Let me know if anything dramatic rears its head.'

Nobby drew his hand to his forehead and gave a Yankee-type salute. Men like Wormsley held no fear for him.

Wormsley placed a firm grip on Stark's shoulder and gave him a rare smile. 'Back to the ranch then, David.'

Professor Disney-Hargreaves was the top pathologist in the area. He was in his early fifties, with greying hair and a drained face. He was a popular man and well respected in medical and police circles alike. He had a businessman's aura of confidence. The green attire that he wore ill suited him. The V-necked T-shirt, baggy trousers and pumps belied his professional status.

Stuart Kirkland from the Scenes of Crime had arrived, and he and Steve Aston had donned white 'Andy Pandy' suits and plastic shoe coverings. The professor stood away from the corpse as Tony began to cut away the clothing from the dead girl. Each article was placed to one side and photographed by Kirkland. Once this was done, Steve gingerly searched through the pockets. Tony was careful not to sever the knot of the ligature that he peeled away, revealing red and blue contusions and an indentation around the circumference of the dead girl's neck.

The four men accompanied Cheryl Towlson into the post-mortem room. There were five slabs and the men heaved the solid lump that was Cheryl on to the one at the far end of the room. An array of tools lay at the feet of the body: metal scissors, knives and a round-edged 'hacksaw' that would subsequently unceremoniously cut through the sternum of the deceased. The electrical trepan was close by, ready to shear off the top of the skull, affording access to the brain.

The men were joined by a rather attractive woman in her late thirties, with tied-back hair and wearing a white coat. She was Disney-Hargreave's secretary, and would take notes at his dictation as he undertook the examination. His cultured and well-articulated voice and the presence of his secretary gave a bizarre feel to the proceedings. Take a letter, Miss Jones! Those assembled huddled close around the corpse in the grim theatre. Today's main attraction: Cheryl Towlson.

The pathologist began by an external visual examination, commenting on any bruising or cuts. He placed a thermometer into the anus of the deceased; Stuart hurriedly appropriated it after the reading had been obtained. The sexual nature of the murder necessitated its seizure in case semen had been transferred on to it via the anal passage. Better to be safe than sorry.

Tony was quick to make a remark, as Stuart released the thermometer from his two-fingered grip into a plastic bag.

'The weather forecast said there would be a drop in temperature!'

Tony's cutting comment was to be followed by cutting of an even cruder nature.

You either liked Nobby Clarke or hated him; there was no in-between. Nobby had a ruddy complexion with peasant-like features. His body was firm and he was as strong as an ox. He was certainly rough at the edges, but life had dealt him quite a few bum hands. He was a former Regimental Sergeant Major in the Parachute Regiment and had undertaken three tours of duty in Northern Ireland. He'd been involved in a stormy marriage that ended abruptly when his wife was killed in a car accident two years before he left the army. It had seemed to him the most natural step in the world to return home and join the police force. That was in the early seventies, a time when a hard man such as Nobby was welcomed with open arms, and when courage and loyalty were high on the list of desired qualities, in contrast to today's concentration on academic achievement. He had quickly been identified as a suitable candidate for the CID, with his steadfast ways and terrier-like determination to see a job through, and was eventually promoted to Detective Sergeant after a spell on the Regional Crime Squad.

He was currently involved in a personal battle with apathy and disillusionment, fuelled by the new breed of officers who were getting promoted above him, men who gave him orders but with whom he would have refused to work in the old days in Belfast; men he would not send to the shops for sweeties, never mind trust with his own life. He did however have a lot of time for David Stark. He had worked with Dave first of all over fifteen years ago at Central police station, and knew him as a man he could trust and relate to. The feeling was mutual.

He had been seeing Detective Policewoman Stephanie Dawson on the quiet now for a good six months. The relationship had done him good and helped to get him out of the rut into which he found himself being drawn. She was somewhat younger than he and she was a 'cracker', to use his vernacular.

He could see Steph near the window as he watched from the

street below. She was pacing the room on the first floor of the flat complex. He was aware that she had been left to talk with the dead girl's flat-mate and decided he would pay her a visit to offer his assistance. Special Operations Unit didn't need him hovering over them; they had their own sergeant to do that. He gave a loud knock on the flat door. Steph answered and greeted him with a pensive smile.

'Come in, Sarge.'

She led Nobby into the lounge and introduced him to Barbara, who puffed on a cigarette. Her black hair had not yet been combed and her hands were still shaking.

Nobby's voice was deep. He never spoke quietly and its loudness was accentuated in the tense atmosphere of grief.

'I'm sorry to hear about what's happened, love. We are doing everything we can. I promise you we'll catch the bloke that's done this.'

Barbara nodded.

Nobby looked at Steph, who excused herself from Barbara and went with him into the hallway.

She spoke first. 'Try and keep your voice down, Nobby, I know it's difficult for you, but she's upset.'

'What's the crack then?'

Steph leaned against the wall and, as always, gesticulated heavily with her hands as she spoke. 'Well, it seems that the dead girl lived here with Barbara. They've only just moved in. Her name is Cheryl Towlson.'

'Yeah, we know that from credit cards in her purse. Has she any idea who might have done it, or haven't you got that far?'

'I've not tried her on that yet. As I say, she's very upset. All she has said is that Cheryl went out to work around ten o'clock and never came home.'

'Let's have a chat with her, then.'

'All right, but go easy on the girl.'

Nobby moved closer to Steph and smiled. 'What do you think I am, some kind of animal?'

She gave him a sideways glance. 'No comment!'

The two returned to the smoky confines of the living-room and Nobby sat down next to Barbara, who was staring vacantly. Nobby noticed an empty cup of coffee next to her.

'Do you want another cuppa, Barbara?'

She came to life and looked at Nobby, her eyes red with tears. 'No, thanks.'

'Listen, love . . .'

Barbara interrupted him. 'I know. I know why you are here and it's just hit me. It's hit me like a bloody steam train.'

'What has, Barbara?'

She pursed her lips and shook her head. More tears welled up in her eyes. She took a deep breath before speaking. 'It's Patrick, isn't it?'

'Who's Patrick?'

Barbara stood up and walked towards the window. Nobby shot a puzzled glance over to Steph, who shrugged her shoulders and shook her head.

'Patrick,' Barbara continued. 'Patrick Dunn, I'll bloody kill him. I will. I'll pissing kill him!'

Both Nobby and Steph got up. Steph put her arm around Barbara and comforted her as she broke down again, her body jerking spasmodically.

'Calm down Barbara,' Steph said soothingly. 'I know it's difficult, love, but we can handle it. Just take a deep breath.'

'I know you can handle it, but she was only a kid. This is going to kill her mum and dad, you know. I just can't believe that Patrick would do this to her!'

'All right. Who's Patrick, Barbara?'

'Her ex, Cheryl's ex-boyfriend. It's just come to me – he rang her up the other night at the party, swore at her, called her a fucking bitch or something. It's got to be him that's done this to her. Why, though? Why?'

'How do you know that it was Patrick on the phone? How can you be so sure?' Steph asked.

Barbara struggled to catch her breath. She swallowed hard. 'Cheryl told me. I asked her the same question, but she was positive it was him. He called her by her pet name, she said – some name he always called her. She didn't tell me what it was, she was too embarrassed, but it was him, it was definitely him.'

'What's his full name, Barbara?'

'Patrick Dunn. He lives in Bulwell. It's him, all right, he threatened her. She was going to see him about it today. Oh my God. Why? You silly sod, Patrick. I even rang him myself last night to

50

ask if he had seen Cheryl. My God, he was as cool as anything. You had better get to him before I do, that's all I can say!'

Barbara wrestled free from Steph's supporting arm.

Steph spoke softly but reassuringly. 'Don't worry. We will sort this out. Don't you bother yourself about that, you just concentrate on resting for the time being.'

'I'm all right, honest. Just you go and get him, you won't need to look far. She was going to see him after work – she told me herself. I never expected this. I didn't know him that well. If I'd ever thought he would do something like this, I would never have let her go, honest I wouldn't.'

The realisation had given Barbara a new resolve. She gave Nobby Patrick's details.

Mr Dunn was due a visit from the nice policemen.

4

'Never forget what a man says to you when he is
angry.'
HENRY WARD BEECHER

Stark had taken over the office at the far end of the Major Incident
Room at Force Headquarters, Sherwood Lodge. He closed the
door, blocking out the chatter of those detectives who had already assembled and who sat around an array of computer terminals and telephones. He scribbled down various points in a
notepad and was checking them over as the door burst open. It
was Wormsley.

'Right then, David, let us have a chat about the investigation so
far, shall we?'

'Yes, okay. I was just jotting down the state of play as you came in.'

Wormsley sat down in the corner and reclined slightly in the
chair. He made himself comfortable and crossed his legs, displaying a frightful inch of bare white leg above his sock.

Stark began, tapping a tube of Polo mints on the desk in rhythm
with his speech, a meagre substitute for his sorely missed pipe.

'Right, the body has been identified as that of Cheryl Towlson,
aged nineteen years, who lived at 16, Buckingham Avenue,
Hucknall. The post-mortem reveals the cause of death as as-
phyxiation caused by a ligature pulled tightly around her neck.
The ligature appears to be her own tights that she had been
wearing prior to the attack. Now, we know that sexual inter-
course had taken place prior to her death, which is roughly
estimated as around teatime-ish yesterday. We assume that she
was raped. I know it is dangerous to assume anything, but I think
we are on fairly safe ground there. She was semi-naked, albeit
there is not much sign of a struggle in the foliage around her

body, and she had been struck in the face a couple of times, prior to death.'

Wormsley stared out of the window, nodding his head occasionally from his seated position as Stark continued.

'The good news is that there are traces of semen in her vagina, none in her stomach. So once we have a suspect, a straight DNA check will tell us one way or the other whether that suspect has done it or not. Once they break the sperm down and any suspect's blood, they can compile the DNA read out and compare the two.'

Wormsley was pensive. 'Assuming it is as easy as that and we fall across the right suspect.'

'Is anything as straightforward as it at first seems?' Stark asked philosophically, before continuing on a more optimistic note. 'However, having said all that, the good news is that we have a prime suspect straight away, a youth called Patrick Dunn.'

Wormsley diverted his attention from the window towards Stark. 'Oh, right. Who's he then, David?'

'He is the deceased's ex-boyfriend. Apparently he made a malicious telephone call to her, and this Cheryl Towlson had told her flat-mate that she was going around to see him after work, at teatime!'

Wormsley raised his eyebrows. 'That sounds interesting, although why would he kill her at the back of her flat?'

'Unless the body was dumped there?'

Wormsley looked heavenwards. 'Christ, I hope not, otherwise we haven't got a crime scene! Go on, what else have we got, David?'

'Well, a neighbour at number 20, Buckingham Avenue heard a scream around twelve o'clock at night, but thought it was kids messing around, so paid it no heed.'

'It sounds a bit late if the pathologist puts the time of death around teatime.'

'Yeah, but we've seen this before, haven't we? The time of death really can only be put down as between the time she was last seen alive and the time she was discovered dead.'

'True. Who was the last person to see her alive?'

'We think it would be somebody at work but we haven't had a chance to check that out yet. We can't say for certain; I thought we could leave that until after the briefing.'

Stark leaned back and tapped his pen on the edge of the desk. He fished out another mint from the tightly wrapped packet. They were becoming addictive themselves.

Wormsley leaned back in the chair and put his hands behind his head, stretching the fibres of his brown suit.

'Yes, fair enough. I think we'll have a quick briefing and then go and arrest Patrick Dunn. I can't see the point in setting up HOLMES* yet. What's the point in calling people out and logging all the information on the HOLMES computers if we crack it in the first day?'

'Okay. We might as well have a quick word with the troops and then go after Dunn. Are you doing the briefings or shall I?' Stark asked.

'You do them, David. I'll sit in on them when I can and I'll pipe up if there is anything I want to say.'

Stark stood up, easing his chair away with the back of his knees as he did so. 'Fair enough. Let's see if they've all arrived yet.'

The telephone rang and Stark promptly answered. He stared at Wormsley as he spoke, feeling slightly embarrassed. It was his old friend and colleague, Jerry Whittaker, from Radford Road CID.

'Yes, thanks for ringing back, Jerry. Listen, will you do me a favour? I'm a bit stuck for time. You probably know I'm in the middle of this bloody murder, and I'm going to get enough grief as it is. It'll only take half an hour. Will you nip into town and get me a present for my missus?'

Stark saw Wormsley raise his eyes to the ceiling for a second time, in obvious disapproval.

'Yes, go down to the jeweller's and get her a gold bracelet, and get her two or three charms for it to start her off, will you? Have you got enough money?' Stark stopped speaking, before continuing. 'I don't know . . . about seventy or eighty quid, and get her a card as well, will you? Nothing too soppy, though.' There was a pause. 'Are you sure? Thanks a lot, mate. Listen – thinking about it, I'll leave the money with the receptionist and just put the present in my top drawer when you've got it, will you? For God's sake, don't forget, otherwise we'll have another murder on the sub-division! . . . Thanks a lot, Jerry. I owe you one . . .'

---

* Home Office Large Major Enquiry System.

Wormsley remained impassive. 'Shall we make a start on more serious matters, then, or is there anything else?'

'No, I think we can make a start now, boss.' Stark smiled.

George Jackson was a postman. He had been a postman for nineteen years, since the age of twenty-two. He liked being a postman, which was a bonus. He enjoyed the mixture of sorting the mail within the confines of the sorting depot and then going out on the firm's bicycle, facing the elements and delivering the letters. Christmas, for obvious reasons, is an exceptionally busy time for the men and women of the postal service, not only because of the hundreds of thousands of Christmas cards, but with the vast increase in parcel deliveries they have to undertake. George did not mind too much. The overtime enabled him in turn to buy presents for his own family and friends, and the pressure lasted barely a month.

It was with a sense of relief that he heaved the two heavy grey bags on to the bicycle in the rear yard of the depot. He always preferred the streets to the banal banter of the sorting office. He was a quiet sort of bloke and an obvious target for the loud-mouths at work who, in such an environment, were quick to harass the likes of George. He put on his bicycle clips and started cycling off towards his area. The breeze flowing through his greying hair added to the feeling of freedom as his face encountered the cool air. He began to hum to himself as he steadily pedalled along. The very nature of the job of delivering letters places the postman on 'auto-pilot'. In any case George was a creature of habit. He dismounted at the bottom of Papplewick Lane at Hucknall, parked his bike and began rustling through the contents of his bag. He took out two large clumps of letters which he had sorted for Papplewick Lane and began his trek down the hill. He would proceed along the odd numbers and then return along the even numbers side, back to his cycle and off to the next street. Unfortunately Papplewick Lane consisted of a mixture of terraced, semi-detached and detached houses with their own gates and segregating walls, which meant George could not cut across the front lawns of the houses to save time, as could be done in the new-style open-plan dwellings. He quickly strode along, in and out of the gardens like a bee visiting different bunches of roses, with a sense of purpose, happy in his work.

As he whistled his way to the top of the street, he saw a figure darting along at the bottom of the road, running at some speed. George stopped momentarily because the frenetic movement of the youth was quite out of the ordinary and he watched in amazement as the figure quite blatantly hopped on to his cycle and rode off in the opposite direction towards Papplewick itself, complete with delivery bags and all.

George shouted a desperate 'Oi!' but to no avail. He even ran a few steps but it was pointless. The youth had nicked his bike, but more importantly the mail within the bags. The dole cheques, credit cards and cheque books that had been entrusted to the post disappeared from sight.

George stood in the middle of the road, hands on hips, and said aloud, 'Well, bloody hell! Would you credit it?'

He began to walk back towards the depot, his bicycle clips, now redundant, still clasped around his ankles. He thrust his hands in his pockets and lowered his head to meet the gusts of wind, which seemed colder than before. He stopped and checked, turning around and looking back in case by some miracle his bicycle was back where he had left it.

'The little sod!'

Ashley Stevens scribbled on to the Record of Interview sheet. He had earphones on and gazed vacantly ahead as he waited for the laborious tape of interview to get to the evidential part that was worthy of record. It was an interview he had done several days ago with a burglar, about his exploits in Bulwell. It was all really quite boring, but he daren't risk fast forwarding it, in case he missed a vital piece of evidence. The interview had taken forty-five minutes to complete. The subsequent written summary would take two or three hours at least. With the stopping and starting and much scribbling of salient points, it was a horrendously tedious affair.

Barry Marsh lifted one of the headphones away from Ashley's ear. 'Concorde to Air Traffic Control. Permission to land. Over.'

Ashley removed the earphones. 'Bog off, Barry, will you? I'm trying to get this tape sorted. There's another six there to do when I've finished this.'

'So terribly sorry, old boy,' he articulated in the fashion of an English gentleman before reverting to his Welsh twang to justify the interruption. 'There's a phone call for you, mate – Post Office Investigation.'

Ashley strolled over to Barry's desk and picked up the phone. 'DC Stevens.'

'Hello, there. It's Derek Cantwell from Post Office ID. I just thought I'd let you know we've had another mailbag snatch.'

'Wonderful! Where at?'

'Papplewick Lane at Hucknall, about three-quarters of an hour ago. I thought you would be interested, seeing as you are dealing with the other one.'

'Yes, I would – I mean, I am. Thanks, Derek. I'll let Uniform know and follow it up myself. Where's the postman now?'

'He's in our office. I think you'll find it's legit. The bloke's worked with us for years; he's as honest as the day's long.'

'All right, pal, let me know when you've done and I'll see him for a statement. Any chance of an ID on the offender?'

'Not a prayer, mate. He's guessing at the age. There's not even anything particularly identifiable about the description.'

'I just thought it might be worth passing out to our patrols.'

'Well, if anybody sees a youth without postal uniform cycling along with two mailbags on the back of the bike, it might be worth a stop and check.'

Ashley laughed. 'Sounds fair enough to me. Two bags, how many letters is that?'

'It tends to vary, but I would say at least a thousand letters.'

'Oh Gawd. All right, Derek, give us a tinkle when you've finished at your end.'

'Okay, then. What time did you have in mind to see him?'

'After dinner, probably – about 14:30, something like that.'

'Okay, then. Cheers.'

Ashley replaced the receiver. Barry passed comment.

'14:30! You'll do well to do that. My watch only goes up to twelve!'

Stark's mini-briefing had left some of the troops rather deflated.

They had been psyched up for a long-running murder investigation and there he was telling them it could be detected in the next couple of hours. He had chosen Charlie Carter and Grant Donaldson to attend Patrick Dunn's house in one vehicle, with himself and Nobby in another. A group of Special Operations men were following in a Transit van behind. They would do the searching after the arrest had been effected.

As arranged, Nobby pulled in a couple of streets away from the target house to ensure that they all arrived together. Once Charlie and the SOU van drew in behind him, he drove off again, around the corner and outside the front of the semi-detached house. The men alighted. Charlie and Grant went to the rear door while Stark and Nobby approached the front.

Patrick Dunn was twenty-four years old. He had fairly long brown hair and a wispy moustache. He tended to wear baggy jumpers with sleeves that extended over his wrists. He hoped one day to have his own business; he was a brickies' labourer, but had visions of a better future, a nice little business, just enough income for a comfortable future for him and Cheryl and perhaps a couple of kiddies when the time was right. But no, that wasn't good enough for her, she wanted to go out 'clubbing' it and living the high life. She wasn't ready for any sort of commitment, now that she had shacked up with that tart Barbara.

Brickies' labourers can have a lot of leisure time during the winter months and Patrick's was spent glued to satellite television and moping around thinking about Cheryl and what could have been. He sat sprawled out on the settee and was surprised to hear the banging on the door. He rose quickly to his feet, and was taken aback to see two burly men on his doorstep.

Stark introduced himself. 'Hello there, I'm from the CID. Are you Patrick?'

'Yes, I am. Is there a problem?' Patrick felt ill at ease. The men appeared serious.

'No problem, mate. Can we come in?'

'Yes, sure. What's up?'

As the two men entered, Stark asked if there were any other people in the house.

'No, just me and two cats, that's all.'

'So you are Patrick Dunn, are you?'

'Yes. What's the matter? Is something wrong?'

Still he got no answer from his quite legitimate question.

Nobby spoke for the first time. 'Can you open your back door, Patrick? There are two of our friends out there and it is a bit nippy out.'

Patrick looked puzzled and ambled towards the rear door to admit Grant and Charlie. Stark controlled the proceedings as Patrick returned to the living-room.

'Patrick, I'm not going to mess about with you. Cheryl Towlson was found murdered this morning. I understand you threatened her the other night on the telephone and in fact saw her only last night. I am therefore arresting you on suspicion of Cheryl's murder. You are not obliged to say anything unless you wish to do so but what you say may be given in evidence.'

Stark had no alternative but to arrest him, because if he asked Patrick to attend the police station voluntarily, he could leave at any time.

Patrick stared at Stark, mouth agape. He blinked several times and swallowed hard. He stammered out a reply: 'Cheryl's been murdered?'

'That's right, Patrick, and we need to have a very serious chat.'

Patrick was agog. 'I don't believe it. Surely there's been some sort of mistake?'

'There's no mistake, Patrick, my old love. You're coming with us.'

Stark had considered breaking the news rather more gently but that would have betrayed to Patrick a doubt that he was the murderer and he felt it necessary to show control from the very outset. Stark laid down the law to the seemingly astonished young man.

'One thing I will say to you though, Patrick, is that the truth will out, whatever it is, and if you are involved, and we think you are, then I think I can offer you some words of advice.' Stark leaned towards him, his face close to Patrick's acne scars, his eyes glaring as he spoke. 'Tell us about it from the bloody start. This is a murder investigation and if it's you, my pal, then we will prove it. People do things for all sorts of reasons and whatever is done is done, and nobody can turn the clock back now, can they?'

Patrick dropped down into an armchair and stared straight ahead. He shook his head. 'No, no way . . . she can't be dead, she just can't be!' He started to cry. 'No way, man. I loved that girl.'

He sobbed, covering his face with his hands. 'It's nothing to do with me, honestly.'

Stark placed a hand on his shoulder. He wanted to show that the hard-faced bastard that he was portraying did have another side to him. 'All right, son, it'll all be sorted out, don't worry yourself. The sooner we get you back to the nick, the sooner this mess can be sorted out.'

He glanced at Nobby, who raised a sneering lip. Nobby smiled over at Charlie. He spoke dispassionately. 'Nip and fetch the SOU lads in, Charlie, will you? Let's get them started. I want this place searching from top to bottom.' He added the final bit for Patrick's sake. 'There's plenty of forensic evidence at the scene and we don't want to waste time now, do we?'

Charlie disappeared out of the front door, while Grant solemnly watched the sorry sight on the armchair, his hands in front of his face as if in prayer.

Stark saw Patrick's breakdown as an opportunity, perhaps the only one that would come his way. An image of the dead girl appeared in his mind's eye, semi-naked, undignified, eaten away at the face. The law said he must not interview the man unless he should happen to 'volunteer' anything, until they were in a position to tape the interview back at the station. He spoke.

'I think I know how you feel, Patrick.'

The youth was distraught. Sobs wracked his body and he drew breath as a crying child might, his bottom lip trembling, his breathing disjointed. He spoke softly. 'I'm so sorry . . .'

Nobby raised his eyebrows. Could it be that easy?

Stark's expectations rose. 'I know, Patrick, take your time. Sorry about what?'

'I'm so sorry for Bill and Norma – Cheryl's mum and dad. Do they know yet?'

Nobby pursed his lips. This was not quite what he had hoped to hear.

Stark answered the question. 'That's being sorted out, Patrick. You just think about the position you're in for now, because it's time for the truth, son.'

Patrick looked Stark in the eye, tears trickling down his cheeks.

'You don't give a shit about Cheryl, do you? You just want an easy admission, don't you? Well, you've got the wrong man, buster. I wouldn't hurt Cheryl. I wouldn't hurt a hair on her head. You lot make me fucking sick. You come in here accusing people, it's easy money for you, I suppose; well, nobody likes you, we all hate you, you're useless! I think it's blood money, living off death and pain, getting paid for supposedly helping people. You don't help anybody; you just cause them grief. You're a joke, you just don't give a toss. You're all fucking parasites!'

Stark could hear the SOU lads approaching noisily as they appeared in the open doorway. Their laughter and conversation stopped in the tense atmosphere. Stark decided to put the lad straight. It might not be professional, but he felt it an appropriate time to establish his authority and control the situation. He placed a finger underneath the confused youth's chin and raised it slightly. Patrick's cheeks were tear-stained and his eyes red. He closed them rather than face the detective's steely glare.

'You're wrong, son, I do give a shit, I've given a shit for twenty-odd bloody years! You haven't got the faintest clue what I have to do . . .' He tapped his own chest with his finger. 'You see, I'm the prat that gets his hands dirty. I don't just talk about it and then forget it, I try and do something about the fucker, and I risk my neck doing it, and I place my family in jeopardy because of the absolute scum of the earth that I have to deal with, and that's why, if you are involved, you will rue the day that I walked through your fucking door!' Stark's index finger pointed and jabbed at the startled youth, but he raised his eyebrows as if in conciliatory mood and softened his voice.

'If it isn't you – and to be honest, I don't know if it is – then you have nothing to worry about; but if it is, know this, my pal, I will ensure that I find as much evidence as you have been stupid enough to leave and you will go to prison for a fucking long time . . . a fucking *long* time!' Stark took his finger away. 'Understand?'

There was silence. Patrick moved his head to one side, his heart beating at an incredible rate of knots. This man was unlike anyone he had come across before. Patrick was scared and he was upset. A week ago he and Cheryl had been together, happy and without a care in the world. They had their whole lives ahead of them, but now he had a sudden glimpse of hell in his own living-room. Cheryl dead and him arrested! Why did she have to finish with him? Why did she have to die on him now? He glanced momentarily at Stark, but quickly diverted his gaze and swallowed hard. He spoke.

'I'll put my shoes on, then.'

Stark smiled. 'You do that, Patrick.'

5

'Everyone is the child of his past.'
EDNA G. ROSTOW

Stark looked at the dusty ceiling of his office. He noticed a cobweb in the corner and made a mental note to knock it down as he held the telephone away from his ear. Life was not going to be easy. Carol was still complaining. There was a tear in her voice as it quavered in a mixture of anger and upset.

'. . . it's always the bloody same, David. Why is it always you, eh? What did I say to you? I bloody told you to book leave, but oh no, because that would leave everybody else in the lurch, wouldn't it? Well, who's it affected now, eh? Us – well, me. I shouldn't think you're in the slightest bit interested, you never have been and you never will be . . .'

Stark spoke softly and tried to remain calm. 'Carol, for God's sake, it's not my fault some poor sod's been murdered, now is it?'

'David, I'm not interested, I'm fed up with it all, fed up with being second best!'

'Carol, don't be silly, you're not second –' He did not get the chance to finish.

'What am I going to tell the kids? They were so looking forward to it this year and I've got to let them down again. What about all the plans I've made?'

Stark was beginning to get annoyed. He had a lot on his mind. He was the DI on call and there was no getting out of it.

'Look, you'll just have to go on your own, Carol. You don't think I want to be stuck at work, do you? Doesn't it cross your mind that I might like to enjoy a Christmas with my family for once, eh, doesn't it? No, it bloody well doesn't, because you're too busy feeling sorry for yourself, that's why.'

There was a silence. Now he felt guilty.

'Carol, I am sorry, love, but there is absolutely nothing I can do about it. I'm as disappointed as you are.'

'Bullshit!'

The persistent buzzing drilled home to Stark that Carol had hung up on him. He tapped out his home phone number but before it rang out he replaced the receiver. His heart was beating fast. What the hell could he do about the situation? Somebody had to do the job. What if it was their daughter who had been raped and murdered? She'd want the police there then, wouldn't she? He sighed. He could only hope they had an early result so that he could grab at least a day off during the festive season. Festive season! What a joke!

The surgery at the police station was too small. It was a room conveniently adjoining the cell block and measured approximately twelve feet by eight. There was a stretcher-bed against one side of the room, a cupboard fixed to the wall and a toilet at the far end.

Stark had decided, quite properly, since Dunn was obviously not going immediately to admit the offence, that he should be forensically examined prior to interview. It was not that long ago since the murder, and they might get lucky. In any case, whatever microscopic evidence was available should be obtained without delay. Dunn's clothing had been seized and he sat on the stretcher-bed swinging his legs over the side. He was garbed in a white wax paper overall. DC Grant Donaldson had been quite pleased to be distracted from Jim McIntyre's soul-destroying company, and embraced with some fervour his task of logging all the exhibits that were seized before their submission to the Home Office Forensic Science Laboratory.

Dunn's solicitor, Ivan Stimpson, of Stimpson and Stimpson, stood in the far corner of the room. He was a man of around thirty with prematurely grey hair, a drab suit and spectacles, which he periodically pushed back on to the bridge of his nose with his middle finger.

The police surgeon on call was a very tall man, with a thick moustache. He wore a suit that appeared to have been slept in, and dandruff speckled his broad shoulders. He wore white disposable surgical gloves that he had found after much ferreting around in his brown leather briefcase. Price had been a police surgeon for some six years and was well accustomed to such an examination. He introduced himself to Patrick and explained briefly what it would entail.

'I will need various swabs from different areas of your body and I shall subsequently need to take blood samples. I have been told that you consent to such an examination taking place. Is that the case?'

Dunn glanced across at Mr Stimpson, who nodded.

'Yes,' he confirmed. 'I've got nothing to hide.'

Doc Price noticed that Dunn's hands were shaking.

'Have you any ailments? Are you under any medication at all?'

'No, I'm in good shape. I've not been to the doctor for over a year now.'

'Who is your GP?'

'Dr Murray at Hucknall Health Centre.'

'Okay. I will start by making a visual examination of your body, starting with your head.'

Price took hold of Patrick's head and fingered through his hair. He raised Patrick's eyelids and looked in his eyes, using a small torch. He then took hold of Patrick's left hand.

'I notice there are a couple of scratches on your left hand. Where did you get them?'

Patrick was quick to respond. 'I'm a brickie, I've always got scratches on my hands.'

Mr Stimpson put in his twopenn'orth. 'Dr Price, we have agreed that my client be examined by you, not interviewed by you. That is for the police.'

Price cleared his throat and continued his examination, without responding to the solicitor. In any case, there were no other obvious marks visible. He returned to Patrick's head, this time producing a comb which he scraped through the curly locks, intermittently examining the comb by holding it up gingerly towards the light.

'Okay, I think we have sufficient loose hair there.'

He placed the comb into a small plastic bag that Grant held open.

He then spoke to Patrick as he placed his hands back on to his head: 'You may feel a slight tug here. Don't worry, it won't last long.'

'Ouch!'

He examined the specimen of hair that he had pulled from the prisoner's scalp. There seemed to be enough, but, better safe than sorry, he pulled at another clump, eliciting a similar response.

Grant again assisted with the plastic bags, placing each completed one next to a small brown cardboard exhibit-label, ready for Price to sign when the examination was complete.

The police surgeon reached for a swab, unlike a cotton bud but slightly larger. He scraped it over Patrick's open palms and between his fingers and then disposed of it in one of Grant's see-through bags.

'Just slip your trousers down, please, Patrick.'

Patrick slowly pulled the overall down to reveal a vast array of pubic hair and a somewhat retracted penis. Doc Price repeated the combing and plucking that he had previously undertaken on the patient's head. Patrick's response to the plucking of his pubic hair was similar, only louder. The doctor again felt it necessary to repeat the motion. Even Mr Stimpson winced at the second tug.

He continued his task in a very methodical and businesslike way, glancing at Grant as he reached for another swab and delivered the legend to Patrick: 'Would you like to pull your foreskin back or shall I?'

'I'll do it.'

'Won't be long now, Patrick. I just need a swab from the head of your penis and then the nasty bit is over . . . Now, let me see.'

The police surgeon, who seemingly had a touch like a blacksmith, took hold of Patrick's penis between finger and thumb and held it in a vice-like grip. He then proceeded to scrape the swab around the circumference of the glans-penis where it meets the shaft.

It started with a sharp intake of breath and culminated in a full-blown yell. Patrick's knuckles turned white as he gripped the side of the trolley, throwing his head back into the bargain.

'Jesus Christ!'

'Just another go around.'

Price didn't wait. He scraped the tender area for the second time. Patrick's painful reaction was almost comical as he wrestled with the doctor for the possession of his own penis.

'Fuck off!' he shouted.

Price tutted. 'There, that should just about do it, Patrick. You must realise that it is a very important part of the examination.'

Patrick cowered against the wall, his hands protectively clutching his private parts. 'You can piss off. You're not having any more.'

'You may be glad to know that I do not need any more, young man,' the doctor responded sweetly.

He requested Patrick to produce some saliva and spit it into a small hard plastic container. After some effort, Patrick managed this. Price then took a syringeful of blood from a trembling arm and separated the sample into two, one for DNA purposes and one for the blood-grouping comparison.

Grant would ensure that the blood for the grouping comparison, the saliva, the combed hair and the hand swab would be placed in a fridge prior to transportation to the lab. The other blood sample, to be used for DNA comparison, would go into the freezer. The paper sheet Patrick had been reclining on was carefully wrapped and placed in a brown paper bag for examination in case there were minuscule traces on it which might provide further forensic evidence.

Patrick rearranged his clothing and was ushered out of the surgery, complaining bitterly to Mr Stimpson, while Grant and Price remained in the room to sign the exhibit labels together.

Grant was a trifle flippant. 'You weren't anything to do with the Spanish Inquisition in a former life were you, doc?'

Price replied as he busily signed each of the labels laid out for him: 'Not that I know of. He's in custody for the murder and rape of the young girl at Hucknall, isn't he?'

'Yes, that's right.'

The doctor glanced at Grant. His expression gave nothing away. 'Yes, I thought he was,' was all he said.

Stark had insisted that the samples obtained from Patrick Dunn were dispatched immediately to the Forensic Science Laboratory by a police motor-cyclist. He wanted the results as soon as humanly possible. Dunn had of course requested that a solicitor be present during any interview, and if this resulted in a 'no comment' charade, Stark would be struggling from an evidential point of view. He did not want to risk letting the youth go before at least some preliminary indication had been received from the lab as to their findings. It was no good hoping for co-operation from the suspect; those days had long gone.

Stark had seen many changes in his years as a detective. He was no fan of the present judicial system and the laws of evidence that restrained and hindered the fight of the police against people who might have broken laws.

He had tried looking at the system from a neutral angle. Nobody wants to see an innocent man arrested, never mind convicted, but surely if a man is genuinely innocent, he will have no problem with talking to the police, saying where he was, or what he was doing, at a particular time, and helping to establish his innocence. He considered the old adage, 'Guilt evokes the right of silence, whereas innocence screams to speak,' more than appropriate to these liberal days.

Stark knew the system inside out. He had stood by helplessly too many times as criminals and their ethically bound, freely supplied legal representatives used the system to their benefit while the victims looked on disbelievingly. He did not need telling that if a man who does not live by the rules of society escapes from the scene after committing an armed robbery or molesting a child, or indeed after committing any offence, there is a high probability that he will also escape prosecution. There is of course a slim chance that someone will provide information to the police which will lead to an arrest. The suspect would then be interviewed with a solicitor present, who usually strongly advises him to make 'no comment' replies. The solicitor may also make a well-timed interruption to break the spell at a crucial point, perhaps when his client is about to make an admission. In the unlikely event of such an admission, the man is then often bailed by the court because his wife is pregnant, his mother is ill, or the cat's on heat. It is not unknown for a hardened criminal to tell his solicitor that he is innocent and only admitted an offence because he felt oppressed when a detective stood behind him, or raised his voice a tad! The same hard man who felt so persecuted by the nasty policeman then pleads not guilty, the court accepts his version, and the jury will not even hear the interview that may have contained an admission with details of the offence which only the offender could know!

Stark was aware that the criminal with perhaps a score of

previous convictions may choose never to take the witness-stand, as is his prerogative, and will sit in the dock in a nice suit with a 'Who, me?' expression on his face and the odd shake of his head.

In every full Crown Court trial, there is still around a seventy per cent chance of the jury acquitting. Stark had lost count of the times he had seen a jury find the accused not guilty, only to hear to their horror that the seemingly respectable man they had acquitted on one count had a string of convictions for offences of a similar nature! Of course it did not necessarily mean that the accused had committed that particular crime, but the result might have been very different if the jury had known that the man in the dock did not have a clean character.

So Stark was somewhat embittered by his experience. He genuinely cared about the victims of crime, and what hurt him most was the apathy or ignorance of the general public who seemed unconcerned until the tentacles of evil reached out to suffocate them or their family. He had been on his soap-box about the subject too often. Everybody he spoke to seemed to agree with him, to the verge of outrage at times, but it was just not done to talk about such things professionally. It was all part of 'the game'. Unfortunately it was a game that affected the lives of victims – not usually malicious or dishonest people, but the young, the elderly, the naïve and those who happened to be in the wrong place at the wrong time. These were the people who suffered, who were scarred irrevocably, who, unlike the people who got rich from the game, never got their pay day, and who were left wanting and alone and bewildered.

Like many policemen, Stark took comfort from the fact that he did all he could. If other agencies failed, he knew he had done his best and could do no more. Sometimes, though, he felt it just was not enough.

So it was with some scepticism that he looked across the interview table at Patrick Dunn and his solicitor. Patrick was not a criminal, unlike a lot of them that play the system. Stark felt no particular malice for the man. He did not know if Patrick was the murderer; he had merely embarked on the task of trying to find out. Every enquiry needs a starting point, and Patrick Dunn just happened to be that starting point. There was evidence to suggest that he had threatened the dead girl and that she had gone to confront him just prior to her death. The buzzing of the tape-machine heralded the interview that would go some way to indicating Dunn's innocence or guilt.

Stark introduced himself, as did Nobby Clarke, Mr Stimpson and Patrick. The prisoner was informed of his rights and cautioned that he need not say anything.

Stark began. 'Patrick, you have been arrested on suspicion of the murder of Cheryl Towlson. Are you involved in that offence?'

'No comment.'

The reply came as no surprise to Stark. He always made a point of asking the question outright at the very start of an interview. You never knew, the man might say 'Yes', in which case GEMAC would take more of a back seat than usual. GEMAC was an interview technique found to be effective in recent years. Its basic structure, hence the initials, was Greeting, Explanation, Mutual Activity, Closure. An interview would consist of Open Questions (Who? What? Why? When? Where? and How?), Closed Questions (inviting a single-word reply) and, most importantly, Spiral Questioning (open question leading to the probing of an answer before going on to the next topic). The psychological theory is that if someone has invented a story, particularly if they make it up as they go along, it is nigh on impossible to maintain the lie under such detailed probing. In addition to eliciting replies to specific questions, it is essential to observe what may be called a prisoner's non-verbal communication. Stress has to dissipate itself somehow and a lie induces a fair amount of stress, which may be revealed in any of a number of ways: shifting in one's seat or brushing imaginary dust off one's jeans, for example. Sometimes a prisoner feels an immense pressure to speak in some way, and the use of silence can be the most powerful tool of all.

Stark treated Patrick's 'No comment' as if he had said nothing. He waited momentarily to give Patrick the chance to answer the question in his own mind.

'Fine, okay. So what were you doing yesterday?'

'No comment.'

He paused again, staring at Patrick and nodding his head, before continuing: 'So how long have you known Cheryl, then, Patrick?'

'No comment.'

Stark again ignored the response. He would not be rushed. The onus was on Patrick to answer.

Patrick spoke again: 'I've told you, no comment.'

Stark replied, 'I know, Patrick, and I'm wondering why an innocent man is not trying to tell me how innocent he really is.'

'Look, you've told me yourself I don't have to say anything, so . . .'

Mr Stimpson tapped his pen a couple of times on the table, a pre-arranged sign that his client should shut up. Patrick stopped abruptly.

'No comment and that's it!'

Stark leaned back in his chair and displayed his open palms. 'Look, Patrick, I am not here to trick you. I've already told you, if you ain't done it, that's it. Tell me how you haven't done it and I will get it checked out. It really is as simple as that.'

Patrick glanced across at Mr Stimpson, who tapped his pen on the table yet again. Patrick looked over at Stark.

'All right, I'll just say this and no more. I didn't see Cheryl last night. I didn't bloody ring her and, no, I didn't touch her. I really wouldn't hurt her, Inspector, honestly I wouldn't. Tell me what time you think she was killed and, if I can, I will tell you what I was doing.'

Mr Stimpson spoke up. 'I strongly advise you, Patrick, to uphold your right of silence.'

Patrick glared across at his solicitor. 'No, I've got nothing to hide. They're not pinning this on me and that's it!'

Mr Stimpson raised his eyebrows.

Patrick sighed and addressed his comment to the brief. 'It's all right, I've not done owt!'

The afternoon was wearing on; the dimness of cloud covering and dusk prompted the yellow street lamps to flicker into life. The rows of council houses gave out a glow of peculiar optimism, as the dancing flames of their coal fires reflected through the windows, giving them a life of their own, a warmth to be embraced and cherished by the occasional passer-by who might glance in at the inviting aura. It had been a busy day for Ashley Stevens and Barry Marsh. They had certainly drawn the short straw and it was only Barry's insistence that dragged Ashley along for the ride to investigate the recent spate of dwelling house burglaries. Barry had drawn the car to a standstill and rustled through some papers, the interior light of the Ford Fiesta barely sufficient as the Welsh detective strained to find the details of the next burglary on the list.

It was Ashley who spoke. 'Well, let's hope that the next victim has less form than the last bogger.'

Barry laughed. 'Don't blame me, they've got to be visited. I don't know how they've got the nerve, though, do you?'

'I know. There he was, bold as brass, moaning and groaning about the bastard that's screwed his house and yet he must have half a dozen convictions for burglary himself that I know about.'

'Come on, I've found it – number 16, Sharon Taylor, rear window smashed between 11 a.m. and 3.30 p.m. yesterday. Another daytime break.'

The two detectives got out and approached the house. The front lawn was patchy; they negotiated a green wheelie-bin that overflowed with household waste and a pushchair left outside the door. The number 16 was painted on the brickwork in white six-inch numerals, a few feet down from the almost obligatory television satellite dish. Barry's stubby fist knocked on the glass door-panel.

Sharon Taylor answered the door. She was in her early twenties, with scruffy brown hair and a pale complexion. If she was five foot two, she was no more, yet she must have weighed around twelve stone. Her large flabby belly wobbled over the belt that strained to support her shabby jeans. The familiar odour of stale urine and excrement wafted out of the door into the detectives' faces, as Sharon leaned against the frame. The origin of the smell appeared also, a young toddler, a pretty little girl of around two years old. The infant was clutching a used disposable nappy, and her grey-white vest flapped around her bare genitals. Her grimy face arched backwards and stared up at her mother.

Barry spoke. 'Hello, love, we're from the CID. I understand you've had a burglary.'

Sharon picked up the kid and turned around, walking down the small hallway and shouting over her shoulder.

'You'd better come in, I suppose.' Her jeans rustled as her fat thighs rubbed against each other.

The two constables stepped on to the threadbare carpet and followed her into the living-room. They saw another woman sitting on a settee smoking and watching the television, which

71

was turned up to a relatively high volume. She was skinny and wore similar clothing to Sharon. Barry watched her stub out the cigarette into a crowded ashtray. Her arms were heavily tattooed and her hair cut close to her head. She did not acknowledge the two men.

Ashley and Barry stood and waited for a response, but Sharon had her head turned toward the television and said nothing. They stood there awkwardly. Barry glanced at Ashley. 'I'm not dreaming this, Ash, am I? I mean, I am actually here, aren't I?'

Ashley smiled. 'Yes, you are here, Barry, I can confirm that.'

The tattooed lady spoke. 'I think they're trying to tell you something, Shaz.'

Sharon bent down and let the kiddie on to the floor. 'Well, what do you want to know then?' she asked tersely.

Barry took the cue. 'Can you show me how they got in, please?'

Sharon flip-flopped her way through the open-plan dining-room and into the kitchen, followed by the two detectives and the child. She stretched out her open palm towards the window and said sarcastically, 'One window.'

'Yes, that's right, madam. I can see it's a window, but was it smashed, or forced, or what?'

Sharon made her way back to the living-room before replying. 'Look on your report,' she shouted to the two men, who were left on their own in the kitchen. 'If you don't even know that, you ain't gonna get my stuff back, are you?'

Although she lowered her voice, they distinctly heard her mutter, 'Soft bastards,' from the living-room. The insult was clumsily echoed by the child: 'Off 'astards.'

Ashley spoke in a soft voice. 'Come on, let's piss off,' he said. 'Bollocks to her. If she wants to be like that, stuff it.'

There was something about Barry that would not allow him to run away from awkward situations. He always stood his ground, and he was not going to scurry away from a scruffy-arsed cow, just because the situation was a little tense. His enthusiasm was, however, starting to wane.

He returned to the living-room followed by his colleague. Sharon was now sitting next to her friend. They were holding hands, fingers entwined.

'What rooms did they go into, love?' Barry asked.

There was another silence before Sharon's friend eventually

answered. 'Just downstairs. They've nicked a Sharp video recorder and rifled through the drawers, but nowt else has been nicked. That's all there is to it. There's been a load of break-ins round here. We try to keep ourselves to ourselves, if you know what I mean, but it doesn't seem to have made much difference.'

'Yeah, well, they aren't bothered whose house it is, are they? They're just interested in what's in it for them. We won't keep you any longer, then. We'll let you know if we get anywhere with it.' Barry smiled at the friend.

Sharon lolled her head to one side, her double chin accentuated as she looked towards the officers.

'You want to pull your fingers out! I'll tell you now it'll be Paul Digby, everybody knows what a thieving little shit he is, but he still gets away with it.'

Barry sighed. 'Paul Digby off Ruffs Estate?' He didn't wait for an answer. 'We'll check him out on fingerprints then, if our Scenes of Crime find any.'

Barry could see himself that there would not be any, but Digby was worth bearing in mind. The two detectives made their way into the hall and as Barry turned to close the front door behind him, the toddler with the mucky face was at his heels. She waggled her fingers clumsily into a wave and squeaked, 'Bye bye.'

Barry gently rubbed her curly hair. 'Bye bye, sweetheart.'

He closed the door behind him with a sigh, and set off somewhat wearily back towards the car. He glanced back at the window of the house and saw the child's face squashed against the glass. This time she did not wave; she just stared at Barry, her face now solemn. Barry smiled a smile that betrayed his heavy heart. The little girl smiled back. Barry could only look on as he watched Sharon stand and draw the curtains, obscuring the image of innocence as if in defiance, robbing her child of a few seconds more of warmth and friendliness from the stranger. A different smile – a cynical, smug one – etched itself on the face of Sharon. Barry shook his head. He felt older than his thirty years.

Stark sat at his desk in his little cosy office at Force Headquarters. He had a pint mug of tea steaming in front of him and he yearned for a puff of his pipe. His abstention was not getting any easier; in fact it was getting worse. Was it worth it? He had only stopped because of the risk to his health, coupled with Carol's intensive nagging and moaning. The phone rang.

'Hello, DI Stark.'

'Hello, David, John Sanderson from Huntingdon Lab. I'm calling about the blood samples you sent for comparison with the deceased Towlson.'

'Yes. Well?'

'Sorry, I'm not going to bother doing a full DNA check. There's no need – he's not even the same blood grouping. I'm afraid it's looking a bit doubtful for you.'

'Shit! Okay, John, thanks for trying for us, anyway.'

'That's why I'm here.'

'Thanks, then.'

'Cheers.'

Stark replaced the phone and rubbed his tired eyes. It was ten o'clock at night, Christmas Eve. He had a murdering rapist running loose and he didn't know who it was. Brilliant! He felt for his pipe in his pocket, but of course it wasn't there. He tutted and then took a gulp of tea from his over-large mug. He opened his drawer to get out his bleeper and noticed several small neatly packaged parcels inside it. He smiled. Carol's Christmas presents. He took them out and placed them on the desk top. He must not forget them, whatever happened; he was bound to be in the doghouse as it was. He tapped out four digits on the phone.

'Hello, Nobby, it's the DI. You'd better kick Patrick Dunn out. Forensic have rung and the semen inside Cheryl isn't his.'

'Shit!'

'Yes, that's what I said.'

'Do you want me to bail him or Refuse Charge him?'

'Refuse Charge him. We can rearrest him if we get further evidence and have another twenty-four hours on him then.'

'All right. Are you going next door for a pint?'

'Yes, okay. Tell the lads I'll see them in there if any of them are going. They've worked hard; the least I can do is buy them a pint.'

'Bloody hell! It must be Christmas!'

'Don't be so bloody cheeky!'

Nobby laughed. 'So much for it being Patrick Dunn. It looks as though we are back to square one again.'

'You said it.'

Stark put down the phone and took hold of a few small cards.

They were illustrated with snowmen and Christmas trees. He took out his pen and began to write. He had barely formed the first word, however, before he halted the movement of the pen. His lips formed a thin line as he stared at his own reflection in the window, completely mirrored now that darkness had fully descended. He studied his own features briefly; they appeared even sharper as the light above him emphasised the ledges of his cheekbones, accentuating his hardened stare. A sense of sadness overwhelmed him. It was Christmas Eve, but still the bastards of the world reached out at him, challenging him, not letting him rest even at the time of peace and good will. He thought about his family, Carol and Laura and young Christopher, themselves sentenced to another Christmas without him. He thought about the likes of Ashley Stevens and Steve Aston, young men, still idealistic and hopeful. They'd got another twenty years to do yet. What would the job be like then? God Almighty! He took a deep breath and tried to throw off his depressive state and self-pity. There were a lot worse off in the world. He knew, he had met them.

He leaned on the desk and finished the words on the card that had triggered off his despair. His writing was small, each word written as if signing a name, with small characters and long tails on the lower cases.

'Have a Merry Christmas, darling, love from Dave.'

He finished the message with three kisses, a tradition he had started on the first card he had ever sent her: one for 'I', one for 'love' and one for 'you'.

As he sat there alone in the dim light, burdened by reflective mood and sentiment, a realisation dawned on him. He was lucky, he was a rich man, because he possessed the most rare of commodities – somebody to love.

The rattling on the window shocked him out of his thoughts. The pebbles had hit the glass and he threw open the slide window and stared down on to the pavement below. The group were huddled together and each had a beaming countenance as they stared up at him. They were all there – Steph, Nobby, Charlie, Ash, Barry, even Steve and Jim. They burst into song.

'We wish you a Merry Christmas and a Happy New Year!'

Stark began laughing. 'You barmy bastards!'

Barry shouted up. 'Put a few pennies in the hat, mister!'

'Piss off!'

6

'We are all born mad, some remain so.'
SAMUEL BECKETT

Laura Stark was really quite beautiful, now seventeen and blossoming into womanhood. She had jet black hair, which cascaded
down on to her shoulders, and sparkling hazel eyes. Her teeth
were white and often displayed by a ready smile. She lay on the
floor at the foot of the Christmas tree, surrounded by presents
and discarded wrapping paper, her eyes wide with joy and
expectation. David and Carol looked on proudly, warm in the
happiness of parenthood. Stark surreptitiously glanced at his
wrist-watch. Laura waited patiently as Christopher ripped open
one of his presents, which was obviously a compact disc. Christopher was a young fifteen-year-old, quite immature really, still
more interested in football than girls. He was a little bit gangly,
tall but not yet filled out, and his hair was brown and straight, cut
to a fringe. He whooped with pleasure at his prize.

'Great! Thanks, Dad, thanks, Mum, that's brilliant – just what I
wanted.'

He reached over to grab another parcel. David intervened.

'No, hold on a minute, Christopher, let Laura open another of
hers.'

Laura smiled. 'Now, which one shall I open?'

She balanced a small present in each hand, one from her
parents and one from her boyfriend. Blood being thicker than
water, she carefully unwrapped the present from her parents.
She opened the black box and let out a gasp. Her mouth opened
as Christopher shuffled around to see what it was.

'Let's have a look then.'

Laura elbowed him out of the way. 'Hang on a minute. Let me get it out of the box.' She tentatively took out the gold necklace and locket.

Carol spoke: 'The locket does open, you know.'

Laura prised open the locket and read aloud the inscription engraved inside: 'We'll always be there for you. Love always, Mum and Dad.'

She walked hurriedly on her knees over to the settee and hugged Carol and David. 'Thanks, Mum, thanks, Dad. It's so wonderful, it really is. Thanks a lot.'

Christopher was getting impatient. 'Can I open another one of mine now?'

Carol answered. 'Of course you can. I'm going to open mine as well.'

She walked over to the small pile of presents on the window sill and took a handful. She was intrigued as to what was in the box that David had bought her. It was nicely wrapped, obviously in the store from where it was bought; she had seen David's attempts in the past, and this had not been done by his hand. It looked like jewellery. She had hinted at a bracelet but she wondered what sort it was. David was similarly intrigued.

There were many tired eyes that Christmas morning, some as a result of childish expectation and excitement, others through an excessive indulgence in alcohol induced by good company and a pleasing ambience the night before.

Norma and Bill Towlson had tired eyes, only theirs were caused by misery and grief. They had slept fitfully in their armchairs, still dressed. It had been a tormented sleep, harangued by the voice of bereavement and sorrow, an inner voice of despair that haunted every image of their tortured minds. On one occasion Norma had awoken Bill, pleading almost hysterically for reassurance that it was all a dream, a nightmare, all a figment of her imagination; but it was a fleeting hope, dashed by the hollow centres of Bill's eyes that had cried too many tears.

Bill was a hard-working man. His excessive toil had begun when Cheryl was a baby. He had grabbed money then, he'd had to, but it had meant he saw too little of his daughter in order to keep hold of their semi-detached house, bought in haste and paid for with sweat and tears. He would do it all again, work all those hours and endure the same mild heart attack, just to have another day with his only daughter, to say the things that he'd never said. The early separation of father and daughter had created an aloofness and insensitivity that had given a false impression of their innermost feelings for each other.

Norma knew that a large part of her had died when Cheryl was murdered. She kept imagining those awful final moments that her daughter must have suffered, fighting for her daughter's life in her mind's eye, frustrated that she couldn't have been there to kill that evil monster who had robbed her daughter of life and who had violated her in the most contemptuous manner. The way Cheryl had died exacerbated the sorrow by a feeling of helplessness and impotence. Hate for the beast who had attacked her daughter was swirling in her head, swarming with the grief and emptiness that festered inside her.

She was sitting on the floor now, her head resting on Bill's legs as he sat in the chair. Her head was pounding with lack of sleep and stress; her face was lifeless and slack and she breathed heavily as she stared into the darkness that was softened by a standard lamp in the corner of the living-room. She reached a hand up towards Bill's. Her hands were creased with lines and her skin was loose. Bill stroked her hand with his and stared into space. He had a hazy image of the Christmas tree, which now seemed out of place, the presents lying redundant beneath it. Neither had spoken for some time. There was nothing left to say. Their only daughter had been taken away from them. She was dead, there was no escape or release and they were left to cope with it.

It was now 6.00 a.m. on Christmas morning and Norma suddenly gave way. She sobbed again and again, whimpering and groaning, forcing tears to well up once more in Bill's eyes. The whirlwind of mourning swelled from the pit of her belly, cascading uncontrollably to the surface. She howled.

'No! Oh God, Bill, please tell me no, it's not true. My baby! Please, Bill.'

'Don't, love, please.'

He gripped her hand, and put his other hand to his mouth in a vain attempt to choke back his own tears. Norma turned and looked at him, searching his face for an answer, for some comfort from the hell she was in.

'For God's sake, why, Bill? My poor baby's dead. Oh God, she never hurt a soul, she didn't deserve this, you know she didn't.'

Her head collapsed on to his knees and her shoulders heaved as the grief flooded through her, her nails biting into her husband's hand with anguish and despair. She called out into the dimness.

'Cheryl . . . Cheryl!'

Beyond her call, children could be heard outside, laughing ecstatically, feverishly chasing one another and experimenting with their new toys. These were cries and squeals of unbounded joy, unaware of the misery that throbbed inside the breasts of Norma and Bill Towlson, and thankfully oblivious to the hate that dwelled within one man who still remained at large, a time-bomb of perversion, probably ready to explode and wreak another hell, in another place, for another person. Cheryl was beyond the call of a mother's love.

Joanne Peters was twenty-two. She had long blonde hair that rested on her shoulders and she had lively blue eyes. She was a pretty girl with pointed features, a tanned complexion and pearly teeth. Her hands were well manicured with long fingers, tipped by painted nails. The fact that this was her first Christmas alone in her little town house did not serve to temper her excitement on this Christmas morning. She wore a long white dressing-gown over her cotton night-shirt and she gabbled tumultuously over the phone, as she leaned on the wall in her compact hallway. There was a full-length mirror behind the telephone-stand, in which she checked her reflection as she spoke.

'Thanks for the bath salts, Mum, and the records, and the skirt. I told you not to spend a lot on me this year. After all, I have flown the nest now, you know.'

'Well, if a mother can't spoil her only daughter at Christmas time, it's a sorry tale. I'm glad you like them, anyway. Thank you for mine as well. I told you not to bother.'

'Well, if a daughter can't spoil her only mother at Christmas time, it's a sorry tale also.' She laughed. 'What time do you want me over for dinner?'

'Come whenever you're ready. We'll be sitting at the table for two o'clock, and then finish for the Queen's Speech.'

'Oh, mother, you and your Queen's Speech! Okay then, I'll go and get ready and I'll see you a little later on.'

She threw her hair back over her shoulder with her right hand and smiled. The tone of her mother's voice indicated that she was smiling also.

'All right, love. Bye.'

'Bye.'

Joanne replaced the handset and began to walk back to the living-room as the phone rang again. She answered it.

'Yes, Mother, what have you forgotten to tell me now?'

The male voice was low and croaky. 'Hello, Joanne.'

There was a brief pause before the gruff voice continued. 'How I long to stroke and caress those ample breasts, to lay my tongue over your gorgeous tanned body.'

Joanne was confused. It took her a moment to register what was happening. There was more to come.

'How I long to tease you with my tongue . . .'

Joanne was getting scared. How could this person know she was tanned, and worse, know her name? Was it a joke? She knew it wasn't and tried to speak over the increasingly louder voice.

'Who the hell is this?'

The question was ignored but the fear in her voice registered a chord with the sick mind, and the hate the caller had for women rose to the surface almost to the pitch of a shout.

'I am going to fuck you, you cow – you're going to get what you deserve and you're going to scream for mercy!'

Before the man could continue, she slammed the phone down and stepped away from the stand. It was silent momentarily, but its further loud ring made her jump, even though she was expecting it. She stepped gingerly past it as though the phone itself could strike out at her, and she ran upstairs. She sat on the bed shaking, her arms folded and her forehead furrowed. After two minutes, the ringing stopped and her every fibre strained as she expected it to resume. It remained silent and she gradually relaxed her tense muscles, relieved that the ordeal was over.

Dave Stark remained seated as he spoke to the assembled detectives at Police Headquarters. An intercom facility was in place and the detectives at the forward post at Nottingham police station were able to hear it and speak themselves, should they wish. He toyed with a pen as he spoke.

'Well, chaps and chapesses, first of all let me wish you a Merry Christmas . . .'

Groans emanated all around.

'I know I'm no substitute for Noel Edmonds but I'm all we've got. I'm sure you'd all like to be somewhere else today, but I fancy Cheryl Towlson would feel the same way too and perhaps we owe it to her and to her parents to keep the momentum of the enquiry going and hopefully achieve a quick result.'

He sipped at his large mug of tea and swept his hand through his wavy black hair that was tinged with streaks of grey.

'You are probably aware that Patrick Dunn has been ruled out, for the moment anyway. We certainly know that he didn't have sex with her before her death and, to be honest, the vibes I was getting from the interview tended to support that view. I think you felt the same way, Nobby?'

Nobby nodded his head in agreement.

'The brief sequence of events are that Cheryl Towlson had a party on 22nd December and during that party she received a malicious telephone call from somebody who used a pet name for her that made her naturally assume it was Patrick Dunn. Now whether it was Patrick Dunn or not, I don't yet know, but it seems strange that the caller should use a name only known to the two of them. Anyway, the following day she returned home from work and she was only a matter of fifty yards from her flat when she was attacked, raped and her own tights used as a ligature to strangle her to death. The attack happened in a clump of trees at the rear of her flat. She was discovered the following morning, Christmas Eve, by an old man walking his dog. I have designated "the scene" as being that clump of trees at the back of the flat complex. The area is currently marked off with tape.'

Stark took hold of some notes he had made earlier and referred to them. 'The suspect parameters are as follows: male, aged between thirteen and seventy years, who may have some knowledge of the deceased and also may have some previous conviction for sexual offences or violence to women.'

He paused and put the notes down in front of him, before

81

continuing. 'We believe that the offender has stolen a gold necklace from the victim, as this still remains outstanding. The offender ejaculated inside Cheryl and this forensic evidence is a
great advantage to the enquiry, as is the missing necklace. Photographs of a similar necklace will be arranged for today so that we
all know what we are looking for. Bear in mind that the necklace
could have been given to an innocent friend or family member by
the rapist, especially with it being Christmas, so ask the right
questions when you do your enquiries. The area was searched
yesterday, but we shall widen it as the day progresses. Nobody is
to say anything to the media, only myself or Mr Wormsley will do
that, but if anybody feels they want to know what we have
divulged, then look in the media log. We aren't going to tell them
a lot. You can get meal tickets from your detective sergeants.
There is mileage available for those that want it, but keep it to a
minimum; there will be overtime for the next few days before
they start pulling the reins in, so make the most of your time. I'm
hoping for more staff after the bank holidays. That should be
about it. Any questions?'

There were none.

'I want you to do PDFs* of each witness along with your
statements. HOLMES is being set up, so everything will be
logged on computer from this afternoon onwards. I don't want
negative statements at the moment – in other words if they
haven't seen anything or heard anything, then don't bother, we
can always return and commit them to paper later on in the
enquiry. Liaise with your detective sergeants for your actions,
and good luck.'

A slight murmur began to grow from those assembled, which
Stark interrupted.

'Oh, and incidentally, there is a bottle of whisky in my office, so
you can all have a snifter of Christmas cheer before you get down
to work.'

A wave of laughter and chatter rose as Stark himself took
another sip of tea.

Ashley Stevens and Barry Marsh still felt a little left out of it all.
Ash poured a tot of whisky into a couple of mugs and passed one

* Personal Descriptive Forms.

to Barry, who lay almost prostrate, with his legs crossed and resting on his desk.

'Cheers, Ash. Merry Christmas.'

'Same to you, Barry. Did Santa bring you anything nice?'

'The normal – jumpers, socks and undies. What about you?'

'Not bad, shirts, ties that sort of thing. I bet the missus and kids are a bit pissed off with you having to come in, aren't they?'

'Yes. She's quite good about it, really, but I must admit that I miss being with the kids. Andrew's two and Kirsty's four, so it's a good time to be with them, and you can't have Christmas Day back, can you? Once it's gone it's gone.'

'True. I've got a bit of an announcement to make, Barry.'

Barry looked puzzled. 'Oh yes, and what's that then?'

Ash took a sip of his whisky. 'Me and Christie have got engaged.'

Barry looked incredulously at Ash. 'What? You are joking, mate, surely?'

'Oh, thanks very much. I thought "Congratulations" was the appropriate thing to say under these circumstances.'

Barry was smiling and shaking his head. 'Yeah, sorry, mate, congratulations, but, you know, *you* of all people – I mean, you have disposed of more crackling than a Jewish butcher.'

'I know, but I was thinking, perhaps it's time to get settled down. I'm twenty-eight years old, you know.'

Barry grinned. 'Well, I wish you all the best, mate. Christie's a smashing girl. Have you set the date yet?'

'I thought this summer. No point in hanging around, is there?'

'Bloody hell, Ash, it's all a bit sudden, isn't it?'

'Well, bollocks to it; in for a penny, in for a pound.'

Grant Donaldson and Steve Aston came into the room and Barry broke the news to them. There was much amusement and surprise, but Ashley was resolute.

'You think I shall be unfaithful to my beloved but you wait and see, I shall be the perfect husband.'

Grant poured himself a tot of whisky and offered Steve some.

'You know I don't drink, Grant.'

Barry chimed in. 'Come on, Steve, it's Christmas Day, for Christ's sake.'

'I know what day it is, thank you very much.'

Ashley made his contribution, relieved that the attention was being diverted from himself: 'Come on, Steve, if they can stop a world war to have a game of football on Christmas Day, I'm sure you can struggle down a small drink of the hard stuff. Anyway, I've just got engaged!'

Grant handed Steve a mug, emblazoned with the name of a local glazier and freely supplied by a grateful firm that were reliant on the police for a lot of business. Steve took a tentative sip and immediately screwed up his face. The room resonated to cheers, followed by the ringing of the phone. Ashley took the call.

'CID – DC Stevens.'

'Hello, Ash, it's Tom in the control room. You are not going to believe this, Christmas Day and all, but somebody has cashed a stolen cheque at the motorway service station and it's one that was nicked from one of your postbag thefts.'

'Oh shit. So much for a quiet day. I'd got a game of snooker lined up with Barry. Have Uniform gone to it?'

'No, I've got nobody to attend. They're all tied up; they haven't got time to swan about playing snooker, you know.'

'Oh, all right then, I'll go to it.'

'There's not going to be a lot to it, anyway, other than seizing the cheque. I took the call from the cashier. The offender was a youth but he was wearing gloves, so it's unlikely there will be prints on it.'

'Wonderful! All right, Tom, I'll give you a reply when I've been.'

'Thanks, Ash.'

Ashley replaced the receiver and took another sip of whisky. He thought about his impending contact with the cashier.

'Anybody got any mints?'

The living-room of the flat was dimly lit. The orange curtains were drawn and smoke hung limply in layers around the room, giving off a stench of stale tobacco that had stained the white paint on the walls and ceilings of the grubby abode. There was a pale-coloured settee and two chairs, on the arms of which were darker patches caused by years of dirty hands and precariously placed mugs of tea. The shag pile of the carpet had long since been pounded down, to give an almost smooth effect which was sticky in parts, with patches of brown littering its surface where spilt fluid had been neglected and left to rot the underlay and fibres.

The man knelt down in front of the settee and splayed the letters on to the floor. He chose the three that most interested him and placed them to one side. The rest would be burnt, they were rubbish. He picked out one of the three, the one with the tan-coloured envelope, and removed the contents. A sickly smile grew on his lips as he read out loud. This one was his favourite. The sender appeared to share with him a similar penchant for such matters.

'Joanne, the minutes seem like hours as I wait for our next meeting, when the two of us can feel each other's skin again, taste each other's love once more. How I long to stroke and caress those ample breasts . . .'

He paused and let out a laugh, remembering the phone call he had made, a sneering, mocking laugh, devoid of respect for the intimate contents of the letter. He began to rub at his penis over his jeans, continuing to read aloud.

'How I long to tease your gorgeous tanned body that I know is mine alone.'

The man spoke aloud again. 'I've got news for you, pal. It's gonna be my fucker now!'

7

'Gather ye rosebuds while ye may,
Old Time is still a-flying:
And this same flower that smiles today,
Tomorrow will be dying.'

ROBERT HERRICK

Inspector Richard Platt had been at Nottingham police station for
five years. He had moved there on promotion from Newark. He
was a small, wiry man with brown hair, cut very short at the back
and sides, and he sported a tightly trimmed moustache. He had
twenty years' service and for most of those he had been disliked
by his peers and subordinates. Inspector Platt had a chip on his
shoulder so big it must have weighed heavily on the two pips
decorating his ill-fitting white shirt. He was basically ignorant
and he hated the CID. Platt had done a couple of years within the
department when he was a detective constable in the 'old days',
but was forced to go back into uniform because of his idleness and
lack of commitment, despite several warnings.

The embarrassment of the move had sparked a wave of antag-
onism that prompted him into action. He bullied his way into
promotion at a time when such aloofness from the lower ranks
was encouraged by some senior officers. Platt was a loner who
did not mix socially with anybody from work and who only had
contact with the CID when it was absolutely necessary. This
suited the CID down to the ground. Detectives like Steve Aston
and Ashley Stevens would be guaranteed a hard time if ever they
had to approach him for overtime, and this would invariably
result in an argument or intervention from Stark to sanction it.
Today was Boxing Day and there was not a hope in hell of
anybody getting overtime on a bank holiday. Platt had already
psyched himself up in anticipation of any battles on that subject.

He was at his happiest alone in his office, his little empire, safe in charge of young probationary PCs and subservient sergeants who had no wish to jeopardise their careers by falling out with their immediate supervisor.

One such probationary PC knocked on Platt's office door and waited the customary few seconds before the inspector condescended to acknowledge the request to enter his hallowed ground.

'Come.'

Tim Spate entered the room and began to speak. 'Sir, as you know, I've got a prisoner in and –'

'Wait a minute, I'm busy!'

Platt continued scribbling on a piece of paper. He had not yet raised his eyes toward the young man, who waited somewhat awkwardly as the inspector slowly rolled his biro on the page. After a long minute, Platt elaborately placed the paper in the tray at the side of the desk.

'Now then, what do you want?'

'As you know, sir, I've got a prisoner in downstairs – Roman Keystone. I don't know if you know him?'

Tim waited for a reply, but all he got was a steely gaze from cold eyes that seemed to suggest that this was an unwanted interruption, void of any merit.

'. . . He's a well-known burglar, and well in with the local toe-rags at Bulwell. He's coughed the burglary that he's in for, and he's currently on bail for another break at Radford Road. The thing is, he is desperate for bail. He's heavily into cocaine and the thought of not getting his daily dose is sending him crackers.'

'Get to the point, Tim.'

'Well, he reckons that he can give us a name for the murder at Hucknall –'

Platt finished off the sentence for Tim. 'If we give him bail. Am I right?'

'Yes, that's right, sir, yes.'

'No.'

'No what, sir?'

'No, he can't have bail. I've heard bullshit stories like this more times than I care to remember. Anything else?'

'Well, surely we should tell CID about it, at least? I'm pretty sure he's being genuine, and I fancy that he'll get bail at court tomorrow anyway – you know what the magistrates are like and this guy is worth cultivating as an informant.'

Platt's lips grew tight across his teeth.

'There is nothing that the CID can do that we can't do . . .'

He broke into a semi-smile, the best he could manage, before continuing. 'Look, I'll tell you what I'll do. I'm not in the habit of bailing burglars, but once he is charged, then it is up to the Custody Officer whether or not the man is bailed, so I'll let you try and persuade him. How's that?'

Tim smiled and nodded. 'Okay, sir. Thanks a lot.'

He hurriedly left the office. Perhaps the inspector wasn't so bad after all.

Platt lifted his phone and tapped out four digits. He spoke to the Custody Sergeant in his normal manner, terse and to the point.

'It's the inspector. Listen to me – whatever happens, Keystone does not get bail. He's a fucking burglar and he goes before the court tomorrow, understand?'

'Yes, sir.'

The Custody Sergeant, who was waiting on a promotion board, had no sooner put the phone down than Tim Spate came bounding in, confident that his request would be granted by the usually more amenable sergeant. He was to be disappointed. If Stark had only known of this pettiness, the walls would have shaken, but of course he didn't know, nor would he find out.

Roman Keystone was five feet eight inches tall and of muscular build. He was black and had a flat-top haircut. He wore a silk shirt and suede jacket. He was eighteen years old and had been committing crimes since he was thirteen. The criminal friends he had grown up with much preferred street robberies to burglaries, but he had regarded burglary as more productive and less conspicuous. This meant that he associated more with the white criminal element, who respected him as a reliable man to do a job with. He had never before grassed anybody up, but his penchant for cocaine and his disgust for the crime of rape gave him sufficient reason to 'help' the police on this particular occasion. All right, he didn't know for certain who the rapist was, but he had heard a whisper from his burglar friends that one youth in particular was very cagey about the newspaper reports, refusing to discuss them, and he was weird enough to be involved. Roman wanted out, and he wanted out now.

He lay on the wooden bench of the cell with his hands behind his head and jumped to his feet as soon as he heard footsteps approaching down the corridor. He peered through the small circular window of the cell door and instantly recognised the figure of Tim Spate through the scratched perspex. The metal of the door was cold to the touch and the noise of the keys turning in the lock made him step back to allow the heavy door to open inwards, as he anxiously awaited the result of Tim's quest.

Roman spoke first. 'Well? Am I getting out, or what?'

Tim appeared tense and Roman could see by his face that all was not well.

'You'd better not be fucking me about!'

'Well, Roman, I've spoken to the Custody Sergeant and there is a bit of a problem.'

Roman pointed an angry finger close to Tim's face. 'Don't you fucking give me shit, man! I don't want to hear about no fucking problems. You promised me bail, you bastard. I've got a name for you and it's fucking straight.'

'Look, you'll get bail at court tomorrow anyway, Roman, it's no sweat. I'll write the court application up myself. I've got to ask for a remand, but I'll make it a weak application.'

Roman stared at the young copper. He was breathing heavily and the bones in his cheeks protruded as he gritted his teeth. 'You bastards make me sick, you're full of shit. Go on, fuck off out! You can't do anything for me.'

'Look, Roman, it wasn't my decision, you know that –'

'I said fuck off! You're getting nothing!'

Tim left the cell and slammed the door behind him. It was pointless trying to persuade the prisoner. He had nothing with which to negotiate.

Roman Keystone had the answer to the case. He had offered a detected murder in exchange for bail. He lay on the hard bed and curled his knees up to his chest. A day isn't a long time, unless you are a cocaine addict in need of a score.

It was not difficult for the man to observe the end terraced house of Victoria Street at Hucknall. The ageing brickwork protruded defiantly, sixty years old but apparently more solid than the newer 'cardboard box' houses on the other side of the street. The alleyway at the side of an empty house afforded the man sufficient privacy and an excellent view of Joanne Peters' abode. He had been watching for about twenty minutes and he was cold. The chill that ran through his bones was caused partly by the temperature and partly by his excitement. He had seen the bitch sauntering around the house in her bathrobe and then eventually enter the front bedroom. She looked pretty as she drew the curtains. He was partial to blondes.

He glanced up and down the street but there was nobody about. It was very quiet apart from the hum of an occasional motor car at the far end of the road. He smiled to himself, drawing on a cigarette, as he watched blue ultra-violet light fill the square of the bedroom window. He stepped silently across the road, like a cat stalking its prey. This was going to be easy. He reached into the inside of his leather jacket and pulled on a pair of yellow rubber washing-up gloves. His eyes widened as the rear door opened to his touch. How careless of her to leave the door unlocked! He stepped cautiously inside.

Joanne Peters' long blonde hair rested either side of her face as she lay naked. She was hot from the rays of the sunbed, which stood flush with the side of her own double bed. She was starting to burn and there was a fusty smell of sweat, of which she was hardly aware. Her eyes were closed but the brightness of the UVA light fought at her eyelids, giving her a fuzzy feeling behind her eyes. She could hear the incessant ticking of the timer behind the music from her radio alarm clock. She lay almost motionless apart from the occasional tapping of her long painted fingernails against the mattress in accompaniment to the music. Her blonde hair stood out against the bronzed colour of her skin.

The mixture of heat and rhythmic pulsations of the music had already started her on a journey towards sleep. A smile played about her lips as her mind wandered to thoughts of her parents squabbling like little children the day before over Christmas lunch, and then being very polite when they spoke to her. Some things never changed.

It did not register at first that the music had stopped. When eventually it dawned on her, she struggled to locate the radio, keeping her eyes closed to avoid the harsh light. It was at the very moment when her hand touched the alarm clock that an over-whelming feeling of being watched came over her, sending a shiver down her body. She slowly opened her eyelids, and horror entered her consciousness. There was a man at the side of her bed! The blue light and her squinting gave him a surreal appear-ance. He was a hazy figure at first, and she concentrated on the movement of his hand. He was wearing yellow washing-up gloves and was masturbating. His penis was exposed through the fly of his trousers, and he had a full erection. The harsh realisation made her move quickly and, rolling back towards the area covered by the sunbed, she let out a scream. The man took hold of her right arm and yanked it hard. Using both hands, he pulled her back across her own bed, causing the quilt to rise and create a temporary barrier between them. His voice was coarse and venomous. His vilification came readily.

'Come here, bitch! Don't struggle or I'll kill you!'

Joanne swung at him with her fist and hit him in the stomach. To her disgust she caught the end of his erect penis. He was strong and quickly took hold of her throat with one hand, press-ing her neck hard into the mattress and restricting her breathing. Instinctively she tried to scratch at the man's eyes. He relin-quished his grip on her neck and held both her hands, either side of her head, and laid his body weight down hard, forcing a knee into her stomach, winding her immediately. His gloating face was contorted and the whites of his eyes were exaggerated in the UVA light.

'I fucking warned you!'

As the effects of the winding registered and she gulped for air, he used his knees to force her legs apart and, despite her weakened efforts, managed eventually to enter her. The revul-sion grew inside her and she cried 'No!', followed by a deep breath that enabled her to scream with all her might. It was an ear-piercing scream that startled the rapist, who at once placed a hand over her mouth. She could smell the rubber of his gloves and she tried to bite into his hand, which he curled into a tight fist and rammed into her teeth, using jerking movements to force it further into her mouth. Joanne could feel him inside her, thrusting away with great strength. She hated this defilement of everything that was sacred to her. She tried to cross her legs and she wriggled and squirmed, but he was strong and the two remained locked together.

His senses were at their peak now. In his imagination he had not considered that she would fight as hard as this. Her recalcitrance had surprised him and he was getting more and more angry, and more and more excited. Her robe was visible in the weird light on the floor and he leaned down the side of the bed and pulled at the cotton belt – a suitable ligature. Unable to pick it up with one hand, he quickly removed his fist from her mouth. She at once arched her back and threw his heavy body upwards, twisting hers at the same time and disengaging the man. She called out with great energy and force, a loud yell that could be heard from the street.

'Help me! Quick, help!'

His fervour pushed him to even greater violence. He straddled the thrashing girl and harshly wrapped the belt around her neck, pulling it tightly. Her hands reached towards it and she managed to insert her fingers between the belt and her throat. As the constriction grew and panic swept over her, she bucked with all her might, her breasts wobbling, her nipples hard with fear. The sight of this and his previous penetration caused her attacker to ejaculate on to her face and chest. He rubbed his hard penis against her breasts and groaned aloud. He could feel a thin necklace rub into his shaft and in his sexual stupor he quickly snatched at it, ripping it from her throat. Such a token of the attack would serve as an aid to masturbation long afterwards, to help him relive the frenetic scene and the feeling of power that heightened his perverted lust. Joanne could feel the vomit about to come, but the tightness of the belt, still around her neck, afforded no release for it as she started to heave.

An anxious voice loudly interrupted her hell.

'Joanne, are you all right?'

She recognised John's voice, her next-door neighbour.

The voice from downstairs hit the attacker like a thunderbolt and his basic craven instincts were laid bare. He jumped off her, in time for her to tug at the belt and vomit over the quilt. In a second the man was out of the bedroom and down the stairs.

John was taken aback by the fleeing figure approaching him,

and the coughing emanating from Joanne's room. He grabbed at the rapist, who fought like crazy, hitting out at the much older man, wrenching free from his grasp and racing out the back door. John managed to shout '*Oi*' and thought about pursuing the younger man, but the sobbing from upstairs sounded more urgent, and he went quickly up the stairs to offer his assistance.

The sight that greeted him was heart-rending and shocking. Joanne was curled up on the bed, her lovely blonde hair matted in her own vomit and her fists curled up near her face. She was waving them about, crying out loud. 'Stop it! Stop it! Stop it! Stop it! . . .'

John spoke from the doorway. 'Okay, Joanne, it's all right now. It's John here, he's gone. I'm here, you're safe now, it's all right.'

'No, keep away, don't come near me. Oh God . . .' She sobbed pitifully and ashamedly and tore at the quilt, hitting her face and chest, wiping the filthy semen off her, which the coarseness of the quilt served merely to smear around, making it grow and creep over her, sticking to her skin. She squirmed as a fly might in a spider's web, trying in vain to free herself. She struggled to her feet and staggered past John to the bathroom, her head bowed. She turned the taps on full, splashing water over herself in desperation, before collapsing on to the bathroom floor. The spray of water rebounding off the sink showered over her and she sobbed. John stood by helplessly, the image of the ruined girl for ever etched into his mind.

The nightmare for Joanne had only just started. Rape lives on. Its ramifications are immense, and no amount of water would free her from the feeling of being dirty, of having been violated and debauched. It would be a long time before she would let herself feel warmth again. At the moment she knew only emptiness, bitterness and fear – an overwhelming fear that would force a happy-go-lucky young woman into becoming an introvert, a loner who would never fully trust another man again, and who would never again want to experience the touch of a man's hand or allow herself to surrender to the promise of true love and affection.

Joanne Peters cried into the pile of the carpet, hugging the harsh fibres, her eyes wide and unseeing. The smell of vomit cursed her nostrils and she began spitting, as if to expel the remnants of vomit and the stench of the bastard who had violated her; but they would not go away. Her heart was racing and her body shaking. She was cold and, despite John's presence, so alone. She could hear John talking, saying something, but all she could do was cry. The cotton belt was still around her neck, loose now, but she had no energy left. She could barely move. After what seemed an age, John turned off the tap, stopping the water. He could not, however, stop her tears.

8

'One should always be in love. That is the reason
one should never marry.'
OSCAR WILDE

The female voice that issued from the speakers of the UHF radio
on the dashboard of the Traffic Patrol car was calm and aloof.

'Observations in the Hucknall area for a suspect for rape,
approximately one zero minutes ago. Description of offender is a
white male approximately thirty years old, wearing a black
leather jacket and jeans, no further details. May be in possession
of a thin silver necklace and yellow washing-up gloves. Repeat-
ing observations for a white male . . .'

Police Constable Mark Fletcher pulled on the steering wheel of
his Ford Granada Traffic Patrol car and turned on to Annesley
Road, doing a steady twenty-five miles an hour as his eyes
scoured either side of the road in response to the Observations
message. He turned right on to Spring Street and then right again
on to West Street.

The wind was getting up and the trees in the gardens were
beginning to rock. Dust and carelessly abandoned litter blew
along the pavement. Mark lowered his speed as he strained to
look out of the windows, into gardens and alleyways. There was
no point in racing around, the offender was just as likely to be
around the next corner as to be fifty streets away.

In the distance he caught sight of a youth crossing the road as it
became Common Lane. He was barely visible in the darkness of
an early winter's evening. Mark pressed the accelerator pedal
and in a few seconds was behind the young man, now illuminated in the headlights of the car. Mark studied his features: he

could see now that he was probably in his late twenties and wearing a black leather jacket and jeans. He was worth a pull.

The suspect did not look at Mark as he drove past and stopped the car some fifteen feet ahead of him. Mark got out and approached the man.

'Hello, there.'

The man stopped in his tracks as he was addressed by the ungainly traffic policeman, who was tall, with wide hips, and wore metal-rimmed spectacles.

'There's been an incident around here, a few minutes ago. Can I have a brief word with you?'

The young man leaned against the stone wall and put his hands in his pockets. 'Yeah, if you like. What's gone off?'

'Well, I'd rather not say at the moment, but you do fit the description of the bloke we want. Do you mind if I take a few details off you?'

'No, not really, but how long is all this going to take?'

Mark fished in his pocket for a scrap of paper and took out his pen. 'Not long. What's your name?'

The man sighed. 'Kevin Kirk, 347 Ruffs Drive, Hucknall, born 6.7.64.'

'Thanks. It sounds like you've been checked before.'

Kevin took out his hands and folded them defensively. He appeared to be apprehensive but attempting to portray indifference. 'Yeah, I've been stopped a couple of times in the past.'

'Have you got any form?'

'A bit for joy-riding and theft, but that's all.'

'Anything else?' Mark scribbled on his scrap of paper, keeping the outline of the suspect within his peripheral vision, just in case he decided to take off.

'Burglary, but that was last year. I've got a job in the pipeline, so things aren't as bad as they used to be, you know.'

'Okay, mate, I'll just check you out. Are you going to sit in the car? It's a bit warmer.'

Kevin tutted. 'Do I have to? All I'm doing is walking down the street, for Christ's sake.'

'I'd prefer it.'

Mark and Kevin walked slowly to the car and Kevin sat in the front passenger seat as Mark spoke into the black handset.

'Tango Mike One Five to NH, over.'

The same female voice replied over the speaker. 'Tango Mike One Five, go ahead, NH, over.'

'Ten nine. Name check please, code seven, Common Lane, Hucknall, over.'

Mark could hear her tapping on her computer as she replied over the mike. 'Ten Four, pass details.'

Mark passed the contents of his scribbled note over the radio and then waited for a reply. He tried to elicit information from Kevin.

'Have you been anywhere good, then?'

'No, not really. I nipped to the off-licence for some fags, that's all.'

'Do you want dropping off home? It's only around the corner, isn't it?'

'Yeah, okay then.'

As Mark drove off, the reply from the Police National Computer, via the female operator, came over the air, confirming Kevin's list of his previous convictions. He was not currently wanted or suspected for any offence.

Mark drew the powerful, liveried car to a standstill outside Kevin's house. As the two got out, he asked to look quickly through Kevin's pockets.

'Bloody hell, do you have to?'

Mark diligently went through his pockets and searched his clothing thoroughly. There was no necklace, and no gloves of any description. All Kevin had on him was a sealed packet of Benson and Hedges, a cigarette lighter, a wallet containing miscellaneous papers, a five-pound note, some stamps and a condom. Mark started to write out a 'Search of Persons' form.

Kevin turned away and walked up his drive. 'Don't bother with that. I ain't going to complain, don't worry.'

Mark returned to the car and started the engine. As he did so, another name check came over the air. He hoped that this one, a few streets away, would be more productive, and he decided to join his colleague and check out that everything was in order.

It was not long before he caught sight of the Traffic mobile on Derbyshire Lane. As he drew alongside it, he could see the youth being checked. He recognised him as David Streets, a well-known 'hard man'.

Mark wound down his window, and was greeted by a tirade of abuse.

'And you can piss off, as well. It's a bastard when you can't walk down the street without getting crap off the likes of you!'

'Good evening, David. I see you are being your normal helpful self.'

David ignored the sarcasm in Mark's voice.

It soon became apparent that David was not going to be arrested and his temperament modified somewhat. He spoke to the officers in a more conciliatory tone.

'All right, I was a bit leery. I know you've got a job to do and all the rest of it, but you get pissed off getting stopped all the time. What's happened anyway?'

Mark's colleague answered. 'There's been a serious sexual assault down the road, that's why we're having to stop people that match the description.'

David's reaction turned aggressive again. 'Well, I'll tell you now, if I find the bastard that's done it, you'll be fishing him out of the Trent and that's a promise.'

Mark smiled. 'In that case, then, let's hope you get the little shit before we do.'

'Can I go now then or what?'

'Yeah, go on, bog off.'

'Charming!'

David's hunched figure set off towards the town centre, the wind billowing in his leather jacket. He looked a comical figure with his flat cap and his yellow translucent socks attracting the eye as he broke into a trot.

Mark laughed. 'Why should England tremble?'

Stark travelled over to Oxclose Lane police station, where rape victims were often taken. It had the best facilities for the purpose, including a specifically designed 'rape suite'. He had been to the scene and was appalled by the account given to him by Joanne's neighbour. The degrading details as they unfolded created a determination in Stark to find the man who had perpetrated such an evil attack. He felt sure that he was looking for the same man who had murdered Cheryl Towlson. All the hallmarks of the MO were present: the ligature, the verbal abuse and the taking of the necklace. It would not take long to confirm his belief through the use of DNA techniques, matching the sperm from the Towlson murder with that at the scene and on Joanne Peters.

Joanne had been taken to hospital and Stark had dispatched Stephanie to see how she was and to ascertain if she was well enough to be examined by a police surgeon. From the police viewpoint the importance of such an examination had to take precedence over everything else. Fortunately, this time the victim was alive. The next few days were vital if the police were to take advantage of this fact to try and capture the rapist before another woman fell foul of him.

Stark knew that Joanne had been very lucky and that only her neighbour's intervention had saved her life; there was no doubt about it. He could feel the pressure building up, with one girl dead and now another within a hair's breadth of it. He threw another Polo into his mouth, his stomach almost retching for a puff of tobacco. His abstinence created confusion in his mind and prevented him, momentarily, from being able to focus on events.

Once at Oxclose Lane police station, he spoke with Steph on the telephone. She had rung from the Queen's Medical Centre, Accident and Emergency Department.

'Yes, sir, she is incredibly calm now. I think most of the hysteria burst out of her during, and immediately after, the attack. She is quiet and obviously badly shaken but she will be okay to talk to.'

'Any injuries?'

'A few minor scratches and grazes, but the biggest injury is in her mind. She wants to come away from here; she doesn't like hospitals. What do you want me to do?'

'Bring her to Oxclose Lane rape suite and I'll see you here. We could do the medical at the hospital, but it's a better environment here, and our police surgeon will know exactly what we want. I can arrange for him to be here within the hour.'

'Okay then. See you in a bit. Put the kettle on, sir, will you?'

'Consider it done.'

Stark waited for the arrival of Steph and Joanne. Scenes of Crime were doing their bit and the lads were taking statements and doing house-to-house. The next few hours would belong to Steph, who was, in his opinion, the best DPW on the sub-division for cases of this nature. The most important stage of this inquiry fell squarely in her lap.

The rape suite consisted of two rooms in an open-plan format. There was a comfortable settee and chairs in one part and then the surgery adjacent to it. The furniture was orange-coloured and a few paintings hung on the walls.

Steph sat next to Joanne. Both women were normally of a similar appearance, with long flowing blonde hair and trim figures. Joanne's face, however, was masked with tears, her hair now unkempt as she sat on the edge of the settee, her body bowed. She stared at the mug of hot tea in her hands, the steam slightly stinging her sore cheeks which were already soaked through incessant weeping. She wore a T-shirt and jeans. The solemnity within the room created a heavy atmosphere.

Fortunately, the police surgeon was a female doctor, a slightly dowdy woman of around forty in a grey two-piece suit and with short hair, who wore somewhat incongruous large-rimmed, fancy spectacles. As the medical took place, she was sympathetic but businesslike. The sooner it was over, then the sooner Joanne could make a start at recovery. Steph packaged all the swabs and the syringes and attempted to put Joanne at ease as the most delicate exterior and interior vaginal and anal swabs were undertaken. Fingernail scrapings were obtained and blood taken. Once the police surgeon had completed her examination and given Joanne a morning-after pill to prevent pregnancy, she signed all the exhibit labels that accompanied each item and left.

Joanne said very little and Steph was becoming concerned that she might close up altogether, so she tried to keep contact with her, in as friendly and special a way as possible. They returned to the settee and she rubbed Joanne's forearm.

'That's the worst bit over, Joanne.' She smiled reassuringly.

Joanne remained silent. The examination had been an ordeal in itself. Steph knew that the idea of being penetrated again, although by friendly hands, so shortly after the violation was stressful in the extreme, but Joanne understood the necessity and had tried to be brave.

'You've done remarkably well, Joanne. I know how hard this is for you, but if we are going to catch the bastard that's done this, and stop it happening to some other innocent person, then we must get through this, but we'll do it in your time, okay?'

Joanne nodded and sipped at her tea. It was cold.

'Do you want another cuppa?'

'Yes, please, if you don't mind.'

'Of course I don't mind. You really are doing so incredibly well. I don't think I would have your strength, Joanne.'

Joanne attempted a smile and muttered in reply, 'Thanks.'

Steph busied herself with the cups and returned with the new mashing. She felt that it was best to keep the victim fully aware of what was about to happen so that she could prepare herself and not be surprised by any event that was to take place.

'Joanne, there are a couple of things we need to do. One is to photograph the bruises on your body. Now, you can wait until tomorrow for that to happen if you like, or we can get it all out of the way tonight – it's entirely up to you. You know how you feel and I will be guided by whatever you think is best.'

'What do you think I should do, Steph?'

'Well, as I've said, it's up to you, Joanne, but I've found it better in the past to get it all out of the way at once; that way you will know that most of the intrusion is over in one go.'

'Okay, then. Let's do it tonight. What's the other thing?'

'Well, I shall have to take a statement from you, but that will just be the two of us.'

'Okay.'

'I'll come and see you tomorrow anyway, but at some stage, probably tomorrow, we will ask you to look at some photographs, and possibly even do an artist's impression, but don't worry – I shall be with you all along the way. Okay?'

'Okay.'

At Steph's request the female Scenes of Crime officer came in and took a set of photographs of the bruising around Joanne's neck and on her face and legs. The first flashlight from the camera caused Joanne to close her eyes and she kept them closed throughout. The SOCO thanked Joanne and then was pleased to leave the charged atmosphere.

Stephanie took her statement. She started off by scribbling down a few notes and then committing them to the proper forms set out by the Criminal Justice Act. Understandably, Joanne's version was stilted and out of sync, but Steph skilfully supported her and teased out the relevant information piece by piece, in chronological order. There were long periods of silence and at one stage Joanne broke down completely and collapsed into Steph's arms, sobbing unashamedly.

Joanne was unlike some of the victims Steph had dealt with on previous occasions, many of whom were low-life slags or prostitutes who, in Steph's opinion, had gone some way towards causing the act themselves, or had even invented the story for a variety of reasons: being late home to a violent husband, adultery that was soon to be discovered or blatant spite. Being a woman she was fully aware of the implications of rape, but she had seen it all and had grown hardened to it in some respects. The circumstances of Joanne's ordeal, however – her lack of a criminal record and her absence from the False or Persistent Rape Allegation file – gave Joanne a credibility that Steph could sympathise with. Despite all her years of service, she could not remain completely aloof and had to fight back tears herself as she cradled Joanne, but she had to remain strong for Joanne's sake.

It was important that Steph got everything right, not only in an easy-to-understand form, but with sufficient detail to be able to match the *modus operandi* with any possible further attack, anywhere else in the country. Minor detail could help identify a suspect who had knowledge of the particular circumstances of the rape. Steph wanted to know how the rapist had approached his victim. Was there anything that attracted her attention before the attack? Was he aggressive, subtle, charming, what sort of things did he say? Did he use threats or intimidation and, if so, in what way? Did he carry a weapon, or improvise one? Did he ever let go of it? Did he use violence and to what degree? Did he ridicule? Did he offer any incentive to his victim to comply? What was his manner like? Was he arrogant, boastful or possibly even remorseful? Did he appear concerned over whether he was going to be identified or injured? Did he betray knowledge of police procedure, or give the impression he had acted this way before?

Did he behave in an unusual manner sexually, or was any particular perversion evident? What did he do without making demands or requests? Did he force his victim to submit to anal, oral or varied sex? Did he kiss her? How did he react to resistance? Was there premature ejaculation or any dysfunction? In what sequence did he make his sexual attack? Precisely what words did he use, and in what accent or tone of voice? Did he change mood quickly or at all? How did he leave the victim – making threats, apologising, or even thanking her? Did he steal anything or take something as a souvenir? What did he look like? Did he disguise himself? What did he wear?

These and similar questions might elicit valuable answers. In Joanne's case the description of the offender was poor and not much better than the one given initially. Apart from her terror, the fact that the rape had taken place under an eerie ultra-violet light had not helped her to see things clearly. It was only when, a couple of hours later, Joanne remembered to reveal the malicious call she had taken on Christmas Day that Steph realised in a flash that they were almost certainly dealing with the murderer of Cheryl Towlson.

In conclusion, Steph arranged for Joanne to stay with her parents and told her to contact her day or night if she wanted. She reassured her that the man would not return; it would be an immense freak if he did.

'You know, love, I can't begin to comprehend what this must have been like for you, but one thing I do know is that you have done the right thing. This man must be caught. We must try and stop him.'

'I know.'

'You did exactly the right thing when you were attacked, and the reason I know this is because you are still here to tell us about it. Rape is always a life-threatening experience and you reacted the way you thought was best, and you have beaten him. I know it doesn't seem like it now, and life will be hell for a while, but you still have your life. He didn't take that away from you, did he? And while you have got your life, Joanne, your life that is so precious, then you have won, haven't you? You've beaten him. His life is pathetic, preying on the innocent; you wouldn't want to be like that, nor would I. You have people that love you and respect you and that won't ever change. You're alive, Joanne. You've won, not him!'

It's a fact. Life goes on. Ashley, Barry and Grant Donaldson had finished for the night at eleven o'clock, and after much deliberation had decided to go to the legendary Blitz's night-club. Blitz's was a favourite for policemen; there was rarely any trouble, the music was good and the women there were often good for a laugh.

The three men stood near the bar and observed the vast elevated 'television' screen, that displayed Diana Ross in the skimpiest of clothes. They were frequently distracted by groups of women parading around them, some offering a smile, others ignoring them. Ashley as ever seemed to warrant more smiles than his colleagues. It hardly mattered whether it was his superior good looks or his overt appearance of wealth that created his success with women. A few beers into the night, Barry noticed a group of four women who stood further down the bar, slightly obscured by the lines of people jostling to be served.

'What about those little beauties over there, then, Grant?'

Grant turned and raised his eyebrows. 'Very acceptable – for this place, anyway.'

'Since when have you had any standards?' Barry smiled as he spoke.

It was Ashley's turn to pipe up. 'Where are we looking?'

'Over there at the end of the bar, there's four of them, look you.'

Ashley caught sight of the objects of desire, one of whom, wearing a tight-fitting silver-coloured Lycra mini-dress, waved at him seductively. She flicked her auburn-black hair over her shoulders and raised her firm breasts, giving him a smile that positively invited a meeting.

Barry shook his head. 'He's done it again. It's bloody marvellous isn't it?'

'She happens to be an old girlfriend, that's all,' Ashley said.

'An old conquest, more like,' Barry observed.

'I'll have you know she's a very nice girl. In fact, I think I'm going to have to go and reminisce about old times with her.'

Barry took hold of his arm. 'Here, hold on a minute, you've just got engaged to Christie, haven't you?'

Ashley removed Barry's hand and patted his mate on the side of his face several times. 'What the eye doesn't see, old love; you know that.'

With that, Ashley strode confidently towards the beauty and immediately struck up such a rapport that she allowed his arm to slip around her waist within seconds.

Barry seemed most put out and sunk the remnants of his pint. 'Fancy another?'

Grant looked at his watch. 'How many have we had?'

'I don't know, two or three, who's counting?'

'Go on then, one more.'

A couple of hours later, Ashley and his newly found friend burst out of the double doors of the night-club. He had both hands around her tiny waist. The two of them were singing and dancing as they stepped on to the pavement: 'Aye aye aye aye, conga, aye aye aye aye, conga, na na na na, oi!'

The three heavily built bouncers standing near the door in bow ties and black suits looked on expressionlessly.

In the distance, unseen, was a Vauxhall motor car with its headlights dimmed. The driver was watching Ashley with disdain. The two revellers got into Ashley's spotlessly white Toyota Celica sports car and he sped off, risking life, licence and employment. The Vauxhall struggled to keep up with Ashley's high-powered car but the late-night city traffic didn't help matters. Ashley's destination was the woman's house, and two miles on he parked right outside it. The pair were giggling and laughing as they got out, slamming the doors and then shushing each other, before breaking out into more laughter.

It was 3.45 a.m. when Ashley left the house. He felt rough, and dehydrated, and he was tired. He had to be up at seven. Was it worth going to bed? Oh, well, it had seemed like a good idea at the time! As he opened the door to his car he noticed a piece of paper folded in half on his windscreen. He removed it and read it in the yellow light of the street lamps. It was written in the thick black lines of an eyeliner pencil: 'I hope she was worth it. You bastard. It's all off, don't come near me ever again. I trusted you, you bastard!'

It was signed 'Christie' – his fiancée, or probably now his ex-fiancée.

'Shit!'

He could see the woman waving through the window. He put on a false smile and waved back. The Celica pulled away slowly – he did not have the strength to speed off – and he was starting to regret ever going to Blitz's. Was it all worth it? The excessive drink, the false chatter and posturing, all to get inside some tart's knickers, and then afterwards, approximately 2.0 seconds after he'd had his wicked way with her, the down side starting to take

105

effect. The struggle to fight off sleep and the pounding of his head. He knew he would suffer all next day, fighting off tiredness and a sore brain, trying to concentrate on his job and undoubtedly failing.

He lit up a cigarette as he turned the corner, and wound down the window. He decided to stick to the back streets in the hope that the late-night patrol cars would stay on the main roads. He would run the gauntlet for the umpteenth time and pray that if he was stopped, the traffic officer was not out to notch a CID officer as another breathalyser victim. He turned down the CD player on the dashboard and began to tap away on the steering wheel. He wouldn't need any rocking tonight. He thought of Christie. She was a nice girl and he had been captured fair and square. Yes, the night had indeed been a mistake.

9

'I shut my eyes in order to see.'
PAUL GAUGUIN

Linda Sykes was a gossip, not out of malice but more through her lacklustre attitude towards life and her limited intelligence. Everybody else's business was of interest to her, probably because her own life was so incredibly dull. She had spent a number of years as a fabric spreader in the local factory until they were hit by a string of redundancies. She had been unemployed for over a year now, and it was during that time that she had really piled on the weight. She had never been slim, but the relative inactivity that being jobless had caused her, and the onslaught of addiction to game shows and soaps on the television, had really taken their toll, especially around the hips and backside. She had a round face that always appeared flushed, and the rings seemed to be bursting off her chubby fingers, but she was a character, and she spoke her mind. The highlight of her day would be when one of her myriad friends and neighbours called around for 'a chat' and 'a cuppa'. These chats were far more informative than anything found in the local newspapers and Linda had become something of an authority on who was having an affair with whom and all the tawdry details.

She was now having a chat with Steve Aston and Grant Donaldson, who sat somewhat bemused as she jabbered away, sometimes apparently oblivious that they were there. She wore a purple smock affair and brown Crimplene trousers that hugged the contours of her fat buttocks and protruding gut. A plate of chocolate biscuits took pride of place on the small coffee table in the centre of the room.

'Cry! I've never cried so much. Of all the people it should happen to, it had to be Cheryl. I've heard another girl has been raped. Am I right? Anyway, I know it's none of my business, but a woman isn't safe on the streets any more. I've laid in bed frightened to death, I have. I mean you never know, do you? But fancy it being at Christmas time, not that there is ever a good time, but you know what I mean, don't you?'

She leaned over, took two biscuits off the plate and began eating one, dropping crumbs on to her lap which she hurriedly knocked off on to the light blue carpet.

Grant raised an eyebrow and refused to look over at Steve, but could feel him staring at him. He spoke quickly as Linda took another breath in preparation to continue. 'It must be upsetting for you, Linda, I'm sure. How did you meet Cheryl?'

'We used to be in the same class at school. She was a lot cleverer than me, though. Do you know, I've applied for well over a dozen jobs in the last year and most of them don't even bother to reply? She did well, though – Cheryl, I mean. I think she got three GCSEs, if my memory serves me right, and well, you've got more of a chance, haven't you? To get a job, I mean.'

'Yes, that's right. How often did you see her, then?'

'She used to come around most weekends, just for a chat – you know what we women are like.' Some more crumbs fell out of her mouth on to the floor. 'Do you want another cuppa? You don't have to stand on ceremony here, you know. It won't take a minute for the kettle to boil.' She finished off the second biscuit and scooped crumbs off her lip with her little finger.

Steve shook his head, and Grant replied, 'No, thanks, Linda. Did she ever mention boyfriends at all?'

'Only that Patrick. Why? You don't think he's involved in all this, do you?'

She leaned back and placed both hands in the air as if in readiness for Muslim prayer.

'Oh, my word ... Mind you, he sounded a bit shady to me, unreliable, you know the sort. I've never met him, though, but you can tell, can't you?'

'Did she mention anybody else?'

'No. She was fed up with him, though, that Patrick feller. "Cheryl," I said, "Cheryl, get rid of him, if he's messing you about now then he always will..."'

'How was he messing her about?' Steve was interested and leaned forward in the chair.

'He wouldn't turn up for dates, cancelled at the last minute to go out with his mates, that sort of thing, the normal, you know. I told her, though, I told her straight. "Cheryl," I said, "Cheryl, he's no good for you, you deserve better..."'

'Have you heard anything about Cheryl from any other quarter?' Grant asked.

'Gossip, you mean? I try to steer well clear of that sort of talk. I'd heard she was enjoying her new life with her flat-mate – Barbara, is it?'

Steve nodded.

She continued before Grant could ask another question. 'Well, Barbara used to go gadding about down town all the while, so they tell me, anyway, and I think that would have had an effect on Cheryl; I mean it does, doesn't it? When you're living with somebody, it has an effect on you...'

'I hear that she was seeing another man, or that's what she told Patrick. Do you know anything about that at all?'

Linda appeared pleased with herself and threw a limp hand out dismissively.

'Don't believe that. She made that up to get rid of him. I suggested it to her. You see, if they think they are going to have problems with another man on the scene, they soon lose their bravado; they tend to keep out of the way if they think they will be scrapping with somebody.'

'So she just made that up to get rid of Patrick, then?'

'Yes. Good idea, don't you think?'

Grant shrugged his shoulders. 'Well, yes, I suppose so. Linda, have you ever heard of somebody called Joanne Peters?'

She scratched her head and pursed her lips. 'Joanne Peters. Let me think, is she a local girl?'

'Yes, she is.'

'Joanne Peters...' She shook her head. 'No, I can't say I have. I might know her by sight, though. Who is she?'

'She's a friend of Barbara's, that's all,' Grant lied. 'She never mentioned her to you, then?'

'No, sorry, I've never heard of her.'

'Fair enough. If anything else springs to mind, let us know, won't you?'

'Of course I will.'

The two men stood up in unison. Steve spoke. 'If you happen to hear anything on the grapevine, give us a ring, Linda, and we can check it out. If it's a load of rubbish, it doesn't matter, does it?'

'No. Okay, then. Drop by any time you're passing; you're always welcome to have a cuppa here, you know.'

The two men left via the back door. As they reached the car, Steve looked over at Grant. 'What do you think?'

'She's just an old gossip, isn't she? We've not learned a great deal and I think if there was anything worth knowing, she would know it.'

Steve turned the key in the lock. 'Yes, you're right. She obviously doesn't know Joanne Peters, though, does she?'

'No, it seems not. Oh well, such is life.'

They had still found no connection between Cheryl and Joanne.

There was something about Claudia Mason that Stark could not quite put his finger on. She was a well-dressed woman, about his age, in a blue two-piece suit and a silk blouse with a large bow, tied at the neck. Her hair was brown and wavy and laughter lines were evident at the sides of her hazel eyes. Stark could not avoid a glance at her well-defined legs, as her stilettos clip-clopped up the stairs of Oxclose Lane police station towards the rape suite. The sitting would take between two to three hours, and he had booked the suite accordingly. Claudia was a little early and, once in the room, the two of them sat, slightly awkwardly at first, waiting for Joanne to arrive. Steph had only just left to pick her up so they had about ten minutes to kill.

Claudia spoke first. 'How is the investigation going, Mr Stark?' She was smiling, almost as if she were taking the mickey.

'So-so, I'm afraid. I'm optimistic, but I would like to get hold of him before he strikes again, because next time we will be looking at another murder. Joanne was very lucky.'

'Yes, I'm sure you're right.'

The smile was still there. Stark looked puzzled. She was a confident woman.

'You don't remember me, do you?' she suddenly asked.

He wagged a finger. 'I know I've seen you somewhere before,

but I don't think you've done any artist's impressions for me, have you?'

She crossed her legs towards Stark.

'No, I haven't. You would have to cast your mind back twenty years, I'm afraid.'

'Oh my Gawd. Go on then, put me out of my misery.'

'Well, I might be Claudia Mason now, but twenty years ago I was Claudia Brown. Does that mean anything to you?'

Stark flung back his head, as his face lit up in recognition. 'My God, you used to be a policewoman at the Meadows police station when I was there. Bloody hell, Claudia, that's going back some time. Here, didn't we, er, have a, you know, a bit of a fling?' He was smiling excitedly.

'Whatever do you mean, Inspector Stark? Yes, it seems I have a better memory of those years than you.' She licked her lips. 'Happy times,' she said.

'I'll say, and stop this Inspector business, it's David to you.'

'Anything you say, sir.' She saluted mockingly.

'I didn't know you were a police artist. How long have you been doing that?' His interest was now heightened by the attractiveness of the woman and the halcyon memories he had of her company.

'About a year. It's not for the money, that's for certain. I just like the idea of helping out if I can, that's all.'

Stark nodded. 'That side of it must be quite rewarding for you.'

'Sometimes, but it can also be very frustrating, depending on the accuracy of the witnesses.'

'So what have you been doing all these years? I couldn't believe it when you left the force. I always thought you were a cracking policewoman.'

'Well, you know how it is, boy meets girl, boy very wealthy, no need to work. He wanted me at home and, like a fool, I thought it was the best thing to do.' Claudia spoke frivolously.

'Hence the now Claudia Mason.'

'Yes. I kept my married name despite the divorce.' A twinge of sadness fleetingly swept over her face.

'Oh, I'm sorry to hear that, Claudia . . .'

'Don't be, it was a long time ago. Money has a habit of attracting young ladies to a man, but I don't have an axe to grind.'

'He must be a fool,' Stark said flatteringly.

Claudia lit up a cigarette. 'You don't mind, do you? It's a filthy habit, but what the hell!'

'No, I don't mind at all. I could kill a smoke myself, but I'm battling with abstention at the moment.'

There was a pause as Claudia blew out a cloud of smoke.

'So what about you? You've obviously done well for yourself. Are you married?'

'Yes, but you know how it is. I'm here more than I'm at home, so things get a little fraught.'

'I see. Oh well, everybody goes through a bad patch. Let's hope that's all it is.'

The intimacy was broken by the phone ringing. Steph had arrived with Joanne and was downstairs. Stark smiled at Claudia.

'Listen, Claudia, I'm going to leave you to it with Joanne and a policewoman. It's been nice to see you again. We must continue our chat together some time.'

Claudia reached out a hand and squeezed Stark's, scratching her long nails through his palm. 'We will, David, we will.'

As Stark closed the door behind him, he caught sight of Wormsley. He shouted over to him and joined him at the far end of the corridor.

'Yes, David?'

'I'm not very happy with this artist's impression lark.'

'Oh, aren't you? Why's that, then?' Wormsley stuck his chin out in surprise at Stark's challenge.

'I'm always dubious about them. I can't remember an impression ever looking anything like the suspect when he's been caught.'

'I certainly can. It depends on the artist and the witness. Claudia Mason is the best artist we've got, in my opinion, and she's had a lot of success since we've been using her. Besides, the Peters girl didn't pick anybody out on photos, so what are we going to lose?'

'Okay, fair enough, but I don't want to be led down a blind alley if the picture isn't very good. We might have somebody who thinks they know who the offender is, but fails to ring us because the bloody picture is nothing like the suspect.'

'I know all about that, but let's not be premature. We'll play it by ear.'

'Let's not release it yet, let's keep it up our sleeve until I think the time is right,' Stark suggested, hopefully.

'Agreed.'

Charlie Carter had been dragging Jim McIntyre around with him all morning. Both men had a similar amount of service on the CID, but whereas Charlie had retained his keenness, if not his trim stomach, Jim's pock-marked face did nothing but whinge and whine about when they were going to stop for a drink. As was the norm, they stood at the bar of the Queen's Head, both gulping at their pints. There weren't many patrons evident amongst the array of brass ornaments and leather riding equipment that for some reason adorned the bare brick walls of the long-established hostelry.

Jim continued his moaning, his Scottish brogue filled with scepticism. 'How many more are there now?'

'Let's see ... We've done Peter Smith, Darryl Renshaw and we've got Craig Newton to do this afternoon.'

'It's a frigging waste of time, Charlie, this is.'

'Oh, shut up bloody complaining, Jim, for God's sake. What do you suggest we do? They are all ex-boyfriends of the girls and they might be able to connect the two for us.'

'They've told us sod all, Charlie, and you know it.' Jim took a swig of his ale, spilling a bit down his dull tie. 'Shit.' He wiped his mouth. 'Anyway, I know Craig Newton and he's just a poser. His mum used to be a cleaner at the nick; we'll get nothing there.'

Charlie smiled. 'I take it you are not an exponent of positive thought then, Mr McIntyre.'

'Talk bloody English; I reckon you're getting brainwashed with all this new thinking. There's nowt different about the job now than there was fifteen years ago.'

Charlie coughed into his pint as he drunk from it. 'You what! Where have you been living? It's all changed and we have to learn to adapt, Jim – if we are going to be effective, anyway.'

'All right, Chairman Bloody Mao, I'm just saying that we are on a fishing expedition and we're no' going to catch a deal.'

Unfortunately Jim was to be proved right. The footslogging was going to get them nowhere. They needed a glimmer of good fortune.

113

Jim was happy in the bar. He felt at home and was warming to the ambience. Charlie was irritated by his negative attitude.

'Hark at Mr Bloody Optimist.'

'Well, what do you expect? Fancy another?'

Joanne was very tired and she was shaking. She had hardly slept. The images of the rapist kept appearing within her mind. Most of the time she would fight them off, aware that they were there but not allowing them to come forward. She had tried singing or talking about anything that came to mind, just to try to keep that face away, but still it hid in the recesses of her mind, hiding behind a rock, ready to jump out at the slightest opportunity. Joanne now had to release the image, set it free and examine it in great detail, to confront it all over again, to relive those horrible moments and to feel the shame again.

After an initial conversation, Claudia had just begun sketching a few lines in pencil on to a pad. Joanne sat next to her, watching her graceful strokes and sipping at a mug of coffee.

Claudia explained: 'The image will initially be amorphous and it is you who must try and guide me, Joanne. Remember I am blind and you must help me to see!'

'Okay, then – his face was thinner than that and more chiselled at the chin, like a flat bottom to the chin, not rounded. That's it . . .'

Claudia sketched and erased and then sketched some more, gradually building up the hundreds of lines into one form. After the face shape, she began to compose the eyes. Witnesses invariably remembered the eyes better than any other feature.

'They were wider than that, staring. The whites were very white, but that would have been the sun lamp, I suppose. His teeth were the same, but two or three of them appeared to be darker than the others.'

'Okay, fine – we'll come on to the mouth in a bit.'

'I only saw his teeth partially when he was grimacing.'

Joanne kept closing her eyes and then opening them again. At first she could only visualise bits of the image at a time, but suddenly she could see his face fairly clearly and remembered studying it, trying to assess the best way to act. Would he really have killed her? She had always been a fighter, she knew no other way, and thankfully this time she had escaped, but if John hadn't heard her screams . . . She put the mug down harshly on the table and stood up. She folded her arms and walked towards the window.

Stephanie joined her. 'It's all right. Take your time, there's no rush. We've got all day if necessary.'

She closed her eyes again and could smell the rubber of his smelly yellow gloves and taste it as she remembered biting into his hand and then felt the panic rise as the fist was stuffed into her mouth, constricting her breathing. It was like a slow-motion replay, and the same sickly feeling started to rise in her stomach. She reached towards her neck, but of course he had ripped off the necklace. He still had that, he still owned part of her. She imagined him laughing at her, knowing what she was going through, enjoying it. She returned wearily to her seat, next to Claudia.

Joanne's memory was clouded in a blue haze, which did not help matters, but Claudia managed fairly well and the pencil image took just over two hours to complete. Claudia's technique was next to use her watercolours to get the feel of the skin complexion. She would paint a light tone at the top of the page and gradually darken it, until the skin colour was about right. Because of the UVA light in Joanne's bedroom, matching colouring was pure guesswork on this occasion, but she gave him hazel eyes and a light tint. She leaned back away from Joanne and held up the picture.

Joanne was reluctant to look at it. She glanced at it, and then away, and then back at it, each time studying it a little longer.

Eventually she nodded. 'Yes, that's very good, that's very like him . . .'

Claudia offered some advice. 'Squint your eyes, almost close them and then look at it.'

Joanne complied and, as she did, her heart began to race. She raised a hand to her mouth. 'Oh my God, that's him!'

Claudia had seen this reaction before, and she placed a hand on Joanne's. She could feel her trembling, goose-pimples raised to the surface of the skin.

'I've gone all cold!' Joanne muttered.

Claudia smiled and squeezed her hand. 'It's all right, Joanne. Are you sure that is how he looked?'

115

'Yes, positive. That looks just like him!'

Joanne was leaning away from the picture as if a few lines and a splash of paint could hurt her.

'Well done, love. That's what we're here for – to make the image look like the man – and you've done very well.'

'Can I go now, Steph?'

Steph nodded. 'Yes, come on. I'll take you home – if that's all right, Claudia?'

'Yes, sure, if that's the closest we can get, Joanne?'

'Yes, that's him. I've already told you.'

She had picked up her coat and put it on as she spoke. Steph opened the door and the two left hurriedly. As the door closed behind them Claudia glanced at the image. It had been a fairly good sitting, but she could never be certain that the likeness was good, based as it was only on the word of the victim who had probably been reluctant to recreate the face of someone she was trying to forget, not reincarnate. Claudia had to hope that Joanne's subconscious had helped her to get the picture right.

Her instinct was that the image was good enough, albeit the eyes were staring a little too much. It was a shame that the UVA light had affected Joanne's ability to describe the skin tone with any great degree of accuracy and the eye colouring was subject to interpretation. The whole appearance was so important, and if the skin colouring was wrong, it could invalidate the entire impression. For all that, the face looked good enough; it looked right and in proportion.

Claudia walked over to the phone and spoke to Stark. 'I've finished now, David, if you want to come and have a look.'

'Okay. I'll be right through.'

She glanced again at the image on her pad. The eyes in the picture seemed to follow her around the room.

10

'You might as well fall flat on your face, as lean over
too far backwards.'
JAMES THURBER

Stark looked into the camera and felt uncomfortable. He knew
that an appeal on television was far more effective and emotive
than speaking to an interviewer, but it was not easy. He concluded his request.

'. . . so I would ask anybody in the Nottingham area who has
received, or receives, malicious telephone calls that seem to
imply a degree of personal knowledge about the recipient to
contact the police in confidence, and we will take the matter on
from there.'

He was happy to return to the office, where he updated himself
feverishly on the progress of the enquiry, reading reports and
talking to Steph, Ashley, Barry, Jim and Charlie.

Suddenly Wormsley burst in through the door. His voice was
raised. 'What in hell's name do you think you're doing, David?'

'I'm sorry?' Stark looked up, surprised.

'You bloody heard. I said what the hell do you think you are
doing, asking people to call in if they've had malicious telephone
calls? There are going to be thousands of them. The switchboard
is already jammed. They can't take the normal calls, never mind
those with information for our job.'

'I didn't say everybody that has had malicious calls, I merely
said those that displayed a degree of personal knowledge of the
recipient.' Stark's voice was becoming louder in his own defence.

'Well, tell that to the thousands of people that are calling the
bloody station, will you? I just can't believe the stupidity of it.'

Stark stood up and pointed a finger at Wormsley. 'Here, just hang on a bloody minute, you don't come in here, sir, and start slagging me off in front of the troops. If you've got something to say, then let's talk man-to-man in your or my bloody office.'

Wormsley turned and walked out, followed by Stark, his face now red with rage. He slammed the door behind him. The detectives looked at each other, embarrassed. Barry broke the awkward silence.

'That's what I like to see, management in action.'

They laughed.

Stark joined Wormsley in his office. The superintendent wagged a finger in his face. 'Don't you ever swear at me in front of the men again! Understand?'

Stark struggled to overcome his wrath. He was breathing heavily. 'Look, if you hadn't come barging in, shouting the odds, sir, calling me fucking stupid, none of this would have happened. You were out of order, damaging my credibility like that in front of everyone.'

'Well, what do you expect? The bloody switchboard's jammed with calls. What do you hope to achieve, eh? I should imagine that anybody that's ever had a malicious call will be terrified that they are going to be the next fucking victim. You could cause mass hysteria, for Christ's sake!'

Stark raised his eyebrows and looked at Wormsley in defiance, scorn etched across his features. 'I think you are over-reacting a trifle, don't you?'

'Do you, now? Well, save it for the Chief, David. You have dropped an almighty bollock here, I'm telling you.'

'Hold on a minute, sir, let's look at this reasonably, shall we? I need to find out how the murderer has personal knowledge of the victims. If we stake out the houses of the malicious calls where the caller has shown a degree of personal knowledge, then we could catch the bastard. At least it's a positive step.'

'There aren't enough policemen in the force to stake out the calls we're getting.'

'Okay, then, we'll have to be selective – choose the ones where there is personal knowledge and the ones where the tone is the same and the words used are similar. It's better than wasting hours knocking on fucking doors.'

There was a silence. Wormsley sat down and stared at his desk. 'It's bloody unorthodox, David. It's very hit-and-miss.'

'But what are we going to lose? If we choose the ones close by, we could pick, say, ten persons and the manpower wouldn't be that much, just for a couple or three days – surely it's worth a try?'

Wormsley was not used to his subordinates using their initiative and, more, arguing their corner. He sighed.

'All right then, but for two days only; and if we get nowhere, I'm calling it off. But if the Chief goes scranny over it, then you had better be able to persuade him.'

There was another silence. Wormsley did not look at Stark.

'Right, then. I'll arrange it with the Support Department.'

Wormsley made no reply and Stark turned to leave. He could not be permitted to have the last word.

'And, David . . .'

'Yes, sir?'

'If you behave like that again in front of the ranks, you'll find yourself with a big hat on, understand?'

'Yeah, all right.' Stark was dismissive.

Steph and Nobby were alone in the CID office. They spoke in quiet, hushed tones, appropriate to the content of the conversation that was taking place.

'Let's just cool it for a while, Nobby, can we? I don't want any hassle, all right?'

'What do you mean, cool it? We only see each other a couple of times a week, if that. I get enough of you at work, for God's sake!' He laughed. Steph didn't.

'Look, I'm not joking, Nobby – and keep your voice down. Stark's only in the next office. I'm fed up with all of this cloak-and-dagger stuff.'

'You're in the wrong job, then, Detective Policewoman Dawson.'

'Oh you, you can never be serious, can you?'

'Life's too short . . .'

Ashley came breezing into the office. 'It's very quiet in here. Somebody died?'

Nobby addressed him. 'Ha bloody ha! You don't understand the pressures we Murder Squad detectives are under.'

Ashley's voice rose. 'Pressure! What about me and Barry?

We're disappearing up our own backsides, covering for the men that've been seconded on to your team.'

Nobby was as understanding as ever. 'My heart pumps piss!'

'You always were sympathetic, Nobby.'

Stark, as was his wont, was listening to the banter from his adjacent office. He smiled to himself.

'Well, it's not that busy at the moment, is it?' Steph said.

'It isn't, no, but there's hardly any of us left to deal with it all. Barry's getting snowed under with all the burglaries on the Ruffs Estate and I'm getting all sorts of grief over those postbag thefts.'

Nobby raised an eyebrow. 'What do you mean, all sorts of grief? They're only poxy thefts, for Christ's sake!'

'Only poxy thefts! You obviously don't realise the problems that a mailbag theft causes. Just think about the ramifications of just one theft of a bag of mail: job applications missing, letters to MPs, opportunities lost, reconciliations squandered, Giro cheques, cash in Christmas cards, love letters, banking documents. It's bloody horrendous, and everybody wants their own little problem sorting out.'

Nobby shrugged his shoulders. 'I'd not thought of it like that, to be honest . . .'

Stark appeared in the office, his face alive. He spoke quickly to Ashley. 'What did you just say?'

Nobby laughed. 'You can't say anything in here, Ash, without the gaffer earwigging everything.' He glanced towards Steph, who met his stare.

Stark was impatient. 'Shut up a minute, Nobby, I'm being serious. You said love letters, didn't you?'

Ashley appeared ambivalent. 'Yes, but that's just a small part of –'

Stark turned on his heels and left the office before Ashley could finish his sentence. He looked at Nobby.

'I'm worried about the gaffer. He's starting to behave very strangely.'

'What the hell do you want?' Patrick Dunn asked vehemently.

'I want to come in, basically.' Stark had expected some resistance.

'Have you got a warrant?'

'Look, I don't want to piss about, Patrick. I need five minutes of your time, that's all.'

Patrick stared at Stark's chiselled features. He was unsure about what to do. 'I think I should speak to my solicitor first.'

Stark raised both his hands as if in surrender. 'Listen, Patrick, this five minutes could get you off the hook for good.'

'I didn't know I was still on "the hook", as you say.'

'Well, you're not completely out of the frame yet, are you?' There was irritation in Stark's voice.

'It isn't me, so why should I worry?'

'Can I come in or not?'

Patrick opened the door sufficiently wide for Stark to squeeze by and into the living-room.

The two men sat down. Stark leaned forward, resting his elbows on his knees, almost on his haunches.

Patrick was puzzled. 'What's it all about then?'

'Patrick, did you ever send Cheryl any love letters?'

'Yes, I did. Why? Not that it's any of your business.'

Stark raised a hand, to stop him short. 'How did you send them?'

'Through the post. I mean, there's not much point giving them by hand. It would be embarrassing.'

'Of course. Now, did you use Cheryl's pet name in the letters?'

'Yes, I did. That's the idea in sending them, isn't it, to say things you might find awkward saying face to face?'

'What was her pet name then?'

Patrick went red in the face and scratched the back of his head. He mumbled something.

'I'm sorry, Patrick, what was that?'

'Honey-bun.'

'Right. How many have you sent to her?'

'I don't know – about four, I think.'

'Think, Patrick. Can you say how many she should have at her flat?'

Patrick stared at the carpet in thought. He tapped his hand on his thigh. 'Yeah, it's four. I sent one about every month and the first one was at the beginning of September so yes, it would be four. Why?'

'I'll explain later when I'm more definite. Can you remember when you sent the last one to her exactly?'

'Not the exact date but it was probably only four or five days before Christmas, because I wondered if it would get there before Christmas Day.'

Stark nodded. 'Great. I thought so.'

Stark visited Barbara after he had finished with Patrick. He searched Cheryl's things, which were still waiting for collection by her parents, and found three letters from Patrick, but the one sent just before Christmas had apparently not arrived. The initial search of the flat had revealed the existence of the letters, but they had not seemed significant at the time and were simply noted at number 167 on a list of her personal property.

Joanne was the next to be visited. Two different men had sent her love letters. She found them romantic and strangely comforting, although Peter's had been quite overtly sexual and something of a turn-on for her boyfriend.

A quick check soon revealed that Peter had sent a letter just before Christmas, which had also never arrived.

Stark had found the connection. It could have been a bizarre freak of fate that two rapist's victims had not received letters, but he knew that this was no coincidence, especially since the girls lived in the same postal area. That was how the telephone caller knew personal details about them, because they were contained in love letters that were stolen from the mail.

It had been another lost Christmas for most of the detectives, who had to make do with stolen moments of camaraderie in the local public houses. There was a sense of euphoria in the Queen's Head as the gang engaged in a variety of chatter. They were getting close to the killer. If they found the postbag thief, he would undoubtedly be the murderer.

Ashley had fully briefed Stark about the state of the enquiry regarding the theft of mail and Stark had seconded him to the murder team, much to the disdain of Barry Marsh, who was only slightly appeased by the promise of two men being drafted over from Radford Road to help him out with the day-to-day crime.

Ashley glanced around the busy pub and was quick to notice a woman in her early forties, in an expensive-looking pale-blue dress and extravagant ear-rings, who was paying particular attention to Stark.

'Is she a friend of yours, then, sir?'

'Who's that?'

'Her over there, in the blue dress, standing next to her fat friend.'

Stark caught sight of Claudia Mason, who waved and smiled.

'Excuse me a moment, boys.'

Stark headed off towards his old friend, leaving the rest of the team slightly bewildered.

Ashley was first to pass comment. 'Well, I never, the dirty old git. I didn't think Stark had it in him.'

Charlie supped at his pint and shook his head. 'Don't worry, he won't step out of line. Unlike a lot of us, he won't stray from Carol, much as he complains about her.'

'Get away, he's no different from anybody else. What's the matter with you?' Ashley was persistent, sniffing scandal in the air.

'Look, I've known Dave Stark for years. I first met him when you were just a twinge in your father's scrotal. I'm telling you that he wouldn't screw another woman. He's not pious about it though, it's just his way.'

Barry shrugged his shoulders. 'Good luck to him, anyway. Hey, Ash, what's the score with you and Christie? Is it over for good now, or what?'

'No, she'll come around eventually. I'm going to give her a couple of days to cool off a bit and then I'll give her a call. She'll be all right.'

It was usual for Steph to jump down Ashley's throat at such a comment, but she and Nobby had drifted to one side and pretended to be choosing a record on the juke-box.

Steph was adamant. 'Nobby, I think it's best that we break up. If you like, we can make it for a three-month period or something and then see what we both think.'

'Don't give me that crap, Steph. We either finish or we don't. I'm not having any of this temporary separation bollocks.'

'Well, okay then, I need more time. You won't let us have a trial separation, so . . .'

'You make it sound as if we were married. It's only a bit of fun,' Nobby said.

Steph was resolute. 'Exactly, it's only a bit of fun, so if you don't mind, love, let's finish it. I've enjoyed it, but I think we should pack it in.'

Nobby couldn't joke his way out of this one; he knew she meant it. He was disappointed, but had known in his heart of hearts that it wouldn't last for ever. There was too much of an age gap and he got the impression that Steph was starting to look around for a permanent partner. Theirs had been a very physical relationship but they weren't suitable to get betrothed. He touched her hand.

'Okay, love, I do understand. I'm a bit disappointed, but so be it. And don't worry, I won't give you a bad assessment because of it.'

Steph laughed. 'Thanks, Nobby, I know you won't, and for what it's worth, you are still an incredible screw.'

Stark had rejoined Ashley and the crowd.

'Are you in there, then, sir?'

Stark smiled. Surprisingly, he felt quite flattered, if not a little awkward at the attention that Claudia had created. 'It's funny you should say that, Ash. I am quite certain that I could take her back to her place tonight . . .'

'Oh, yes.' Ashley glanced at Charlie.

'However, I won't be doing so. Much as it is tempting and all that.'

Barry looked at Steve Aston with interest. He was standing holding a gin and tonic in one hand and a pint of bitter in the other. He seemed distant.

'Are you all right, Steve?' Barry asked.

Steve was not all right. Using Christmas as an excuse to drink, he was beginning to feel the effects. His speech was drawn out and slurred. 'Yes, I'm fine. Why d'you ask?'

'No reason. You are very quiet, that's all.'

'No, no, I'm fine . . .' he repeated. 'I've been studying Steph. You know, she is a cracking piece of stuff, isn't she?'

Barry winked at Ash. 'She is that. I'm sure she's got the hots for you, you know, Steve.'

'Don't be daft.'

'I'm not being daft, I'm just saying, that's all.'

Ashley wasn't going to miss an opportunity to get involved in a wind-up. He said his piece. 'That's right, Barry. Can you remember when she was on about Steve, yesterday?'

Barry smiled. 'Can I, bloody hell? You couldn't shut her up,' he lied.

Steve swayed slightly as he puffed out his pigeon chest. 'Why, what was she saying?'

Stark shook his head, and giggled to himself.

Barry continued, mocking Steph's voice. 'That Steve isn't like you heathens, he's got something about him, he's a gentleman.'

Steve downed the remnants of the G and T. 'Get away, did she really? You lying bastard!'

'I am not lying. I'm just telling you what she said, that's all. I'd go for it if I was you.'

'What's she doing over there with Nobby?'

'Why don't you go and ask her?'

'All right, then, I will.'

The group were giggling and Barry nudged Ash as they watched Steve stagger over to Steph.

'You know, Stephanie, I've always thought you were a very nice woman, do you know that?'

She looked over at her colleagues and sensed something was afoot. 'It's very kind of you to say so, Steven. I think you are very nice also.'

'They said that, them lot, those bloody heathens, but I thought they were joking.'

Steph put her arm around Steve's waist and squeezed hard, pressing her breasts into him. He spilled his ale over his hand and it dripped on to the floor.

'I've always had a soft spot for you, Steve, you know that. The thing is, I do expect a lot from my men ...' She clutched his buttocks firmly with her hand and squeezed. '... staying power, I mean.'

'Bloody hell.' His Dutch courage was starting to wane and he excused himself. 'Sorry, Steph, I'm going to have to go for a piss.' He staggered off towards the toilet.

Raucous laughter echoing in his ears, Nobby did not find it humorous at first, but then saw the funny side and burst into laughter also. Steve stopped short of the toilet door and shouted back at the group.

'What's up with you lot? What are you laughing at?'

Joanne Peters was not fully asleep; neither could she be described as being awake. She was in a sort of semi-slumber as her brain ebbed and lilted gently into darkness. Images periodically flitted into her mind's eye as she tossed and turned. Inspector Stark, Steph Dawson and Claudia Mason all paid a call to her subconscious, their mouths moving but the words indecipherable. The face on the artist's impression appeared and she curled into a ball, clinging on to the light blue quilt that had ridden up, exposing her knees. The image grew larger, as if floating, looming over her and then moving quickly back and forth as a falcon swoops down for its prey and then back again for the next swipe. Suddenly the face became real and moved towards her again, the eyes widening and the mouth opening. She could feel the man's lips on her own. They felt and smelled of rubber. He was sucking at her mouth, pulling the tender flesh of her lips in between his teeth, tugging at the thin layer of skin that connects the lips to the gums. This was hurting her and she thrashed around, but still he sucked with immense power and then he bit right through. He had bitten her lips off, and blood gushed out of the ripped flesh. Now the man was laughing and chewing away as blood flowed down his chin.

She forced herself awake and jumped out of bed, quickly running to the light switch by the door. She pawed at her mouth as she stared into a full-length mirror. Of course her lips were intact, but the nightmare had seemed so real. Her skin was goose-pimply and a shiver chased down her spine as she scanned the room for the man and picked up a shoe ready to hit him. After a few seconds she sat on the bed, still clutching the shoe. Her body was cold and clammy. She put a sweaty palm on to her forehead and bowed her head in despair and embarrassment as she sobbed. Still she was taunted by the bastard. She was a prisoner of her own mind and experiences and did not know how to escape. The fear of the nightmares had made sleep anathema to her, yet she was so tired, so weary and so darned scared.

Malc Abrahams had the thin end of the wedge. He strolled quietly around the back of Station Street at Hucknall and stared out at the railway track, trying to make out images in the darkness. Malc was a very tall man at six foot four. He had short-cropped black hair and wore white training shoes. He came back around the side of the houses and sat on a low brick wall, swinging his feet and knocking a tune around his head to relieve the boredom. Malc had been on the Support Department two years and usually enjoyed his work, but he didn't fancy hanging around the street all night, just because some old tart was getting heavy breathers every now and then. He noticed a light go on in an upstairs room of a house across the street. It was the bathroom light and he watched with some interest as the naked form of a woman in her mid-forties appeared behind the frosted glass. This made him uncomfortable as he found himself watching; he was himself in the position of a voyeur, not dissimilar to the man he was there to catch. Initially he looked away but his eyes were drawn towards her. He checked that nobody was watching him and he calmly sat, 'gamekeeper now turned poacher', observing the buxom woman's contortions. At one stage she seemed to lean across the window for a toothbrush and her breasts squashed against the glass, revealing large nipples. He felt a stirring in his loins and by now was becoming well confused with himself. Malc was only human, and she did have well rounded breasts and a seemingly heavy bush of pubic hair. It wasn't as though he was hanging around purposely to peep at women. He was stuck there, and she should be more careful where she roamed in that state. The boredom now relieved, despite the conflict of emotions, he studied her brushing her hair and wondered if she was aware of her public display. She must know, a woman of her age!

After a couple of minutes the light went out and the tedium returned. He adjusted his jeans and jumped down off the wall and kicked at a pebble close to the railway track. He could feel his hard penis forcing at his jeans and surreptitiously flicked it to one side so that his erection would not have been apparent to anybody else. As he kicked at the stone, his excited state began to wane and the cold bit once more at his bones. He pulled out a rolled-up newspaper that he had read twice already and looked through it, searching for some trivia that he might have missed. He struggled to see in the dark, averse to standing too close to the light in case he should be seen by any would-be attacker or heavy breather, and 'show out'.

'Gary to Malc.'

The radio in his black leather jacket was set on a vacant channel, allowing them to use less formal radio procedure.

'Go ahead, Gaz.'

'I'm at number 15. The woman's on the phone now, talking to our man. Can you see anything? She's keeping him talking.'

Malc ran to the front of the houses and noticed a youth illuminated in the telephone kiosk at the end of the street. He threw down his newspaper and raced over, his eyes glued to the youth chattering away. When he was a couple of feet away he saw the youth turn and freeze in astonishment as fourteen stone of muscle charged towards him. Malc pulled open the door of the kiosk in an instant and grabbed hold of the phone. He held the startled youth against the wall within the confines of the booth and spoke down the telephone.

'Who's this?'

'Hello.'

'Hello, who are you, please? I'm a police officer.'

The woman appeared startled. 'You're a police officer? What do you mean? What's going on?'

A male voice came on to the line. 'Hello, who's that?'

Malc recognised the voice and grinned as he breathed heavily, trying to get his breath back. 'Gary, it's me, Malc. It looks like we've got our man. I'm in the telephone booth at the end of the street.'

'Good man. I'll come out to you.'

Malc replaced the receiver and glowered at the quivering young man who was squashed up against the glass. He was no more than fourteen and he was scared.

'It was only a joke, honestly.'

Gary, accompanied by Terri Jarvis of number 15, arrived at the booth. It quickly became apparent that the boy lived a few doors down from Miss Jarvis, that he had indeed made a 'joke' call to her but he was not a rapist and murderer.

The result was a very sore ear for a fourteen-year-old youth from his irate father. As far as the police were concerned, there was one less house to observe.

11

'Never forget the most powerful force on earth is
love.'
NELSON ROCKEFELLER

Dave Stark abandoned the idea of eating his bacon sandwiches in
the kitchen. It was much more comfortable in the living-room
with the television as a focal point. His mind was cloudy, both
with the beer he had consumed the night before and the tiredness
that was forever with him. He wasn't sure if it was his age, or the
dreaded stress, or what it was, but he couldn't remember the last
time he felt really sharp, when he had time on his hands, when he
could totally relax. At work in his suit and tie, he looked immacu-
late. As he sprawled out on the settee in his navy blue robe,
however, he did not cut much of a dash. He was convinced he
was getting greyer by the day, and was faintly aware that bags
were beginning to develop under his eyes. He put this down to
the demands of work and the demands of his wife and family. He
used to like an occasional game of golf, but it was over a year since
he had last hacked around a course. He made a mental note to
arrange a tee-off with one of his friends, just as soon as he had
cracked this case. He had been playing for fifteen years and was
pleased when he managed to play to his handicap, which
remained at twenty-six. The same handicap he had had for the
last ten years.

Despite the noise of the television, he could hear Carol singing
to herself in the kitchen. She wasn't a bad old stick. They had
been through a hell of a lot together over the years, and there
weren't many women who would have put up with the life. His
job had become like a drug to him, his dependency increasing
with habitual usage. It was forever in the background, no matter

what was happening in his private life. He had always intended to slow down a bit before his retirement, to increase his leisure time and ease off on the pressure. He had seven years to go yet, but he wondered how he could possibly take things more easily if he remained a detective inspector.

Often when he got home, he was too tired to do anything but fall asleep as soon as he got to bed. It did not bother him too much, but it was not knowing how much it bothered Carol that caused him concern. There was a time when it had been quite an issue between them, which had created a barrier and made matters worse. The only saving grace was that when the two did get together, their lovemaking was extremely heated and passionate.

His daughter Laura sat in the armchair, her foot tapping to the rock music issuing from 'the box'. She wore a white dressing-gown and looked fresh and lovely. She really was blossoming into an attractive young woman. Dave found it quite difficult to treat her as an adult, and she was at the stage where she so desperately wanted to be treated as such. He often felt like laughing when she started a conversation, in what she considered a mature way. She would say something out of the blue, like: 'The Middle East situation is so volatile, don't you think, Daddy?' or 'I notice the Dow Jones has taken a bit of a slide.'

He reasoned that if he treated her like an adult, then hopefully she would behave like one. That was the theory anyway.

He bit into his crispy bacon sandwich as he spoke to her. 'Are you still seeing that lad, then?'

Laura tutted. 'Dad, do you have to talk with your mouth full?'

'Oh, I beg your pardon. Perhaps I've regressed back into child-hood. Perhaps I'm really only nine years old and only think I'm a detective inspector?'

She laughed. 'Well, what do you expect? Yes, "that lad" happens to be called Mark, and I am still seeing him.'

Stark knew his name. He always made it his business to find out who she was dating and he could not resist checking the boy out on the Police National Computer, just to make sure he had no previous convictions! This Mark seemed a nice enough lad. He didn't have much 'get up and go' about him, but he appeared harmless enough.

'Is it a big love job then, or what?'

Laura blushed. 'Dad, what do you think I'm going to say to that? It would shock you if I said it was, and that we were getting married at the Register Office on Saturday, wouldn't it?'

Stark swallowed a lump of bacon before continuing the verbal horseplay.

'Don't worry about that. I've been trying to give you away for years.'

She pulled a face at him. There was a slight pause as the music drew their attention to the screen. After a minute or so Laura spoke again.

'How's the rape case coming along, Dad? Have you any idea who's done it, yet?'

'We're getting there. I don't have a name yet, but it's coming together nicely. You see, I've found out how the two girls are connected...'

Laura held up her hand. 'Ssssh, oh brilliant, it's got to number one, just let me listen to this, Dad, and I'll be right with you.'

Dave shook his head. For a minute, it had appeared that a member of his family was actually interested in his work! Laura, understandably, was far more interested in the cavortings of some heavy rock megastar.

Once the racket had ended, she spoke. 'Sorry, Dad, yeah, what were we talking about? Oh yes, I saw you on telly, asking for people to come forward if they were getting cranky phone calls or heavy breathers, is that right?'

'Yes, something like that. I'm wondering now if that was a bit of a mistake. I actually said come forward if the caller appeared to have some sort of personal knowledge about them, but that part seemed to get lost. Anyway, we are getting inundated with calls and it's becoming a bit of a distraction in some respects, but we can only hope that they'll dwindle down as the days go on.'

'Oh right, that sounds a bit of a bummer.'

'A bit of a bummer! What sort of talk is that?'

He threw a cushion at Laura, who threw one back. Carol walked in.

'Come on now, David, it's about time you were getting ready for work. You'll be late.'

'Okay, Mummy, anything you say,' he responded. 'Please don't send me to bed early.'

131

Laura joined in. 'Yes, go on and get off to work while the going's good. You're outnumbered now, two against one.'

'You're right there.'

Dave stood up and walked over to the door, deliberately positioning himself between Laura and the television. She dodged her head around, trying to see either side of him, before she realised it was purposely done.

'Dad, will you bog off to work, please.'

He spoke to Carol. 'Have you met my charming daughter?'

The Royal Mail offices on Yew Tree Avenue, Carrington, had a sixties feel about them. They were housed in a flat-roofed building with a small car-park at the front. Nobby and Charlie strolled towards the premises and spotted a window to the left and black rubber 'draught-proof' double doors to the right. A notice outside the window read: 'Customers Reception Area'.

Nobby tapped on the window, which was opened by a man in his mid-thirties, with short wavy brown hair and long sideboards. He was clad in Royal Mail uniform. He was a PHG – Postman Higher Grade – and his manner was relaxed.

'Hello, my duck, what can I do for you?'

Nobby spoke to the man. 'We are from the CID. We want to speak to the boss, please, mate.'

'Which boss is that? There's plenty of bosses around here, I'm afraid to say, but it just depends which one you want to see.'

'Well, who runs the place?'

'That's Mr Pearson. Have you got an appointment?'

'No, but it's fairly important that we see him.'

The man with the sideboards drew in a sharp intake of breath and winced. 'It always is, my duck. I'll give him a ring, I can't do any more than that.' He glanced down at a piece of A4-sized paper that was Sellotaped to the desk in front of him. 'You'll have to bear with me, they've just changed all the bloody extensions . . .' He plied a finger down the list of numbers. 'Let's see, Cluster DOM – Delivery Office Manager, 2679. Hold on a sec.'

He tapped away at the telephone, received his instructions and pointed the way to the two detectives. 'Just go through them double doors, them rubber uns, and turn left. It's the bloke in the suit you want.'

Nobby waved. 'Cheers, mate.'

They pushed open the heavy doors and saw a room about forty foot long and fifty wide immediately in front of them. A number of postmen were busily monitoring the metal pigeon-holes that were the heart of the sorting office. A jolly-looking gentleman with grey hair, in his fifties, approached the detectives with an outstretched hand. Both Nobby and Charlie shook it.

'You are obviously Mr Pearson,' Nobby observed.

The man had a red face, and closer scrutiny revealed small purple veins on his cheeks. He wore a suit that was a little drab, in need of a dry-clean, no doubt caused by mixing white-collar work with manual.

'I am he. What can I do for you gentlemen?'

'I'm Detective Sergeant Clarke, and this is DC Carter. I'd like a few minutes of your time, if I may.'

'Let's go in my office, then.'

Nobby and Charlie followed the man, avoiding several large trolleys scattered around the entrance door.

'Mind those coffins. I've told them a hundred times not to leave them like that.' He shouted up toward the far end of the building. '*Cyril*! Get these bloody coffins shifted, will you, they're a bloody hazard to all and sundry!'

Cyril gave Mr Pearson the thumbs-up and sauntered down towards him.

The office was a little sparse: three chairs in a row down the side of the wall, a wooden desk that had seen better times, a metal filing-cabinet and a token picture that appeared to be the tail fin of a killer whale somewhere in the Arctic Ocean.

Nobby spoke as he handed Charlie a chair. 'That's quite a cheerful name for a trolley, isn't it – a bloody coffin?'

'I suppose it is quite macabre. They've been referred to as that for as long as I can remember.' Mr Pearson was not used to the company of detectives and felt uncomfortable. He attempted a joke in an effort to disguise his unease. 'Anyway, it isn't the cough that carries you off, it's the coffin they carry you off in.' Pearson stared at the men, who smiled politely.

'Quite,' said Nobby.

Pearson was starting to sweat. His guests were not helping his already high blood pressure.

'We've come to ask about the system that is used to deliver the mail to the various houses in Hucknall. There have been a few thefts of mail and we are involved in trying to track down the offender.'

Nobby might have been economical with the truth, but he was not lying. The fact that this was part of a murder enquiry was irrelevant. On a need-to-know basis, Pearson did not need to know.

He used a handkerchief to wipe away the beads of sweat now rapidly appearing on his forehead. 'Well, one of your officers has already spoken to the postmen, but the system is no great secret. Anybody that is observant could see how it works by the way their local postman operates. Not that I'm implying you aren't observant, I meant . . .'

'I know what you meant, Mr Pearson. I wondered if you could explain to us in some detail how the system works?'

'Well, it's simple enough, really. The footmen take their sacks out and deliver the letters, and when one sack is empty, they go to a pre-designated spot, which could be a newsagent's, or even a porch doorway, and collect a second bag. That sack will have been dropped there by a postman in a van who must wait until the bag is collected, and that's about it, really. It's very basic.'

Charlie was curious. 'Surely that takes the man in the van a heck of a long time if he's waiting for a dozen, or whatever, men to arrive at different collection points.'

Pearson swallowed hard. 'Yes, it can take a long time, but there's no way around it, is there?'

Charlie nodded. He put a hand to his mouth in thought. 'I was interested when you said that the vanmen dropped off the sacks. Why did you say that, Mr Pearson?'

'It was just the way I put it, that was all. You know what I meant.'

It was Nobby's turn to force more sweat out of the poor man's brow. 'We aren't here to get anybody into trouble, Mr Pearson. It's just that we need to know what really happens so that we can make any arrangements we need to; that's all, it won't go outside this room.'

'I've got nothing to hide. I can show you in the regulation book how it's done; there's no problem with it, I promise you.'

Nobby raised a hand. 'There's no need for that, Mr Pearson. I know about regulations and how things should be done, but what interests me is how things are actually done. Are you with me?'

'Yes, of course, but I would imagine that the men comply with the regulations. I always did. It's a very serious disciplinary offence if you don't, it can mean the sack, if you'll pardon the pun.' Pearson again tried to raise a smile but was met with an even lesser response by the two men.

Nobby continued. 'You see, the other thing that puzzles me is that when you described the ''drop-off'' points – your words, not mine – you said a porchway or a newsagent's, something like that.'

Pearson nodded.

'Well, what I can't understand is, if the vanman has to wait anyway, why not keep the bag in the van until he sees the footman?'

Pearson shifted in his seat. He shook his head, his loose jowls eventually catching up with his face as it stopped. 'I . . . I don't know. I don't make the rules up, you know, I just see that they are carried out.'

'You see, if it was me, and I was a vanman, then after the novelty had worn off, or perhaps if I was getting reprimanded for being slow, I might just consider the easiest thing to do would be to drop off the sack at the designated point, knowing that the footman is going to pick it up anyway. Instead of it taking me four hours, it might take me two hours or less. What do you think about that?'

Pearson sighed heavily and began clicking the top of a Biro pen that he had picked up off his desk. 'I think that I am ready for early retirement soon and I could never tolerate such behaviour by my men.'

'I understand that, Mr Pearson, but I don't want to have to find out through other means, like the Post Office Investigation Department, or by checking with the postmen themselves. We are not here for a witch hunt, we just want to know the system. Now, does my theory have any validity or am I just a cynical detective?'

Pearson scrutinised the eyes of the two men. Could they be trusted? Did he have a choice? He wiped his forehead again. 'I would say that your theory would have a great deal of validity in some quarters.'

Nobby smiled. 'Thank you, Mr Pearson. Now we know.'

Worried that he had gone too far, or that perhaps the conversation had been tape-recorded, he was quick to add, 'Not that it would happen with my staff, do you understand me?'

Nobby nodded. 'We understand perfectly, thank you. Don't you worry.'

The two men got up and bade farewell to Mr Pearson.

As they made their way to the car, Charlie spoke. 'It's not taken us very much further, has it?'

'No, not really, but at least we know that it's common practice for the van drivers to leave the mail unattended.'

'Yes, but the last guy had his bag pedalled away on a bike. It wasn't a case of a discarded bag going missing, so what relevance does it have?'

'Probably nothing, but I remember two other thefts of mail at West Bridgford last year in which bags were stolen that had been left. I'm going to have to backtrack a bit and see if the two are connected in any way. Mail thefts are extremely rare and it just seemed a bit coincidental, that's all.'

'I doubt if they're the same people involved, anyway. We've probably been wasting our time.'

'It wouldn't be the first time.'

Nobby grinned at Charlie as they reached the car.

Jim McIntyre had not pulled out any stops during the enquiry. He was an idle man with a miserable expression. Everything was an effort for him. His days were numbered and it would not be long before his back would go and he would retire, comfortably off, on a medical pension. It was just a case of him deciding when his back should happen to 'go'. He plodded through any enquiries that were given him, using the telephone wherever possible. At Stark's request, he had checked out the most recent suicides in the unlikely case that the murdering rapist had had a fit of remorse. It was all pure routine. Jim preferred this way of working. Everything was written out for him to do, each task was there to see in black and white. All he had to do was complete each one, as best he could, in his own time.

He glanced at the next action sheet and rang the Force Intelligence Bureau. They could only find one other recent offence of rape where the offender had removed jewellery from the victim. That offence had occurred at Leicester, and he jotted down some of the details, before dialling Leicester Central CID office.

'CID, DC Morton.'

Jim had a Glaswegian lilt to his voice. 'DC McIntyre from the CID at Nottingham. We are investigating a rape and murder on us and we notice that you had a rape where jewellery was taken from the victim. That matches the MO of our rapist as well. Can you give me some details about it?'

'Yes, I know about your man.'

'Oh, you do? That's good.'

'Yes, we got your circulation about him, but our offender committed his crime on us on the same day and around the same time as your second offence took place so he can't be the same man, unless he can manage to be in two places at once. Anyway, we have a fingerprint at our scene and it matches a bloke who was locked up at the time of your first rape, so there's no way it's your offender, I'm afraid.'

'Oh right, okay then. Cheers.'

Jim replaced the receiver. He omitted to record that the time and date had been the same when he jotted down the information from FIB. The truth was that he was not particularly interested. It was getting close to four o'clock and he fancied an early-doors drink at Radford Road police station bar. Some things appeared to be more important to him than rape and murder, like quaffing a pint down his loose-necked gullet.

Lying on a bed with your hands behind your head and your eyes closed does have a tendency to send you to sleep. However if you happen to be a seventeen-year-old girl and think that you are in love, then you are apt to let your mind wander into the realms of the unknown. Laura Stark had adopted such a position. She wore black denims, a white T-shirt with a 'Hell Rider' motif and pink furry slippers.

Her mind explored the future as she lay alone with her thoughts. It was all ahead of her to map out for herself, and why not? Her mind drifted in the sedate confines of her own room.

When will I get married? I think twenty-five is a good age, or is that too old? God, it's ancient! Perhaps twenty-two … Yes, twenty-two is a good age to get married. It's got to be a white wedding, though, all the trimmings. Horse and carriage – the lot – well, you only do it once, don't you?

Will I really stay with Mark for the rest of my life? I don't know, I really do love him, but I suppose we are young. Other people do, though, don't they? Why not us?

How many children shall I have? A boy and a girl would be nice, or it could be twins! Yes, twins would be great, but you have to be realistic. A girl first and a boy a couple of years later, then she can do his hair for him when they are older and help him choose the latest fashions. You can always tell the lads that haven't got older sisters, they dress so normal!

I wonder what it's really like giving birth? She could see herself there as clear as day, legs akimbo, straddled up on the stirrups, fighting the pain, not screaming, being extremely brave – and suddenly, there is the baby. It's got Mark's face. Poor little bogger! She smiled to herself.

Carol's voice invaded her private world. She was shouting from downstairs.

'*Laura*! I thought you were supposed to be cleaning your room? I can't hear much movement up there.'

Laura muttered out loud to herself. 'Christ almighty!' To Carol, she shouted, 'Yes, Mother, I'm doing my room. Don't panic.'

With a sigh, she reluctantly swung her legs off the bed and opened her bottom drawer. She extracted her diary from under her lingerie and removed the elastic band that was holding all the loose odds and ends inside it. There were a few birthday cards, scribbled notes and, most sacred of all, Mark's love letters. She opened one, her favourite, the first he had ever sent. The excitement it had wrought when she first read the letter always returned when she scanned its contents on subsequent occasions. He was so base in them, using words like 'fanny' and 'cock'. It was wonderfully disgraceful. If her mother ever found them, or worse her father, it just didn't bear thinking about!

The Major Incident Room at Sherwood Lodge, Police Headquarters, looked more like an office for computer programmers. Several computer terminals complete with visual display units

138

were unattended, but three police officers in uniform tapped away on others. In the centre of the room were larger tables where readers and researchers studied numerous documents in relative quiet. There was none of the occasional high jinks that occurred at the forward post at Nottingham police station. A library-type atmosphere was the order of the day. There was a large map on the wall with two circles drawn on it in thick red pen, depicting the two designated crime scenes.

Stark stood in front of the map and scrutinised it. Steph appeared at his side.

'I suppose you are wondering where the next one will take place, sir, are you?'

'They are very close together, aren't they?' Stark mused.

'Yes, that's because of the mail deliveries. There's no doubt in my mind that is where the answer lies.' She pressed a long red fingernail on to the map, before continuing. 'I just hope the next attack isn't around there.'

'Why's that, Steph?'

'Because that's where I bloody live, that's why!'

'Nobody's exempt, are they?'

Stark appeared philosophical. He sat down at a vacant table and Steph joined him. He appeared quite morose.

'You look tired, sir.'

He rubbed his hands into his eyes. 'I feel tired, Steph.'

Jim McIntyre came into the room, clutching a large bundle – more reports of malicious calls to sift through. He planted them down heavily at the side of one of the computer operators, who groaned out loud and threw his head back.

Stark spoke quietly. 'We are going to have to hit the area of the two attacks really hard now, Steph. I'm going to have detectives visit every household. They are going to have to interview each male thoroughly, and if they match the suspect parameters, they can interview the women as well. I find it difficult to believe that a loved one doesn't know or suspect something. I might even start obtaining blood from all the males within the area.'

'Sounds fair enough to me,' Steph observed.

'All alibis will have to be checked and double-checked. He's out there somewhere and he must be about ready to strike again. The Regional Crime Squad are covering the local mail deliveries. You've got your own little commitment tonight, haven't you?'

'Yes. There's me and a couple of lads from Support Department on it.'

'Good luck with it, anyway. It's worth trying.'

She nodded. 'Anything's worth trying.'

Jim sat at the far end of the office with a copy of the *Nottingham Evening Post*. The picture on the front page was the artist's impression that Claudia Mason had done. Stark rose quickly to his feet.

'Give me that paper, Jim.'

Stark practically snatched it out of his hand and stared at the headline above the photograph in disbelief. It read: WANTED FOR RAPE AND MURDER!

He marched towards the top office, where Wormsley was visible through the glass façade. Stark did not bother knocking. He threw the paper on to the desk in front of the detective superintendent.

'What the hell is this?'

Wormsley leaned back in his chair and smiled. 'I would say it's the *Nottingham Evening Post*, David, at first glance.'

'You know what I mean. I thought we had an agreement.'

'Have you ever heard the phrase "circumstances alter cases"?'

'Come off it, sir, you never even had the common courtesy to tell me it was going in the paper.'

'I was going to mention it tonight, but I've been busy. I've alerted the switchboard staff and the HOLMES men.'

'You've what? So every fucker in the world knows about this apart from the officer in the case, namely me!'

Wormsley pointed a finger. 'You see, that's where you're wrong, David. On paper I'm the officer in charge of this case. You report to me, not I to you. I'd appreciate it if you'd remember that from time to time. It may serve you well.'

Stark nodded. He should have expected this. Wormsley's autocratic reputation had preceded him, but he had given him the benefit of the doubt and he had been let down badly. 'Surely it is bad practice to take such an important step and tell everybody bar me, for heaven's sake?'

'Listen, David, let's go back to basics, shall we? I call you David and you call me sir – that's because I'm the superintendent and you are the inspector. Simple, isn't it? Now I may not always be right, but I am always the superintendent, okay?'

'But the left hand doesn't know what the right hand is doing. And don't talk to me like I'm some sort of probationer PC!'

'David, I am not going to consult you over every little decision. Now, this conversation is going around in circles. Close the door behind you.' Wormsley threw the paper in the bin at the side of his desk and continued writing.

Stark was frozen to the spot. He had been sorry to see Wagstaff go but he had never envisaged this sort of carry-on. He really couldn't see himself sticking with this obnoxious little shit for very long, and the feeling was probably mutual. Stark slowly turned and closed the door behind him. You can't argue with somebody who pulls rank.

At the back of Linby Terrace is a small copse with a well-worn path at the side that leads towards Buckingham Avenue, near where Cheryl Towlson was murdered.

The woman was attractive and dressed to kill. She wore a skirt that was just above the knee, and black stockings. It seemed a bit cold to be wearing just a tight-fitting, waist-length jacket and her shoulders were slightly hunched, apparently underlining this fact. A heavy black shoulder bag hung limply at her side. She appeared to be waiting for someone as she stamped her feet to try to keep them warm. She glanced at her watch. It was twenty past nine.

She had noticed the youth some distance away, near the end of the street. He was leaning against a telegraph pole and smoking a cigarette. Occasionally he would glance towards her but look away if she met the stare. He made her feel decidedly uncomfortable. She glanced at her watch again.

The young man stubbed out his cigarette on the pavement and walked quickly towards her. That was sufficient for her to turn and walk towards the gladed area. She had no option other than to walk straight towards him. He broke into a jog, and in a matter of seconds attacked her. He pulled at her shoulder bag, but she clung on harder, and the momentum of his run and her strong grip flung him around. Her knee met him fairly in the groin. He was poleaxed, and stumbled towards the ground. She followed up swiftly and knelt across his throat, tugging at his hair and raising his head.

'Don't struggle, twat, or I might get annoyed.'

He had no such intention. He was in too much pain and decided to cover his sore testicles in case of a further onslaught.

She was quickly joined by two men who appeared from nowhere.

Steph Dawson was smiling. 'You took your bloody time, didn't you?'

The taller of the two men spoke. 'Sorry, love, it all happened so quickly.'

'It's not our man. He was after my handbag. He didn't touch me at all.'

'Yes, I can see him now. It's Derek Thraves, he's always nicking bags . . .'

Steph was on a high. She laughed as she spoke. 'Well, this bag's just nicked him!'

The policeman from Support Department directed his observation towards the choking youth, still prostrate on the ground, his throat obscured by a very shapely knee.

'You've made a bit of a mistake tonight, old love.'

'Just get this mad bitch off me, and get me to the nick. She's fucking crackers.'

Steph laughed. 'No manners, some people.'

12

'I know an undesirable character when I see one.
I've been one for years.'
CHRISTOPHER FRY

A smile tickled Stark's face as he read the morning briefing sheet. He was reading about the arrest of Derek Thraves by Steph. He had the utmost respect for her as a police officer, but she never failed to surprise him. His brow furrowed at the thought of his next task. It was no good putting it off; better to get it out of the way. He bellowed through the open door towards the CID office.

'*Nobby!*'

Stark popped a Polo into his mouth as Nobby Clarke sauntered into the office, his collar undone and his tie askew.

'Shut the door, mate. Sit down.'

Nobby complied. 'This sounds a bit ominous.'

Stark put his hand to his mouth and blew through his fingers. He winced. 'It is a bit. Nobby, how long have we known each other?'

'Christ, over twenty years, why?'

'I've always trusted your judgement, Nobby, and you know what I think of you as a detective sergeant. You're the best in my book.'

Nobby folded his arms and raised an eyebrow. 'This sounds a bit heavy, boss. What's up?'

'I'll come straight to the point. It's you and Steph.'

Nobby looked puzzled. 'I'm not with you, mate. What about me and Steph?' His instinct was not to admit anything.

Stark tried hard not to laugh. 'Nobby, don't make this any harder than it already is. It's me you are talking to, Nobby to Dave – I just want to know how serious it is between you and her.'

Nobby released his arms and leaned back in the chair. He sighed. 'I didn't think it would take long. Who's been talking?'

Stark shook his head. 'Nobody at all, I promise you. Bloody hell, I've known you long enough, mate, it's fairly obvious to me. I don't think the others have twigged yet, but it's only a matter of time.' Stark continued before Nobby could speak. 'Look, I know it's none of my business in some respects, it's none of anybody's business, but having said that, I do have a CID to run and I just wondered what you proposed doing about Steph? I mean, is it a heavy scene or what?'

Nobby smiled through his hard features, his high cheekbones reflecting the light from the tube above. His forehead wrinkled, as he pointed a finger at his old mate. 'You know, if it was anybody else asking me this shit, you know what I'd tell them, don't you?'

'I know, all right. But it isn't, is it? It's me that's asking you, so what's the crack with it?'

'Right. Well, for what it's worth, we've just finished the relationship, if that's not too strong a word for it. It was just a . . . you know, a fling, I suppose you might call it. Anyway it's over. She finished it. Okay?'

Stark sighed and scratched the back of his head, ruffling his wavy black hair. 'Was it an amicable separation?'

'Yes, of course it was. I'm a grown man, Dave. Bloody hell.'

'Do you think there's any likelihood of you getting back together?'

'No, don't worry. It's over. There's been no arguments and it won't affect the smooth running of the office, I assure you.'

'Okay then, subject closed.'

Nobby shook his head. 'Nothing gets past you, does it?'

'Not really.'

Nobby rose to leave but stopped to pass comment. 'I noticed the artist's impression in the paper last night. Do you think that was wise, David, at this stage of the game?'

Stark stared at him with a deadpan face.

'No.'

'Oh, I see. Don't tell me Wormsley's struck yet again.'

''Fraid so. You know the git never even told me, never mind consulted with me.'

'That is bang out of order,' Nobby rightly observed.

144

'Tell me about it. Anyway, it's done now and, who knows, perhaps it will work. We'll see.'

'Yeah. Listen, going back to that other thing, none of the gaffers know about it, do they?'

'No, and they're not likely to either, mate.'

'Cheers, Dave.'

Stark was pleased that there was no scandal in the offing but he did feel sorry for Nobby. He gazed at the long list of enquiries he had scribbled down for his men to pursue in an attempt to find a witness or an offender. It was vast. The man-hours it would require would be immense. It included enquiries with local informants, newspaper deliverers, milkmen, water board, electricity and gas men, workmen, window-cleaners, bin-men, reps, door-knockers, pedlars, charity collectors, mobile libraries, pools collectors, religious canvassers, Neighbourhood Watch, CB operators, vagrants. The list appeared endless – and those were just the normal routine actions, without the more specific tasks relating to the theft of mail and individual aspects of the rapes themselves.

He leaned back in his chair and muttered to himself, 'Prioritise.'

The phone rang. It was Laura.

'Hi, Dad.'

'What's the matter?'

'That's a nice greeting. Nothing's the matter, why?'

'Well, you hardly ever ring me here, I just thought . . .'

'Well, you thought wrong. I've just rung up to tell you that I'm going to stay at a friend's for a couple of days. She's having a New Year's Eve party and I said that I'd give her a hand to get it organised.'

'Has your mum said it's all right?'

'Yes, but I had to promise to ring you out of courtesy.'

'I'm glad somebody's showing me some courtesy. Okay then, don't get too drunk. Who's the friend?'

'Heather.'

'She's not been round for a while. I thought you two had fallen out.'

'No, it's just with seeing Mark and that, I've not seen so much of her, that's all.'

145

'Okay, darling, have a good time and don't forget to ring your mother every night.'

'I won't. Byeee.'

He replaced the receiver. 'Oh to be young again.'

Ashley appeared in the doorway. 'Talking to yourself again, sir?'

'No, it was my daughter. Anyway, don't be so bloody cheeky.'

'Sorry. We're ready for the briefing when you are, sir.'

There was a tuft of hair sticking up on the top of Steve Aston's shock of ginger locks. He had put some water on it from the sink in the toilet, but that served only to make it stick out in a clump as opposed to separate hairs. Steve had a pale complexion and his eyelashes were barely visible, being so light in colour.

He peered through the perspex window of the cell door and studied the youth lying on the mattress. It was true: he did have a resemblance to the artist's impression, and the young PC who had alerted Steve had done the right thing.

Carl Pitchers was in his early twenties and had brown hair. His teeth were quite white, apart from two on either side of his mouth which were slightly discoloured. He had been arrested the night before for a Breach of the Peace. He was not a criminal in the proper sense of the word. He had a couple of previous convictions, but they were some time ago for ABH and Public Order offences. His neighbour had rung the police last night. He was fed up with the screaming kid and the adults screaming louder. It was some dispute or other, something to do with whose turn it was to change the kid's nappy. Anyway, it was the catalyst to start off another blazing row and to go over old wounds that were not yet healed. Carl was very excitable at the best of times but when the police arrived, he met them at the gate and told them what they could do, in no uncertain terms. He would not be calmed down at any cost, so the officers decided to arrest him and let him simmer down in a cell overnight. His release was now imminent, but it was worth Steve having a look at him before he was allowed to leave.

DC Aston unlocked the heavy door and swung it open. The man inside appeared surprised to see him as he swung his legs off the hard bed and sat on the edge. Steve introduced himself and informed the man that it was a matter of routine that all prisoners are spoken to by the CID, which was a blatant lie, and Steve was not a very good liar. Carl looked at him somewhat incredulously. In the corner of the cell were a couple of old newspapers and the plastic coverings of the microwave meal he had eaten, most of it still inside the tray. Two Maxpax plastic coffee cups also littered the floor.

'Well, what do you want to speak to me about, the weather?' Carl asked sarcastically.

'No. Unlike your good self I am aware of what the weather is like outside. I'm more interested in what you were doing the day before Christmas Eve.' Steve had not obtained any sort of rapport with the man at all, so he went straight for the jugular, metaphorically speaking.

'I don't know. I can't remember.'

Steve sat down on the bed and leaned against the cold wall. He put a foot on the mattress. 'Well, try and remember, will you?'

'I've told you, I can't remember. Now what?'

The man was smiling. He obviously had no fear of the likes of Steve Aston. He wore a look that Steve had seen before and it irritated him. The more Steve tried the hard-man image, the more ridiculous he appeared. Someone should have told him a long time ago to just be himself.

'What do you mean, "Now what?" I think you ought to try and remember; it could be important and save you a hell of a lot of inconvenience.'

'You aren't threatening me, are you?' Carl was still grinning inanely.

'No, I'm trying to explain something to you, but while ever you continue this cavalier attitude, there doesn't seem much point.'

'Cavalier, oh excuse me!'

'What about Boxing Day – is your memory clearer about that?'

Carl looked puzzled. 'The day before Christmas Eve, Boxing Day, what's this all about?'

Steve tutted. 'Carl, can you remember or not? I'm not going to prat about all day.'

Carl stood up quickly. 'Hold on a minute, I know what you are talking about now; it's those bloody rapes, isn't it?' He laughed. 'You are way off beam talking to me about those, my old mate.'

'I'm sure I am, but until you tell me what you were doing, I can't check it out, now can I?'

'This has got to be some kind of a sick joke. Don't tell me that you ask everybody who has been arrested what they were doing. Christ, you must be clutching at straws.'

'Carl, it has obviously escaped your notice that you bear quite a resemblance to the artist's impression of the murderer.'

'Do I? It's news to me. Look, I don't want to waste your time even bothering investigating me. I've got no time for perverts that rape women. What do you take me for? Hold on a minute, just let me have a think and I'll tell you.'

'That's very big of you, Carl, thank you. Now what were you doing on those dates?'

'What times are you talking about? Christmas is a very busy time, you know.'

'What about teatime-ish on the day before Christmas Eve?'

'I'm not sure about that. I think I'd be at home. What time on Boxing Day? I should be able to remember that a bit better.'

'Early evening?'

'Early evening, let me think; yes, I was at home then definitely, because there was a James Bond film on, wasn't there?'

'Probably, there usually is. Who were you at home with?'

'Jackie would be there, that's my missus. The little one would be in bed but I feel sure that Jackie was with me. She'll tell you, nip around and see her.'

'I will do. Why couldn't you have told me that before?'

'Well, you know how it is.'

'No, I don't actually. I'm afraid you won't be released until I have checked it out.'

Steve slammed the door behind him and pounded down the corridor back to the cell complex. He spoke to the young Custody Sergeant.

'Can you hang fire releasing him until I can check out his alibi for the murder job?'

The sergeant looked at Steve disbelievingly. 'You're joking, aren't you? He's got to go, mate. You've not arrested him for it, have you?

'No, but it won't take me an hour. I just want to nip and see his missus, that's all.'

'I can't keep him that long. The other job has been dealt with and there are no reasons to hold him for anything else or to put him before a court. His review is due in ten minutes, by the inspector.'

'Shit! Let me give her a ring then, from your office.'

Steve took Carl's phone number from the custody record. Carl had already rung Jackie to tell her they were keeping him overnight. There was no reply to Steve's dialling. He reported back to the Custody Officer.

'I'm sorry, Steve, I'm going to have to release him. He's been in sixteen hours already. My hands are tied.'

Steve would have to feed Carl's details into the HOLMES computer in case there was anything that might tie him into the enquiry more strongly. It might be necessary to try to obtain a blood sample from him voluntarily to prove or disprove his involvement in the crime.

Jim took the call.

'CID, DC McIntyre.'

'Can I speak to DC Marsh, please?'

'DC Marsh is out of the office at the moment. Oh hang on, he's just walked back in. I'll put you on to him.' Jim pressed the mute button and spoke to Barry. 'Phone call for you, mate.'

'Who is it?'

'He didn't say.' Jim shrugged.

'DC Marsh.'

'Yes, it's Freddy here.'

'Ehup, mate, what can I do for you?'

'I want you to do me a favour. I've got some info about all the burglaries on Ruffs Estate, if you're interested.'

Barry took a pen out of his jacket. He sat on the desk and prepared to write on the white blotter.

'What sort of favour?'

'I got nicked the other day for a break-in at Bulwell, and got a load of grief. Anyway, they wouldn't let me talk to you then, so I thought I'd give you a ring now.'

'What sort of grief? Who dealt with it?'

'Forget it, it doesn't matter now, but the info I've got is dead straight and I want a bender when I go to court. What's the chances?'

'It depends on what the job is and whether the info turns out to be good.'

'It's spot-on. There's a youth on the estate, I don't know his name, they call him Dillon, but that's not his proper name. He's got a stack of gear in the house. He keeps it in the loft, under the insulation, between the rafters, but he uses some of the stuff he nicks. I reckon the video is knock-off.'

'I'll see what I can do for you about a suspended sentence. If nothing else, I can get you some dough for it. What's the address of this bloke?'

'347 Ruffs Drive. See what you can do about the bender, will you? I couldn't stand another stretch, it would do my head in.'

'I'll see what I can do. Give me a ring in a couple of days.'

Barry finished scribbling on the blotter as he put down the phone. So much for the day he had planned. It was time to get a warrant.

The man was married. The simplest thing would have been to finish it, just to walk out of the door and never return. But he was a proud man and she was okay most of the time. It was only when they went out, or were among his family or friends, that she would start. He found it so humiliating, all the jibes and clever quips, nothing sexual, just continual 'put-down' comments that caused everybody within earshot to laugh. It had got out of hand. He was now the butt of everybody's jokes, and he hated her for it.

They had argued about it time and time again. She would try and goad him into hitting her, thrusting out her chin defiantly and pointing at it, but he dared not, and she knew it. Her father was a massive man, a former coal-miner, who would rip him limb from limb if he saw the tiniest mark on her. So the mockery and scorn festered inside him without a point of release. The ridicule was forever with him, the comments reverberating around his head, the laughter grating on him.

The first girl had taken him by surprise in some respects. He had fantasised about rape before, but he never believed he could go through with it. They had been in the pub all day, drinking, and she had started, hadn't she, his missus.

'The only thing he's good for is bringing the dole in; he hasn't got anything else in his favour.' She had looked at him with

150

disdain, mockery in her voice. 'Mind you, at least you've learned to pull the chain now, haven't you, dearest? All these years and I've just got him potty-trained!'

She had tweaked his cheek and he had shrugged her off, before walking out with the sneering laughter echoing behind him in waves.

'Fucking cow, the whore.' He muttered abuse to himself, which soon became: 'Fucking cows, fucking whores, they're all the same. Who the fuck do they think they are?'

It was then that he had waited on the footpath for Cheryl Towlson, the route she always took home. He thought at first that it would stop at the telephone calls, which were just to frighten them; yet looking back, it seemed a natural progression to meet them head on. He wasn't satisfied with just the calls, he needed to see the fear, touch it for himself, show them who was really the boss.

Now as he stood at the side of the house, he could see the young woman quite clearly from where he was standing. She had turned left out of the smart detached house and was walking towards him. He couldn't believe that she hadn't seen him yet, daft cow!

He was only a matter of twenty feet away from her, but she walked slowly, as she was carrying a small suitcase, which he found curious. She had not spoken at all when he had telephoned her, but he could sense that she had been there on the line, shivering in fear.

Opposite to where he stood was an old factory with the wire fencing pulled down. It would do. Not many people around, stuff it, let's go!

The man walked quickly across the street. He was only ten feet away when the woman shouted and waved straight ahead.

'Yoo hoo!'

He noticed another woman approaching, so decided to abort the attack – for now, anyway. He continued walking, right past her. She paid him no attention at all.

The two women embraced, exchanged greetings and began walking off together arm in arm, giggling and laughing together, oblivious to the dirty-looking individual who followed them with his eyes.

This was exciting. He decided to follow them. The suitcase

bothered him. The girl was obviously not going to be at home that night. Where was she going?

Laura and Heather turned left at the end of the road towards the bus stop. They were still completely unaware of the casually dressed man walking slowly some distance behind them.

The young cashier at the Lloyds Bank at Hucknall had a pasty face and acne. He also had a strange wispy moustache that for some reason seemed to slant across his top lip. His suit was cheap, dark grey with lighter grey and white specks; he wore a white shirt with a thin red tie dangling from the collar.

The two uniformed officers in front of him were an odd couple also. The younger one had blond hair and freckles. He looked only about seventeen, yet his partner, greying at the temples, was considerably older, probably in his early forties. It was apparent that the older man was tutoring the youngster in the ways of being a police officer.

The cashier explained the reason for his manager's call.

'This guy came in, I've seen him before, he's got an account with us, and he gave me a cheque to put into the account. Well, it was for £1500, so I thought I'd better check it out, because he's a scruffy devil and I think he told me once he's on the dole. Anyway, it turns out that the cheque was from a book that was reported stolen, so the manager called the police and that's it.'

The older policeman spoke. 'Where is the man now?'

He looked around the bank: a considerable queue was forming. Most of those in line stared at the officers, pleased that there was some entertainment to relieve the boredom.

'Well, by the time the manager had rung head office and then rung you, the bloke had gone.'

'Why did the manager ring head office first?'

'To double-check it was stolen. Apparently they sent it out to the account holder just before Christmas, but he never received it. It was stolen out of a mailbag or something. I can't believe how stupid the chap is, putting a stolen cheque into his own account.'

The older of the two policemen spoke again. 'It doesn't surprise me at all. The sort of criminal element we come into contact with are not strong on brains, I assure you.'

'No, I shouldn't imagine they are. Still, having said that, if it had been a cheque for a smaller amount, we may not have spotted it until it went to head office.'

'Yes, but it would be detected eventually, wouldn't it? What a plonker!'

'It's hardly the crime of the century, though, is it?'

'No, it isn't. What's the man's name?'

'Paul Digby.'

Neither of the officers realised the importance of the seemingly everyday occurrence, which was dealt with in a fairly lackadaisical manner. It was only when the CID were informed about the theft and deception that it was discovered that the cheque book was probably in the bag that had been stolen by the bicycle thief – the same bag, perhaps, that had contained the love letters that never reached Cheryl Towlson or Joanne Peters.

Stark was informed and the excitement grew as the detectives began to muster in the main office of the police station in anticipation of the swift end to a murder enquiry.

13

The room was brimming with detectives. All of Stark's men were there, plus other officers drafted in for the enquiry, including six Support Department officers in overalls and a Dog Section man. The more experienced officers had seen it all before and leaned back in their chairs, seemingly unaffected by the underlying buzz of excitement that charged the atmosphere. Smoke issued forth from cigarettes and a hush lay over the room as Stark entered, clutching a clipboard.

Charlie was quick to make a joke. 'The Gas Board have already checked the meters, sir. There's no need to do it again!'

Nervous laughter greeted the remark.

Stark smiled and responded: 'Thank you for that, Charlie, the first constructive comment of the day.'

None of the officers knew what their role would be. Despite Charlie's flippancy, they were all aware that arresting somebody for suspected murder can never be treated lightly. Would there be a fight? Would the man have a weapon? Would he even be at home?'

Stark placed the clipboard down and sat on a desk at the front of the room. He began his address.

'Okay then, folks, this is going to be a quickie, we can't afford to waste time. I'm not going to need all of you just to effect an arrest. We are going to hit the house straight away. I'm not going to mess about getting a warrant. We know, because of his doing a runner from the bank, that the bloke is probably expecting a pull, but hopefully he won't realise that we have twigged the connection between the theft of mail and the rapes and murder.'

Ashley piped up. 'What if there's nobody in when we get there, boss?'

'Well, we are going in whatever happens; but if it's empty, then one of the officers can go and get a warrant and we'll sit on the house until we get it, and then break in.'

One of the Support Department spoke. 'It's all right, sir, I've got the big key with me.' He produced a sledgehammer and waved it menacingly in the air.

Stark smiled. 'All being well, we won't have to use it – somebody will be in.'

Ashley spoke out again. 'I'm not being negative, boss, but just so that we all know, what if somebody else answers the door and says that Digby isn't in and refuses entry to search, we have no power of entry then, do we?'

Stark liked enthusiastic officers but he wanted to get out there and nick the man while the going was good, rather than answer unnecessary questions. He remained calm and answered the young officer in the best way he knew how. 'If that happens, Ashley, then we are going in no matter what. Either the person who answers the door will give us consent, or they will be arrested, and we then have a power to search the premises anyway.'

It was the Dog man's turn to ask a question. 'If that happens, what will we arrest them for?'

Stark grinned. 'Bloody hell! I'll think of something. We can't just leave the place or they can telephone Digby or get in touch with him and alert him. They'll know it's not for a poxy theft when we arrive mob-handed. Leave that to me, anyway. I'll nick them on suspicion of handling stolen goods. It's a bit thin but we could claim reasonable suspicion that the property must have been in his house at some time. I don't anticipate any problems there, anyway. I'll let Ashley use his charm to get us in if it's a woman!'

Stark glanced at his clipboard. He was a little self-conscious of it after Charlie's Gas Board quip.

'Right then, listen in, the runners and riders are as follows: myself, Ashley and Steph will go to the front door. Charlie, Steve and Nobby go to the back door and the Dog man can be, let's say

155

at the side of the house, ready to come to the front or back should anyone produce a weapon or whatever. The Support lads will stay on to do the searching after we have brought the prisoner away.'

He glanced towards the Support Department sergeant. 'You might as well stay in the van until we come away. I'll shout you on the radio when I want you to make a start. You should have a list of relevant property and clothing regarding the rapes and murder. The rest will be down to your discretion, obviously bearing in mind the theft-of-mail side of things.'

The most important objects to locate would be the jewellery taken from the two victims. Any clothing likely to have been worn at the time of the offences might be of use forensically.

Stark wanted the detectives working at the nucleus of the murder to be in at the kill. He could have used the Support lads to cover the back door, but his men had worked hard and he didn't want to rob them of the glory. He continued the briefing.

'Jim, you can stay outside the premises in a CID car in case our man happens to turn up while we're inside and do a runner on seeing the police there.'

Jim's secondary role did not go unnoticed by the lads who had worked the hardest and shown most commitment.

'All being well, Digby will be there and we can get him straight back to the nick and make a start on him straight away. Nobby can bring him back in his car. All right, Nobby?'

Nobby smiled. 'Yes, fine.'

'And then we can get him on tape once we land back here. Mr Wormsley has asked to be in on the interview with myself, but I shall want you all to be available should we need any matters checking out as the interview progresses. Any questions?'

Charlie had no inhibitions about speaking his mind. 'Yes, I've got one, boss. How come Wormsley is going to be doing the interviewing? He hardly ever has to interview as a detective superintendent. Surely the most skilful interviewers are those that do it every day. Nobby would be a far better choice than Wormsley.'

The detective superintendent's words came back to Stark: 'The superintendent may not always be right, but he is always the superintendent! Any more questions?'

There were none.

'Okay, then. Let's go.'

Digby's abode was a semi-detached council house. The front garden was surprisingly neat and tidy with a few bushes scattered around the borders of the lawn and a row of fir trees adorning the bottom edge. They were swaying fitfully as gusts of wind buffeted at the branches. There were spots of rain accompanying the flurries, making the weather decidedly uncomfortable to stand out in. The front door was painted red but wood was exposed on the frame through neglect and parts of it were eroded. The glass door-panel had a crack in it from corner to corner and a yellowing net curtain hung on the other side.

Stark could feel his truncheon digging into his spine. He had secreted it by stuffing the bulk end down his belt, leaving the ribbed handle in the small of his back, underneath his suit jacket. He was beginning to wish he had brought his overcoat, as the heavy spots of rain splattered on his head and the wind tore at his curly locks. He could hear a television on inside the house, but the curtains were drawn. He hammered on the door. There was no reply. After a few moments he hammered again, a more prolonged banging. He was about to knock once more, when he heard a shrill, female voice.

'Who is it?'

'It's the police, love. Can I have a word?'

'Just a minute, I'll have to get a key.'

Stark could have sworn he heard muffled voices inside and frenetic movement. He glanced at the Dog man and his beast. It was an exceedingly big dog that he had with him, low on its haunches, with shaggy, long fur. It was whining and pulling at the leash. The officer tugged at it and it half sat down and half squatted in compromise. The dogs could always sense the excitement of the officers at moments like these.

Stark heard the tapping of metal on metal as the female inside fiddled with the key and eventually opened the door. She was a skinny woman with peroxide-blonde hair that hung limply on her shoulders. Her eyes were black with excessive mascara and several freckles were pitted over the bridge of her nose. Most of her teeth were yellowing, but she exposed them readily as she smiled falsely at the big men on her doorstep.

It was at this moment that Stark heard a shout from the back of the house. The Dog man needed no telling, and by the time he got to the rear of the premises he could see Nobby forcing a young man against the wooden fence, which seemed in danger of collapsing. The kitchen window was swinging open. The man was quite tall, with short brown greasy hair. He was not well built, medium really, and his black leather jacket had ridden up behind him as he was squashed against the wooden panel. He drew back a large fist, the venom behind the intended blow etched in his face.

The dog was tugging with all its might at the lead, its teeth bared and saliva dripping from its mouth on to the soil. All eyes focused on the beast. Its handler spoke.

'Can I introduce you to Flash? He's hungry and it's teatime!'

Paul Digby relaxed visibly in submission. Nobby handcuffed him roughly and steered him past the dog, who was now growling very loudly indeed.

Once they were at the front of the house, Stark spoke to Digby in a calm but sardonic manner. 'Good afternoon, Paul. How the devil are you? I am arresting you on suspicion of murder and rape.'

Digby's mouth dropped open and he gasped.

'Oh, and theft as well.'

Digby was cautioned and Stark diverted his gaze to Nobby.

'I'll see you back at the nick then, Nobby.'

'Okay then, boss.'

The Dog officer slipped a chew into Flash's mouth, and patted his mane: a meagre substitute, but sufficient.

Now was the time for the hard work, obtaining some kind of proof.

Searching a house for stolen articles is no mean feat, especially when the articles are small and could have been secreted anywhere. It does not help matters when there is a young woman in the flat, moaning and complaining and generally hassling the officers all the way through the search. She could be annoying the searchers for one of two reasons: either she hated the police or she was attempting to distract them from finding anything. Fortunately the Support Department men were used to this sort of tactic and generally ignored what she was saying, or continued searching as they replied, without looking at her.

Stark had not ordered all the floorboards to be lifted up at that stage unless it was apparent that they had been tampered with, but despite that, it was to be a thorough search. There were four men involved in the exercise, two downstairs, and two upstairs. They were all in boiler suits with a black leather belt tied around the middle, and each pair had a small metal box full of tools, should they need them. They also had access to a large 'Dragon' light, a very high-intensity torch.

They had established that the woman's name was Mandy. She hovered between the two pairs, trying to irritate them as they worked. She wore a beige cotton one-piece dress, which was high on see-through, revealing her small bare breasts and tiny circular nipples. She had on no stockings and black hairs were visible on her bony legs, underlining the fact that her yellow hair was dyed.

PC Gareth Childs was working in the main bedroom as she directed her verbal onslaught at him. 'What do you expect to find, eh? Come on, you tell me what you think you are going to find. I have a right to know!'

Gareth gingerly pulled the mattress off the bed and checked that it was intact. A fusty smell filled the room. It was a long while since the mattress had been exposed to air.

'I'm talking to you! You can't just come in here and take over. This is my house and my personal stuff you are throwing around!'

Gareth grunted. 'Can't we, duck? You just watch us.'

'I'm going to ring my brief up about this.'

'Ring him, then. Just shut up!'

Gareth pulled out some drawers, checking the contents and the space each drawer had left.

'Anyway, what's this crap about rape and murder? You've got to be off your rockers, the lot of you. For a start, Paul hasn't got a fuck in him – well, he has, but it's holding him together.'

Gareth laughed.

'It's not funny, you know. How long are you going to be?'

He ignored her as he scanned through a pile of documents that he had found at the bottom of the wardrobe.

'I asked how long you were going to be. Are you deaf as well as daft?'

'As long as it takes, Mandy. Just keep your hair on, will you? It's worse than being at home with our gert, you nagging all the time.'

'Well, what would you do if a group of blokes came marching through your house, ripping it apart?'

She received no reply. The carpet was loose and he pulled it up at each corner before dropping it down. A cloud of dust rose each time. Mandy was certainly not particularly houseproud. He walked towards her. She had been standing in the doorway of the bedroom throughout.

'Excuse me, please.'

He smiled exaggeratedly, and she stood aside.

Once out in the hallway, he shouted through to his colleague in the other bedroom.

'Have you done the bathroom yet, Terry?'

'No, I haven't, mate.'

Gareth went into the bathroom and started his search. Mandy stood in the doorway, her heart pounding. She lit a cigarette and blew the smoke towards him. Surprisingly, it relieved him of the smell of urine that emanated from the toilet and surrounding carpet.

'What the hell are you going to find in a bathroom? I've never seen anything so ridiculous; and before you ask, we have got a loft, do you want to look in there as well?'

'All in good time, Mandy.'

There was not a lot to search. He lifted the cistern and tapped the wall tiles, which were not hollow. He then came out and Mandy relaxed momentarily. 'See, I told you there was nothing in there.'

Gareth bent down and fished inside the tool-box. He produced a small crowbar and returned inside the bathroom.

'What do you think you are doing with that?' Mandy exclaimed.

Gareth placed the end of the bar into the corner of the blue plastic side panel of the bath and gave it a twist. It came off fairly easily and he shone the torch inside. At the far end, underneath the curvature of the bath itself, was a bundle of letters. He stretched and took hold of them.

He looked through them as he sat on the thin carpet. Several were unopened but there were a couple in particular that contained credit cards addressed to two people on the same street in Hucknall. Gareth glanced up at Mandy, who at last had quietened down. He held the letters aloft, touching them at the sides to preserve any alien fingerprints, should there be any.

'Ever seen these before, Mandy?'

'No, I bloody haven't.'

'In that case, then, if they aren't yours, they must be Paul's.'

Still she tried to wriggle out of it. 'They must belong to the people that used to live here before us.'

Gareth appeared puzzled. He shrugged his shoulders and scratched his head exaggeratedly. 'How long have you lived here, Mandy?'

'About five years. Why?' She sucked on the filter tip of the cigarette.

'Well, the date-stamps on some of these letters are for last week! So are they yours or are they Paul's?'

She stared at the floor and a length of ash fell on to the cheap turquoise carpet. She averted her gaze as she mumbled a reply.

'Sorry, Mandy, what did you say?'

She raised her voice. 'I said, they're Paul's.'

If a solicitor was assaulted by a person who was in police custody, there would be hell to pay. That is why the architecture of the cell complex allows for a designated room, adjacent to the Charge Office, where solicitors can consult with their clients behind a transparent partition. Solicitors however do not, as a rule, like such an arrangement. They seem to find it difficult to create their own rapport with clients, to give them a cigarette, to reassure them and to speak in a hushed tone. Stark often wondered whether this preference was because they wanted to maintain client-solicitor confidentiality or because they were embarrassed by the way they went about their business. Or was it because they were afraid that the police would overhear any indication or admission of guilt; at which point they should withdraw on ethical grounds? It was undoubtedly for the most honourable of reasons.

Mr Roe did not care whether the police could overhear him or not. He was a tall man, in his mid-thirties, with a round face and an almost perpetual smile, even when discussing the most im-

161

portant and serious of issues. He had straight red hair that was cut to a fringe, and he wore a brown suit and an antique wristwatch with a yellowed face and barely visible Roman numerals. He had a real opportunity here to make a name for himself. It was the first time he had represented a man who had been arrested for murder, and he was going to ensure that this man was not convicted, because of course he believed him to be innocent.

Stark stood in the Charge Office. Wormsley sat in the rear of the block next to the female cells, reading the statements regarding the mail theft, so that all the facts were fresh in his mind. Stark could overhear the conversation between Digby and the solicitor, albeit muffled by the consultation room door. Should he put his hands over his ears? Roe was doing most of the talking.

'I know you are innocent, Paul, and that is why you must answer "No comment" to every single one of their questions. I can't stress the importance of that too much.'

Digby was fatalistic. 'Look, all I want you to do is get me out of here. Why can't I just tell them that I haven't done it, and be done with it?'

Paul's head was pounding; he was not the most intelligent of men and he had found himself with a real problem. It was easy for Roe to talk. He wasn't the one sitting in the hot seat.

'It's not as simple as that. They can twist your words around, and make you believe yourself that you've done it, even if you haven't. They can't be trusted, but you can trust me. That's why I'm here, to protect you.'

Paul blew out a breath of air. He was leaning forward on the wooden bench and resting his forearms along the length of his thighs. He stared at the floor and only briefly glanced at his solicitor. He was under great pressure, with a whole array of emotions swirling around his troubled head. Should he listen to the man? What was in it for Roe? Why couldn't he just tell them and go home? What would Mandy tell him to do? All he wanted was to get away from this place.

'But I don't like saying "No comment" to everything. It does my head in.'

'Listen, Paul, do you realise why you are here?'

'Yes, I know. It's serious, but bloody hell!' He swept his grubby hands through his greasy hair. He was shaking.

162

'Well, what would you say to them if you did speak?' Roe asked.

'I'd just tell them.'

Mr Roe let out an exaggerated sigh. 'Yes, but tell them what?'

'Tell them I hadn't done it, for Christ's sake!'

Paul began to chew at his nails in a near-frenzy.

'Okay, so where were you when the crimes took place?'

Paul stared hard at Roe. 'I don't even know when they are talking about, do I? I'm not bullshitting you, I haven't done no stupid rape or murder. Christ, you're worse than them!'

Roe's brow furrowed. 'Paul, I'm just asking you what they are going to ask you, to try and convey to you that what I'm saying makes sense.' Roe looked down at his notepad. 'We are talking about the evening of 23rd December and during Boxing Day.'

Paul shook his head. 'I don't know. I can't think straight. I need more time.'

Roe dropped his pad on to the floor and threw his head back melodramatically. 'Can you see now what I'm saying to you? That's only the first real question I've asked you, and you can't even answer that. Think what it would be like in an interview! Question after question that you would fumble over, and it would all be taped for a court to hear.'

'All right, I know you're right, but I just fucking hate all this shit.'

'Right. Are we agreed that you should say "No comment"?'

'Yes, all right.'

Roe raised a hand, displaying the palm to his client. 'Don't let me influence you. It is your decision. All I can do is offer you my advice.'

Paul seemed to be getting annoyed. 'Look, I've told you I'll say "No comment". All right? Don't keep going on about it!' He chewed some more at his fingernails. 'What evidence do they reckon they've got?'

'I don't know. They've not told me a lot. Something about you trying to pay a cheque into your account.'

Paul managed a laugh. 'No comment!'

Roe grinned more than usual. 'Now you're getting the idea.' The solicitor leaned forward in his seat, his eyes sparkling with excitement. He was rising to the challenge that lay ahead. 'Okay, listen to me then. Every question, no matter what it is about, just repeat "No comment" after everything. They will try to get you talking, to say anything – stick to "No comment". They will ask you what you think about the weather, what football team you support. They might ask you about your family, anything – no matter how daft it sounds, just say "No comment" to everything, okay?'

'Yes, okay.'

'They will go on and on about what evidence they've got. Let them prove it. If they've got any evidence, then the time to produce it is in court. Don't listen to what they say. They will make it sound as though there is overwhelming evidence against you. Don't believe it. We can work on that when we get the depositions.'

'You're making it sound as though I'm going to get charged, no matter what happens. I just want to get out of here. If they want to charge me with the theft, let them get on with it – fair enough – but I don't want a fucking murder charge, Mr Roe.'

'It's not the charge you've got to worry about, it's whether you get convicted, Paul.'

'It's all right saying that, but I'm going to get remanded for this if I'm charged. It could be a year before the trial gets going and I'm stuck in the bloody pokey.'

'Do you want to be in the pokey for life, Paul?'

Paul put his head in his hands, the yellow nicotine stains evident on his stubby fingers. Already he was becoming just a legal pawn in a game he couldn't really understand. He shook his head and pleaded with the solicitor.

'But I haven't done it, Mr Roe!'

Jim McIntyre had shown unusual common sense. In fact, he had saved Steve Aston quite a lot of work. Carl Pitchers had readily brought in his medical card and blood donor's documents, which quite clearly indicated his blood group as O. It was known from semen at the scene that the rapist's blood group was A, so it no longer seemed necessary to submit blood from Carl to Forensic. Had anybody else in the office been dealing with these matters, pressure would most certainly have increased, but Jim McIntyre worked at his own pace and, anyway, they'd nicked somebody, so what was the rush? There were now two very large piles of

164

paper in front of him on his desk in the Major Incident Room. One pile was the ridiculous response they had had from the malicious phone call request, the other was the now-increasing inundation of suggested persons who bore the slightest resemblance to the artist's impression that had been emblazoned on the *Evening Post* front page. Some suggestions were born of neighbourly dislike or pure malice, others were given with honourable intent. One in particular related to a certain burglar from Ruffs Estate at Hucknall. Jim filed it with all the others.

The interview room was already shrouded in a pall of smoke and as Stark pulled the chair up to meet his backside, he let out an exaggerated sigh. It had not escaped him that Digby matched the description that the service station cashier had given to Ashley. He also had far greater proof that Digby was the man who had attempted to cash the stolen cheque at the bank. He was itching to take the interview one stage further and prove the rapes and murder, in addition to the theft of mail. He glanced across at Digby, who turned his head to avoid looking at the detective inspector.

Despite the thin layer of confidence established by his consultation with Mr Roe, Paul Digby did not feel fully at ease with himself. He had gained some initial assurance when Wormsley had forgotten to inform him of his right to silence, but this was quickly corrected by Stark. Paul sensed the apparent dissent between the two officers from the look that Wormsley had given Stark. This brief cushion of hope was quickly dissipated, however, when the searching questions drew out droplets of sweat from his body, making his mouth parched and his senses reel. Even with Mr Roe close by his side as a mute comforter, Digby was no match for the articulate, experienced officers, and the 'fight or flight' reaction of a cornered animal was beginning to creep into the way he responded to the questions. He couldn't flee so he would have to fight. The interview had been under way for over thirty minutes and there was real aggression in Paul's tone as he dealt with yet another question from the square-chinned officer sitting immediately in front of him.

'No fucking comment, now be said, will you! Just stop the interview now!'

Wormsley's voice remained calm and collected. 'No need to be like that, Paul. It was quite a simple question, and I'll ask it you again. Who can we speak to who can alibi your whereabouts on the times we have spoken about?'

'You're fucking sick, can't you get it into your head! No comment, all right?'

Stark spoke. 'Look, Paul, I understand why you are getting a bit annoyed, but you can solve the stress you are undoubtedly feeling, yourself, simply by talking to us. Tell us what you were doing. If you haven't done the murders, then tell us, and let us examine what you say; and if it's true, then that's the end of it, but I fancy that you can't do that, can you?'

Paul almost forgot himself. 'What do you mean I can't? No comment!'

Stark leaned forward, and rested his elbows on the desk. 'What I mean is that of course you can't tell us, can you? Because, you see, you were alone at those times, Paul, weren't you? You can't give us a name, can you? Because you were raping and murdering a young girl, weren't you, Paul? Perhaps she asked for it, perhaps it all went wrong, perhaps you didn't mean it. But we don't know if you don't tell us, do we?'

There was a brief silence. Paul glanced noticeably at Roe, who avoided eye contact. Remembering Roe's insistent advice, he said again: 'No comment.'

Stark laughed. 'I'll tell you what, Paul. Let's meet each other half-way, shall we? I don't think there's much doubt that you produced a stolen cheque to a cashier at Lloyds Bank at Hucknall earlier today, now is there?'

'Leave off, will you?'

'Well, there isn't, is there? The bloke behind the counter knows you by sight, he has served you several times before, your handwriting is on the paying-in slip, and you are on video doing it! What else do you want?'

Paul made no reply. He lit up a cigarette kindly supplied by Mr Roe from the packet on the small desk in front of him.

Stark continued. 'Now you don't need a degree in law to realise that you are bang to rights for that cheque deception, do you? I suppose you could argue that you bought the cheque book off a man in a pub, but did you buy these as well?'

Stark showered on to the desk the letters and additional cheque cards that had been found behind the bath panel in Paul's house.

Paul almost surreptitiously glanced at the letters that were scattered in front of him. He made no reply. Again he looked at Roe; again there was no acknowledgement. He wished that he had ditched the Giros and cheques instead of separating them from the bulk of the letters and hiding them in the bath panel. Why hadn't he left them in the bags with the rest? It was too late now, he was well and truly in the mire.

Stark continued. 'These were found behind the bath panel at your house. Now, I know that will not surprise you, Paul, quite simply because you knew they were there, but you aren't talking to us, are you? And unless you do, what are we to think? There are so many questions that are unanswered. Is your wife involved, for instance?'

For a moment Paul forgot his instructions. 'No, she isn't. Leave her out of it,' he snapped.

'How can we, Paul? It's her house as well. Are you telling me she didn't know about them? In which case you must know about them. Now which is it, Paul?'

The young man sighed. 'Look, I'm not daft, I know you've got me for nicking that stupid fucking postbag, but I ain't done no frigging murder or rape or any of that kind of shit.'

Roe looked at his client anxiously, but before he could intervene Stark was already asking his next question.

'Tell us what happened then, Paul. How did you steal the bag?'

'I just rode off on the bike, bag as well, but I don't see where you get a fucking murder from. It's beyond a joke.'

'You don't have to tell me it's beyond a joke, mate! I've seen the hell it's caused that girl's parents on Christmas bloody Day. I've seen her lying on the slab, pal! And the other girl as well. She is left picking up the pieces of her ruined life because of you, Paul.'

Roe tried to butt in. 'I really must ask for a consul –' but his client shouted above him.

'Just fucking shut up about that, will you? It isn't because of me at all.'

'Well, if it isn't you, mate, who is it? Were you with somebody else? Nobody else was seen nicking the bag.'

'How does me nicking a bag of mail get me nicked for a fucking murder? You've got all the answers. Answer me that!'

'I will. It's quite simple, Paul – because inside that mailbag were letters to both those girls, and the person who raped both those girls spoke about details that he could only have known from the contents of those letters, and that person is you, Paul, isn't it?'

There was a deathly hush in the interview room. All eyes focused on Paul as he stared at the floor, his cigarette shaking in his quivering fingers. They would never believe him; they would think he was just trying to cover his tracks. His lack of intelligence, coupled with his confusion, made him revert to basics. He would stick to Roe's advice now. They couldn't prove something he hadn't done, could they? Finally he spoke.

'No comment.'

Roe smiled. 'I really must ask for another private consultation with my client, Inspector Stark.'

Stark was obliged to acquiesce, by law, and he reluctantly turned off the tape recorder. Paul looked at the ceiling and let out a loud sigh.

14

Stark and Nobby both leaned on the Custody Suite counter with
their arms folded, elbows resting on the pine finish, like a pair of
bookends. Stark's cufflinks flashed gold in the false light while
Nobby's biceps protruded through his suit, straining at the ma-
terial. Wormsley had been quick to excuse himself after the interview. He returned to his office to listen to the tape to see if he had
missed anything Paul had said that might have been of some
consequence when heard in a more sedate atmosphere. Digby
had not admitted the murder but Wormsley's disappointment
was tempered by the admission to the mail theft. There was a lot
of work to do and more interviews would undoubtedly follow.

Nobby broke the silence between the two men by stating the
obvious. 'He didn't cough it, then?'

'No.'

'Has he said anything about the murder or rapes at all?'

'Just that he hasn't done them!'

Nobby managed a laugh. 'Fine.'

The silence resumed. The uniformed Custody Officer was busy
writing out various entries on the Custody records of the seven
other persons currently detained at the station. He had just fed
and watered them all.

Nobby spoke again, flicking his head towards the closed door
behind them. 'Who's in there, then?'

'I've got Ashley doing the medical exhibits. I don't think it's
going to take us a lot further. That's why I had the interview first.
The DNA evidence isn't going to go away.'

169

'No, I suppose not. What vibes did you get off him? Is it our man?'

Stark sighed. 'It's difficult to say. He volunteered readily enough for the medical, and he's coughed the mail job, but there is something about him. He's either lying or he's holding something back from us. He's a bit thick, to be honest.'

'Yes, but is it him?' Nobby pressed Stark for an answer.

Stark shook his head. 'I honestly don't know, mate, it's a bit early to say. Wormsley is convinced it is and I can't see how it can't be, fuck it! It's him, he's done it, and that's it; all we've got to do is prove it and the DNA samples will soon sort that out for us.'

Nobby and Stark moved away from the counter. Stark put his hands in his pockets as Nobby lit up a cigarette.

'Yes, that's true enough. What about the Peters girl? Will she be able to identify him, do you reckon?'

'I don't know, but seeing as the clock is ticking away, we had better get an ID parade jacked up. Can you sort that out for us, Nobby?'

'Me and my big mouth! Where the hell am I going to get twelve stooges from at such short notice?'

'Well, I want it doing about half seven tonight, so you'd better get a move on. Try Basford Hall College, there's a list of volunteers in the inspector's office.'

'It's supposed to be his job to arrange the ID. Why do I have to do it?'

'Just give him a hand, Nobby. I want it doing in a couple of hours, not in a couple of weeks. That's why.'

'Okay.'

Stark spoke out loud. 'What's the police surgeon doing in there? I only want him to do a medical, not a triple by-pass operation.'

After he had finished assisting with the medical examination of Paul Digby, Ashley found a deserted witness-room at the far side of the police station. He wore a fashionable double-breasted suit that must have cost £300 since it fitted him beautifully, but all his suits were made to measure. His tie was speckled with large splashes of grey and red with a secondary pattern woven into the silk. He sat with his brogues resting on the table, in a reclining

170

position, with the telephone to his ear. He waited patiently for the ringing tone to be answered. He knew Christie was off work today and he was confident she would answer. He smiled as he heard her voice.

She was obviously still annoyed with him.

'If it isn't Casanova himself! What do you want?'

'Don't be like that. You never gave me a chance to explain. Even the worst criminal is allowed a fair trial.'

'Is that right? Well, you've taken your time to attend court!'

'Listen, Christie, I think it would be a travesty if we ended over a simple misunderstanding.'

'I haven't misunderstood anything, Ashley. You were the one that misunderstood me.'

'In what way?'

'You thought you could just walk all over me and that I would come running to you whenever you clicked your fingers, just like all the others. Well, you were wrong, weren't you?'

'I didn't think that at all. Surely you have made your point now. Don't you think we should get back together again? Let's go to Reno's again. We can have a lovely Italian meal, a bottle of bubbly and I can reassure you, and tell you what I really feel about you. This has hurt me, Christie, it really has.'

There was a long pause. Ashley spoke again. 'Come on, Christie, what do you say?'

'You've not even tried to explain why the hell you went off with another woman at the first opportunity.'

'Wouldn't that be better said over a nice bottle of champers?'

'No, I want to hear it now.'

Ashley removed his feet from the desk and concentrated hard. 'Okay, then, if you insist. That girl was an old flame, I'll grant you that, but I saw her down Blitz's and she had a problem. You see, her brother had got himself in a bit of bother with the police and she wanted some advice. She was really upset, Christie, waterworks, the lot; and then when I come out of her house, I find your bloody note on my car and I'm well chuffed, aren't I?'

There was another pause and Ashley strained to listen, as if that might give him an indication as to whether she had bought his story.

She spoke quietly. 'I'm glad you called, Ashley. I must admit it has put my mind at rest.'

'That's my girl . . .'

'You see, before you rang me, I was beginning to have second thoughts about what I did, but now you've rung and I've heard your pathetic, bullshit story, it has made me realise what an absolute bastard you are! Don't bother ringing again, just go and screw yourself!'

She hung up.

Christie's tirade of abuse and her unforgiving tone had forced Ashley to hold the earpiece away from his head. He looked at the blue scoop in his hand and grimaced at it, before replacing it with some force. He tapped his fingers on the phone and tutted.

'Ah well, you win some and you lose some. Perhaps it's for the best!'

Steph Dawson was not sure if it was significant, but Joanne Peters wore a long black dress that covered her from her neck down to her ankles. The two women sat in an annexe room at Oxclose Lane police station. Joanne was rubbing the palms of her hands down the dowdy dress over her legs. She was visibly shaking and seeked reassurance. 'Are you sure he won't be able to see me? I mean, how do you know he won't?'

Steph smiled confidently. 'Because I know, that's why. All they can see is a mirror image of themselves. I promise you that. I've stood in there myself and experimented. Would you like me to show you? I can get them to wait a bit until we have had a look.'

Joanne shook her head. 'No, I believe you, Steph. I don't want to go in there until I have to. Anyway, he's going to know it's me, isn't he? Who else can it be looking at him?'

Steph took hold of her hand. 'I'll come in with you. There is absolutely nothing to worry about, I assure you.'

Joanne forced a smile, but visibly jumped as the door burst open. It was Nobby.

'Ready when you are, Steph.'

The two women walked unsteadily out of the room and down the corridor. Steph wondered if Joanne would make it. She held her trembling arm as she tentatively walked along. Nobby let the women into the room before closing the door behind them. He was not allowed inside. It was a long room. There was a uniformed inspector at the far end and a man she did not recognise –

the solicitor, Mr Roe. Joanne was aware of the line of men illuminated along the length of the room behind the two-way glass partition, but she did not look at them. The inspector smiled and spoke to her.

'Hello, love. I am Inspector Palmer and this man is a solicitor.'

Roe averted his gaze.

'I would like you to walk along the length of the room and see if you can see the man who attacked you. Do not say anything until you have walked back down again and then I will ask you if the man is there. I must tell you that the man may or may not be present at this parade. Have you any questions?'

Her mouth was dry and her answer almost incoherent. 'No.'

'Off you go then.'

Steph let go of her arm and Joanne realised that she must make the journey alone.

Mr Roe spoke. 'Inspector, I object to the fact that a detective policewoman has ushered her into the room.'

Inspector Palmer was resolute. 'I will note your objection and ask that you note my reply, which is this: the witness is finding this identification parade most traumatic, which I'm sure you can understand, and her welfare must be paramount along with the smooth running of the parade. You will see that there is no impropriety taking place; the policewoman is only here for moral support.'

Roe did not reply, but scribbled a note of the inspector's response.

Joanne walked down the length of the room and glanced at the line of men opposite her. She began by flicking her eyes at their faces but grew more confident as it became apparent by their demeanour that they were unaware of her. The men each had a number pasted on the wall above their heads. Digby had chosen to stand about half-way down the line and he struggled to appear diffident. The stooges seemed to be more nervous than he was. When Joanne returned to the inspector he asked her a question.

'Have you seen the man here?'

'Yes.'

'Would you like to tell me which number was above that man's head?'

'Number seven.'

The inspector smiled again and Mr Roe made another note.

Steph ushered Joanne out of the tense environment. Once back in the witness room, Joanne collapsed on to the chair and began sobbing. Steph put an arm around her.

'Well done, Joanne, I'm proud of you. That was very courageous. Well done, love.'

Nobby came back into the room. 'Can I have a word, Steph?'

Steph rose from the settee. 'I'll be back in a minute, Joanne.'

Once outside, Nobby gave her instructions. 'Right, take a witness statement off her, will you, Steph?'

'Of course. Good result, eh?'

Nobby remained impassive. 'Not really. She picked out one of the volunteers. Our man was number five!'

Barry Marsh had done his best to keep out of the way. The CID office was crammed with detectives all talking about Paul Digby and he felt redundant. He had decided to get himself a piece of the overtime and, acting on the information he had received, he had obtained a warrant to search a house on Ruffs Drive for the stolen gear from burglaries in the area. There was nobody from CID to assist him, so he had arranged to meet the patrol 'panda' car at the end of the street. It was already in position as he approached. He pulled alongside the two uniformed officers and wound down his window in the light drizzle. Jerry Wilson was a young officer, a weight-trainer with muscles to match; Fred Selston, in contrast, was of slight build, more wiry, about forty years old and with Brylcreemed hair.

Barry greeted the men. 'Hiya, Fred, Jerry. Thanks for giving me a dig out, lads. I know you're busy but it should only take half an hour or so.'

Jerry spoke. 'What number are we doing, Barry?'

'347, it's about half-way down, a lad called Kevin. I can't find him on the voters' register, so we'll have to play it by ear. Just leave it to me. I'll sort it out when we get there. I've got a warrant, so there'll be no probs.'

'Famous last words,' came from Fred.

Barry put the Escort into gear. 'Come on, then. The sooner we strike, the sooner it's done.'

Both cars were driven the couple of hundred yards up the road and they all got out and approached the yellow front door. After four knocks and obligatory shouts, it quickly became apparent that there was no one in. They had drawn a lot of attention to themselves by the banging and shouting and to walk away now would mean that any stolen property inside might be disposed of before they were able to return.

Barry spoke. 'It's no good, the door's going to have to go in. Have you got a sledgehammer or a crowbar in the car?'

Fred answered, 'No, have you?'

Before Barry could reply, Jerry stepped forward. It was time for his favourite occupation, breaking doors. 'No need to ponce about with it. Let the dog see the rabbit.'

Fred and Barry stepped aside and Jerry caressed the door, pushing it at the top and bottom. There were no bolts, just the mortice lock. Jerry took a step back to give added momentum to his kick.

'Just a minute,' Barry intervened. He pulled down on the metal handle and the door opened. All three men laughed as they stepped inside.

'Now that could have been embarrassing!' Barry observed.

'Damn, I was looking forward to giving that door some oomph!' Jerry exclaimed dejectedly.

Barry shouted as they all got into the hallway, 'Anybody in? Police!'

There was no reply.

It was no surprise to Barry that the door was open. It was not uncommon for some people to leave their doors open, often because there was not much worth nicking inside, and usually criminals did not make a habit of screwing their own kind, unless they were desperate and wanted something in particular. There were plenty of strangers' houses with more apparent wealth.

The officers quickly checked every room, but nobody was at home. They then got down to searching the house more thoroughly. Barry started to get a bad feeling about this job. There was hardly anything there and there was certainly no video under the telly! Fred did the kitchen while Jerry searched upstairs. Barry concentrated on the living-room.

Stark had ordered two pints of bitter and awaited Wormsley's return from the pub toilet. The small stocky superintendent strolled back into view, rubbing his hands together. He was smiling as he approached Stark, slapping him on the back and taking hold of his pint.

'Cheers, David.'

Stark took a sip of his beer also. 'Cheers, sir. You know, I'm a bit disappointed about the ID parade.'

Wormsley shook his head as he finished his gulp. 'I'm not. I never expected her to pick him out, did you?'

'Well, I was hopeful – obviously.'

'No. She isn't a particularly good witness, is she? Her description of the bloke was crap from the outset, so to me it was just a matter of routine to have to go through the ID parade. We had a witness who had seen the man and we had a suspect, so we had to do an ID parade – I don't think we've lost anything particularly. But I agree it would have been nice.'

'I don't suppose the ultra violet light of the sunbed helped matters for the poor girl.'

'No.'

'It would have just put the icing on the cake, though, if she had picked him out. We are still struggling to get any real hard evidence on him for the rapes. He doesn't look like the artist's impression much, does he?'

Wormsley was in high spirits. 'David, don't be such a bloody pessimist. We will get the evidence, don't worry about it. What's the matter with you? The good thing is we have got the bloke. There won't be any more rapes and murders from him, that's for certain, and there is a similarity with the artist's drawing.'

'Do you really think so? I don't.'

Wormsley nearly choked on his ale. 'David, it's him, I can feel it, I can see it in his eyes. He's guilty, and we'll prove it. I'll get Steph to work on his missus; she knows more than she's letting on.'

'What about time, though? We are going to have to apply for an extension before we charge him with the murder and rape.'

'That's okay. We'll get an extension up to the full ninety-two hours if necessary, but there's one thing for certain: he is getting a charge at the end of the day and we'll find the evidence. We've got to!'

Barry Marsh had found nothing. He was sweating and yet again swore to lose a few pounds. As he opened the last drawer, he was joined by Fred and Jerry.

'Have you found anything?' Barry asked.

Fred shook his head and Jerry answered. 'No, sorry. Looks like you've been given duff gen.'

'Either that or he's got rid of the stuff.'

'Well, that's about it, then.'

Barry placed a copy of the warrant behind the cheap wooden clock on the fireplace.

'What about the telly?' Jerry asked.

Barry sat on the settee and wiped his sweaty brow. 'I've had a look at it, but I can't find a serial number anywhere. We'll have to leave it.'

'I've got an ultra violet lamp in the car. You can scan the telly to see if it's been post-coded with one of those invisible marker pens. If it's been nicked, it might have been. Do you want me to get it?'

'You're bloody optimistic, aren't you? Yes, go on then, you might as well. We've got bugger all else.'

Jerry hurried back from the car with an oblong tube encased in a metal surround. Barry struggled to his feet and tried unsuccessfully to plug the lamp in the vacant socket next to the telly.

'What's up with this bloody thing?'

He got on his hands and knees and fiddled with the plug.

Jerry was smiling. 'It's not been your day today, has it, Barry? Perhaps it wasn't such a good idea after all!'

There was no doubt about it: the plug would not go in at any price.

'Hold on a minute,' Barry said. 'Three plug sockets. One has got the telly plug in, so that obviously works. Let me try this other one.'

He plugged in the lamp and it emitted a purple beam. 'That one works.' Barry unplugged the lamp and looked at the third socket.

Jerry was becoming puzzled now. 'It's not very often you see three plug sockets together like that, is it?' he commented.

'My thoughts exactly, Jerry. Have you got a knife on you?'

'Yes, just a minute.'

Jerry handed Barry a bunch of keys which had a penknife attached to it.

Fred was concerned. 'Don't bloody fry yourself, will you, for Christ's sake!'

'Don't worry, I won't!' Barry plied the knife around the edge of the socket, trying to lever it a little. It was loose. After a couple of twists, the end of the white socket came off. He handed the knife back to Jerry.

'Sorry, mate, I've bent the end a bit.'

'You're all right, don't worry about it.'

Barry bent his head down and peered into the vacant space. 'I bloody thought so! It's one of those security safes, a dummy wall-socket. You can buy them in any catalogue, and what's more there are some goodies inside.'

Barry reached his fingers in and pulled out the contents. There were two necklaces and a small wad of letters held together with an elastic band. Barry's heart started to race. He was fully aware of the state of the murder enquiry and the significance of his find.

'This is incredible. I don't believe it!'

'Why, are they nicked?' Jerry asked.

'It's more than that. These necklaces are nicked from those girls that were raped, and these are probably the bloody love letters that were sent to them!'

'Fucking hell!' Jerry's eyes lit up and the two officers gathered closer. Barry clicked his fingers.

'Can I borrow your gloves, Jerry?'

Jerry passed him the gloves which Barry put on before removing the elastic band. The letters sprang open and one fell on to the floor. He glanced at them quickly. One was addressed to Joanne Peters, another to Cheryl Towlson. This was some discovery! His eyes grew wide as the realisation of what his discovery meant quickly dawned on him. Suddenly he let out a shriek, taking his two colleagues completely by surprise.

'Oh my fucking goodnight. Shit!'

'What's up?' Fred asked.

'Christ, what's the matter?' Jerry enquired at almost the same instant.

'There's a letter here,' Barry replied, 'addressed to Laura Stark. That's DI Stark's daughter!'

15

'The offender never pardons.'
GEORGE HERBERT

Kevin Kirk had tasted the power that rape had given him. It was true that the day afterwards he did feel a little guilty, but only to the degree that an adulterer might the morning after an assignation. Kevin was of low moral standing, and he found it no more difficult to justify rape than he did his other crimes, like burglary. After all, the women were tarts, they asked for it, and they deserved it! It didn't take long for the brief twinges of remorse to fade and the quest for power to grow within his distorted mind yet again. The need for his inadequacies to be offset by yet another feeling of complete control was always near the surface. Even the smart comments his wife made to him had less impact, because he knew he was winning; he had a secret that she would never know: the women he attacked were not real people to him, they were her, the bitch. He couldn't touch her, but each attack was another blow in her sneering smug face.

Kevin was becoming careless because he was brimming with confidence. The last one had fought like a wildcat but he had still got it up her, still made her cry, still beaten her, and he had not been arrested, although he was almost caught in the act. He was really pleased with the way he had stayed calm when that copper had checked him out. Fortunately he had stuck to his plan of getting rid of the necklace within minutes of leaving the girl's house. He had been worried when he first saw the drawing on the front page of the papers. It did look like him, but closer scrutiny showed the features to be too vague; the eye colour was wrong and the hair too short. He had told himself not to get paranoid and to carry on as normal.

Kevin was first and foremost a burglar. He had spent a couple of spells in a Young Offenders Institute and learnt quite a few tricks. He thought the cleverest by far was the postal drop, which he had used to good effect when he committed his burglaries and now rape. The surest way of getting a charge was to be found in possession of property on one's person. You could talk your way out of almost anything else. So as soon as he came away from doing a job, he would simply pop small items of stolen property into a previously stamped and addressed envelope and post it to his home. That was why he had the added confidence when the traffic copper had stopped him. He knew the man would find nothing on him. The necklace was already in the pillar-box in a small padded envelope. It was ironic really that he was using the Post Office in two ways – the stolen mailbag and by posting the goodies to his home address.

Kevin had never liked Paul Digby, mainly because his wife was of a similar ilk to his own, full of shit and smart-arse comments. Perhaps it was because he could see himself in Paul, submissive and afraid to challenge his spouse. Paul offset his compliance by boasting. It really used to wind Kevin up, the way he would shoot his mouth off about his latest job, and when he started going on about turning over the postmen in Hucknall, Kevin just thought he was a prat. It was later that it occurred to him that perhaps he too could have a piece of the cake. All he had to do was screw Paul's house and nick the proceeds of the mailbag thefts, which is exactly what he did. When he started reading the stolen mail, he was astonished at what he found, especially the love letters. He began to masturbate over their contents in the bathroom, and it was during those sessions that the women in the letters became real to him. He knew who they were, where they lived, and the descriptive detail of the letters helped him create pictures in his mind. His imaginings increased. He was curious about these women. It occurred to him that they would be in the phone book, and when he heard their voices, it sent him reeling with excitement and spurred him on to greater aspirations. He could sense their fear over the telephone. He had caused them to worry about him for a change and there was no reason why he couldn't take it further. Why couldn't he reach out and touch them, taste them, have them?

Perhaps if he hadn't argued with his wife and stormed out of the pub and waited for Cheryl Towlson, it would never have happened – or might he have attacked any woman who happened to catch his eye?

He certainly enjoyed the letter from her boyfriend to Laura. Kevin visualised her as an absolute beauty, and that very night he intended that she was to be his. There wasn't a damn thing anybody could do to stop him. He wanted them to be in bed first, ideally he wanted her to be on her own, away from her friend. He could get in without being heard easily enough, and if he could just get to her mouth and cover it, instil enough fear to keep her quiet and then . . . this one was going to be wonderful! He knew from the moment that he followed the two girls to the house that this occasion was going to be special.

He knew it was a risk with another tart in the house at the same time, but he was becoming invincible. Women didn't scare him any more – he was the one who scared them! He had thought about waiting until she was on her own, or until she was outside, but stuff that – he had waited long enough. It was time to make his own opportunity. It was time for Laura.

He couldn't be seen in the darkness at the back of the girls' house and he crouched down low, his screwdriver held firmly in his hand that was covered in his new pair of yellow rubber washing-up gloves. He could hear the girls talking excitedly from the upstairs room. He had calculated from their chatter that Laura was to sleep in the second bedroom at the back. It seemed as if they would never turn out their lights – still, the waiting, the apprehension, the chase was all part of the experience. He could wait.

The darkness of the garden was shattered by light bursting out from the door of the adjacent house. He froze. His muscles were taut and he dared not breathe. He couldn't see the man but he could hear him.

'Go on, out you go.'

He could hear the dog sniffing at the hedge and then start to whine. It was only about fifteen yards away and his hand tightened around the long red-handled screwdriver. He heard the dog

181

urinate and observed the cloud of steam billow out. The dog began whining louder. It let out a yelp.

Kevin thought about running. He tensed up, ready to scarper. He heard the male voice gruffly shout, 'Oi, you!'

He started to move slowly to the side and was just about to run for it when the voice continued. 'Get back inside this house, you daft mutt – you'll wake the bloody neighbours up!'

A reprieve. The game was still on and Kevin bathed welcomingly in the cloak of darkness that returned with the closing of the neighbour's door.

Stark burst open the cell door and picked Paul Digby off the bed in one movement. He held the startled youth against the wall by the scruff of his neck.

'Why the fuck didn't you tell us about Kevin Kirk, you stupid bastard?'

Digby could hardly speak because of the vice-like clench of Stark's fist crushing into the side of his neck. 'What the fuck's up with you? What about Kevin Kirk?'

The Custody Officer appeared in the doorway, followed by Nobby Clarke, a hulking figure silhouetted in the lighter cell corridor.

'Come on, sir, please cool down, don't let's be silly,' the Custody Officer pleaded.

Stark released his grip and Paul slumped to the ground. Stark's heart was pounding in his chest and his breathing heavy. 'Now listen to me, you little shit! You've got exactly two seconds to tell me how Kirk got those letters, or I'm going to plaster you around this fucking cell.'

Digby could see the wildness in Stark's eyes. He had never seen it before, and knew the man was serious. For the first time, reality dawned on him. Sure, he knew his house had been burgled and the letters in the bags stolen, but he couldn't very well have reported that to the police. He'd had no idea it was Kevin. The bastard! He stammered out a reply.

'I didn't know it was Kevin, honestly I didn't. I was confused. I knew you wouldn't believe me if I told you about the letters being nicked from my house, I just thought . . .'

182

Stark turned on his heels. 'I'll be back for you, you silly little twat!'

He brushed past Nobby and the Custody Officer and out of the cell complex. His mind was reeling as he ran up the stairs two at a time, thoughts about his daughter chasing around his head. Now where did her friend live? He fought to remain calm. He had to think clearly: his daughter's life was at stake. He grabbed hold of the phone and dialled the digits with great speed.

Carol answered. Stark tried to disguise his loss of breath. 'Hello, love, are you all right?'

'Yes, fine, I was just going to bed. What's the matter?'

'Nothing. Listen, I need Heather's telephone number. Have you got it?'

'Yes, somewhere. What's up? You sound out of breath.'

'No, I've just run up the stairs. I guess I need more exercise. Do you know where Heather lives?'

'Only that it's on Vaughan Estate. Why?'

'I need to get in touch with her urgently, that's all. There's nothing to worry about. Just give me Heather's phone number, there's a love.'

'You aren't going to ring the girls up at this time, are you? I bet they'll be in bed by now.'

'I doubt it. Look, love, I need the number. Where is it?'

'Just a minute, it's in the pad somewhere. What do you want it for anyway?'

'Just get me the fucking number!'

There was a pause.

'It's 637 8967. David, will you tell me what is happening, please? I have a right to know.'

'I can't. Don't worry, it's probably nothing. I'll ring you later. Bye.'

Stark replaced the receiver and quickly tapped out Heather's number. He listened impatiently to the ringing tone.

'Come on, for Christ's sake answer it.'

Still he waited. He scribbled the number down and passed it to Nobby. 'Get me the address of this number, Nobby, quick! Do it through British Telecom.'

He put the phone down and rushed into the CID office. The concern on his colleagues' faces was evident as he entered.

'Come on, the lot of you. I've tried ringing Laura at her friend's but there's no reply. Nobby will have the address for us by the time we get downstairs. I just pray to God that we aren't too late!'

Kevin Kirk was excited. Entry to the house had not posed much of a problem and he stood silently at the bottom of the darkened stairway, listening for the slightest sound from above. His first job as an experienced burglar had been to create a quick escape route. He had done this by leaving the rear door wide open, once he had entered through the kitchen window. The key had been on the inside of the lock and he had released both bolts. As he stood at the bottom of the stairs, he pulled at the rubber gloves so that the ends of his fingers protruded beneath the rubber, as a surgeon might before an operation. He began to massage his penis over his trousers in preparation and once it was semi-erect, he began carefully to negotiate the stairs, one at a time. There was no hurry. When at the top, he took a deep breath and opened the bedroom door slowly. The hinges squeaked slightly as it moved.

He was taken aback slightly to discover Laura sitting upright in bed, her hand to her mouth, and her eyes wide open in horrified anticipation. She let out a scream and he dived on to the bed, punching her hard to the face and covering her mouth.

She offered no resistance at all and took the punch heavily. She had gone limp in submission, not knowing what to do.

It was then that Kirk was covered in light, thrown on by the hall light switch that Heather pressed as she appeared in the bedroom doorway. Kevin turned with some speed and ran towards her, clubbing her to the head and knocking her sideways into the bathroom. She turned instinctively and locked the door behind her with the small bolt. Kevin's preconceived idea of how the rape would take place had already gone dramatically wrong and he pulled out the screwdriver from his belt.

He shouted to the young girl in the bathroom, whom he could hear crying and whimpering, 'Shut the fuck up, you stupid cow! If you try to move, then she's fucking dead! Understand? It's down to you, so shut it!'

Heather had never before been confronted with extreme violence and she found the experience terrifying and debilitating. Her sobbing lessened at his command. Laura remained motionless on the bed. She dared not scream again and she just sat there with a pitiful expression on her face. It was at this point that the telephone rang.

'Who's that? Come on, who is it?'

Laura was too astonished to react.

'I asked a question. I said who the fuck is it?'

Laura choked out a sob and started stammering. She could not get her words out. 'I . . . I don't know, honest.'

She held out her arms as if to ward the man off. He jumped on the bed and took hold of her fiercely by the hair and smacked her head against the wall.

'I asked you a fucking question, slag! Now who is it?'

The phone stopped ringing and the man smiled, a sneering obscene smile that distorted his face. His breath stank and droplets of saliva splattered her face as he continued his reign of terror. 'Well, whoever it was has gone now, and we are all alone, my little bitch!'

The assault had rocked her head and paradoxically brought her to her senses for a moment. She found her voice, albeit tremulous and strained. 'Take what you want, please, then go. We won't tell anybody, honestly.'

It was the first time she had thought about her father, and she even contemplated keeping it all from him, as long as the man went away.

'What if I wanted *you*?'

Laura had regressed into a submissive, almost childlike state, and she blurted out the first thing that came into her head, naïvely hoping it might have an effect on the man. 'Please, no. Don't. Listen, my dad's a policeman. He'll get you, but I won't tell him if you go away, I promise.'

Her eyes pleaded with the man. She was too young to have experienced true evil and believed that reasoning was an option with such a fiend.

He stood up and walked towards the door. 'Your dad's a copper, is he? Well, in that case I shall go now then, but you had better not say anything to him.' He pointed a finger as a warning.

She shook her head from side to side. 'I won't, I promise.'

He dived on the bed again and held the screwdriver to her neck. He pressed it hard into the soft skin and laughed – an evil mocking laugh. 'I got you going there, didn't I? Well, tough shit, baby, 'cos I'm going to fuck the arse off you, and your daddy can't do fuck all about it, can he?'

Laura realised that her veiled threat had been a mistake and she clumsily tried to reverse her error of judgement. 'I didn't mean it. I was joking. He isn't a policeman at all.'

'Oh, a lying bitch as well, eh? Well, it's too late now, you are going to have to die for that, you cow! But when I'm ready, that's when I'll do it, when I want to. Understand?'

She lay still on the bed, trembling with fear. He pulled down the quilt and revealed her tanned legs. She remained motionless as he drew back her nightgown and gazed at the triangle of pubic hair. He manipulated the screwdriver around the entrance of her vagina, and she felt the cold steel against her skin. She sqeezed her pelvic floor and her anus as she feared she might defecate.

'No knickers, eh? You horny cow! Let's see what you can do with this.'

He took out his penis and she started to retch as he masturbated frantically, without achieving a full erection. His eyes, all the time staring at her body, had grown wild. She knew there was no escape. She dropped her head back on to the pillow. She did not want to see what was about to happen. She was preparing to relax and shut herself out, to go to some other place in her mind, to blank out the horror. She let out a last-gasp plea.

'No, don't. Please don't.'

It fell on deaf ears.

Stark and his men drew up outside the house. He was in near-panic as he tried the front door, which was locked. He raced around to the back, knocking Ashley and Charlie aside. He was still hoping that the bastard hadn't struck yet and that his baby would be okay. His heart sank when he saw the kitchen window ajar and the rear door open. He charged through into the kitchen followed by Nobby, Ashley and Charlie. Adrenalin pumped around his taut body as anger raged inside him. Within seconds he had vaulted the stairs and burst through the first door he saw.

The sight that met him made him freeze initially. Everything then appeared to happen in slow motion, although in reality it all happened so quickly. The image he saw would haunt him until his dying day. He would never shake off the mental picture that had transposed itself on to his brain for ever.

He could see Laura lying on the bed, eyes wide and fixed, staring at the ceiling. He thought she was dead. And there was this disgusting apparition thrusting into her, rocking her body upwards with each motion. Stark was a strong man anyway, but the horror of the scene before him increased his power to massive proportions. He kicked the man full in the head, just as his leering face turned in surprise, knocking him off the bed. Before he had landed, Stark was on to him, punching him repeatedly with both hands about the head, swinging him around like a rag doll.

Stark had lost it completely. He was no longer a police officer; he was a father who had discovered a maniacal murderer attacking his daughter. Every primeval instinct rose to the fore to beat off the attacker. He was oblivious to Nobby tugging at his arm, as he rained punch after punch into the bastard's head. Ashley and Charlie joined in trying to pull him away. He threw them off and placed his hands around the man's throat, lifting his head off the ground. Stark was breathing heavily and he screamed at the man.

'You bastard! That's my fucking daughter!'

Stark squeezed hard, his thumbs pressing into the man's windpipe with great force. He saw terror in the man's bleeding face.

Charlie threw an arm around Stark's neck and dropped down, taking Stark with him. They both crashed backwards on to the foot of the bed. 'For fuck's sake, leave it – you'll kill him,' Charlie pleaded.

Nobby saw his moment and dragged Kirk to his feet by his hair, away from Stark. Nobby glanced at Laura, still lying there motionless. She was now starting to blink her eyes, and a feeling of revulsion welled up inside him. Images of Laura as a toddler sitting on his knee jolted into his mind and he himself punched Kirk in the stomach, making him double up with pain. He dragged him down the stairs by the collar of his leather jacket.

Charlie released Stark and watched as he put his arms around his daughter, pulling her limp body upwards and cradling her in his quaking arms. He was gasping for breath as he spoke.

'It's okay, baby, Daddy's here, it's okay.'

He rocked her in his arms, as he had when she was a tiny baby, and a tear trickled down her face as she began to come out of her almost comatose state.

Ashley heard crying from behind him and tried the bathroom door. It was locked.

'It's okay, it's the police. You're safe now, open the door.'

He could still hear the sobbing, but there was no movement to open the door, so with a thrust of his shoulder he forced it open. He raised both hands towards Heather as she lay in a curled-up ball on the floor, in the corner of the room.

'It's all right. It's over, sweetheart, he's gone now, we're here.'

She shied away from Ashley as he took a pace forward. He crouched down, still some distance from her.

'Take your time, love. Nobody is going to hurt you.'

Heather spoke for the first time. 'Where's Laura? Is she all right? He said he was going to kill her.'

Ashley attempted a comforting smile. 'She's going to be okay, don't worry.'

The pent-up emotion Stark had felt, especially now as he embraced his daughter, forced a few tears from him, as she sobbed terribly in his arms.

'It's all right now, darling, I've got you.'

Laura raised her head. Her eyes were red. She had always believed in him. Right from being a small child, she had always felt safe whenever he was near. Her eyes searched for an answer. 'Where were you, Dad? You were too late! Where were you?'

She began sobbing again. Stark gritted his teeth and a tear fell off his cheek. All he could manage to say was: 'I'm sorry, love. I'm so terribly sorry!'

Dave Stark paced the living-room of his house. The realisation of the enormity of the situation had now really hit him hard. Carol had coped remarkably well and was upstairs comforting Laura. Dave had played down what had happened when they arrived home. It is difficult even for a woman sometimes to comprehend completely what rape can mean.

Charlie stood somewhat awkwardly near the curtains and watched, concerned, as Dave walked around with his fists clenched.

'You should have let me kill the bastard, Charlie.'

'You know I couldn't let you do that. Christ, for a minute I thought you had!'

'He doesn't deserve to live, that bastard.'

'Don't get me wrong. If it was left to me, you could do whatever you liked to the shit, and I'd give you a hand, but . . .'

'Yes, I know, Charlie. I'm not blaming you, mate. I suppose I ought to be thanking you.' He was gradually beginning to think again like a police officer.

'Don't be daft. You know he'll complain about police brutality, don't you?'

'I don't give a shit, mate. As long as he goes down for life, I just don't give a shit. Anyway, what would you do? What would anybody do under those circumstances. I mean, fuck me!'

Charlie sat down on an armchair. 'He'll go down for life, all right, what with the forensic from the other rapes and us catching him . . . you know.' Charlie wanted to finish the sentence with the words 'in the act', but could not bring himself to say it.

'Yeah, I know, but it's not enough, Charlie, it just isn't enough.'

'I just hope you don't lose your job over it, that's all.'

'That's the least of my worries at the moment, pal – as long as she's all right, that's all I'm bothered about.' He pointed to the ceiling.

'Don't worry about her. She's like her dad, strong as an ox.'

'Yeah, but that's the point – she isn't, Charlie, that's just it, she isn't. It's going to kill her, this is. Why couldn't we have been just a few minutes earlier? Why the hell couldn't we have got there before . . . before . . . ?'

The telephone rang. Stark answered it.

It was Nobby. He sounded serious. 'How are you, boss, how are you coping?'

'I'm okay, thanks, Nobby. Listen, thanks for everything . . .' Stark began to get a little emotional and he had to choke back the tears.

'That's okay. How's Laura?'

'I don't know. Carol's with her upstairs, but I can only hope she'll pull through it all. What else can I do?'

'She will, Dave. I've booked the bastard in, and he's in the cell. Wormsley's travelling to the nick now. It looks like the youth's got a broken nose and two black eyes, David. They've sent for the police surgeon for him.'

'That's tough shit, isn't it? It's done now.'

'Don't bother about that side of things – we were all there. He was armed with a screwdriver. We'll square it up. You just concentrate on getting Laura okay.'

'I will, mate. Thanks again.'

'There's one other thing, Dave.'

'What's that?'

'Kirk was in possession of a locket that was engraved with a message from you and Carol.'

'The bastard! Keep me updated, won't you, Nobby?'

'Of course, cheers. Oh, hold on a minute, sir, Mr Wormsley's just come in. He wants a word.'

There was a brief pause and Wormsley's strident voice took over the conversation. 'Hello, David. Sorry to hear about what's happened – at least he's been caught now, anyway. Listen, I could do with . . . Laura, is it?'

'Yes, it's Laura.'

'Right. I could do with Laura being taken over to the rape suite at Oxclose Lane. Can I leave that one with you?'

Stark's grip on the phone tightened. 'No, you fucking can't! She's going nowhere. If you want her examined, then I'll let a police surgeon come around here to the house; but if you think I'm taking her away from here, you are very much mistaken, all right?'

'Well, I don't know . . .'

'Well, it's up to you. Either he comes here or there's no examination and that's the end of it!'

Stark rattled the phone as he slammed it down.

Charlie bade his farewells as the police surgeon arrived. He was a relatively young man, with longish hair and round spectacles. He and Stark went upstairs and joined Carol and Laura in her bedroom. Stark winced visibly at the bruise to her cheek. He sat on the side of the bed and held her hand gently.

'How are you feeling, love? Any better?'

Laura forced a smile. She was very sore and her whole body ached. She felt exhausted, but was happier in the calm atmosphere of the room and the comforting hands of those who loved her.

'A bit better, thanks, Dad.'

'This is Dr Smith. He's a police surgeon and he will need to have a look at you. Do you feel up to it?'

She sighed. 'I don't know. Does he have to do it now?'

'I think it's for the best. Let's get it all out of the way then you can have a long rest. What do you think? Mum will stay with you. It's up to you, though; he can come back another time if you like.'

'No, let's get it over with.'

'Right. Good girl. I'll leave you all alone.'

Laura clasped his hand and stopped him getting up. 'Dad, you know earlier on?'

'Yes, love.'

'I said you were too late, didn't I? Well, I'm sorry about that. I didn't mean it. I know now that you weren't too late at all, because I am still alive, aren't I?' She broke into tears, but fought through them to continue. 'You weren't too late, Dad, you saved my life and I shall never forget that. I love you, Dad.'

He held her tightly in his arms again. As she had spoken, he had noticed that glint of determination in her eyes that he had seen when she was a child. He knew she was a fighter: with love and time she would beat this. They would have to remain strong as a family, but they could do it.

Stark of all people knew that rape was not a crime that ever ends completely. It can fester and grow and torment, its memory eating away and destroying from the inside. The memories and their effects are the worst part of all. The act may be over but the nightmare still remains. One terrible night could determine the whole of the rest of Laura's life, her entire future, haunting the happy times, a ghost that would never leave, ever-present and grotesque. She would never be the same again, he knew that. She had been violated and her character would change, inevitably, but he was going to be there to help her fight the ghost, to chase it away by exposing it, talking about it and laying it to rest as best they possibly could.

It was only the start of a long struggle, but those few words of love from Laura and that look of grim determination had shown him that it was a fight they could win if they fought it together.

He pulled away from her and left the bedroom. His body ached and his head was throbbing as he walked wearily down the stairs. He poured himself a whisky, and with trembling hands, threw it down his throat. The harsh liquor burned him and he winced.

Dave Stark, detective inspector, husband and father, sat on the settee and placed his head in his hands. He began to cry, sobbing like a child. The daughter he had once known was lost for ever, taken from him suddenly, and in the most foul of ways, by somebody who was not fit to kiss her boots. He cried alone. His tears were for his loss, and for the suffering of his child, and for all the other children of the world who were feeling pain and suffering that cold December night.